FO

THE ⊃ʀE

TG WINKFIELD

Footprints in the Future
Copyright © 2017 by T G Winkfield

ISBN 978-1981333233

www.pintogrant.com

Contents

To time travellers everywhere

PROLOGUE

Tuscany
1475

He stepped forward resolutely and did not look back. There would be no regrets.

His ears were ringing and the world shimmered. Gradually his senses attuned to the sound of songbirds and cicadas and the familiar heavy perfume of the palace garden at dusk. In the distance he could hear someone playing a lyre. He recognised the tune Leonardo had written for him before he had left; he could picture him bending intently over the instrument, beautiful as ever and, as always, totally absorbed in what he was doing. Mark threw the medallion containing the homing device behind a bush.

He went into the palace via a small back door and made his way to Leo's quarters deep in the labyrinthine depths of the building, hoping fervently that Leo had kept his clothing for him. The chinos and T-shirt he had put on this morning would have drawn unwelcome attention in the company gathered in the garden. He had promised to return and sworn that their tearful parting the week before would be the last, even though in his heart he had known he couldn't guarantee it. But come back he had, burning his boats in London. If Leo hadn't kept his clothes the implications hardly bore thinking about but he was sure that after the two months they had spent together, his lover would have been faithful for at least this long. His clothes were still there, hidden in the corner of the room behind the wooden door with the sketch of the lute players nailed to it. Why hadn't he asked if he could take that sketch home with him? A genuine Da Vinci drawing, even unsigned, would have set his parents up in comfort for the rest of their lives.

Mark had walked out of his flat in London that morning leaving one letter for his parents and one for the Professor at St Jude's hospital. He had then got into the store room using the key he had copied and hot-wired the machine. After that had come the tricky part. The codes were in a file by the machine but if he picked the wrong one God knows where he might have ended up. But his memory hadn't let him down and he had arrived exactly when and where he had planned.

He intended to be in Florence for good now – or Milan – or wherever Leo's work might take him. At this point in time, though, Leo was insisting that the Medici court was still the place to be. Lorenzo de Medici was the sun: around him orbited giants of art, music, science and conversation. Mark had gone along to his local library and read up all he could about the Medici court while he had been in London. The achievements of the dissolute bunch of friends he had known and with whom he had laughed and drunk, frequently to excess, were astonishing. They were famous!

Officially, he was Leonardo's workshop assistant in this world although people generally (and correctly) assumed him to be the artist's lover; but Mark's deeper role as collaborator and muse was, of necessity, their secret. Leo's genius and all-consuming curiosity carried him soaring into stratospheres of possibility – he needed Mark to keep him in touch with the ground and to help him realise his dreams. Otherwise, he just might burst into flames. That was yet another reason Mark had to come back. How could Leo achieve all that his lover knew he would achieve without an anchor and support?

Mark knew that he had gone too far on more than

one occasion. Transgressions of the 'no footprints' rule had been the reason he had fallen out with the researchers in London and why he had been booted off the programme. The bicycle had been the last straw, apparently, coming after the submarine as it did. He had acknowledged the enormity of what he had done, of course. The Professor had made him go through facsimiles of Leo's work page by page to point it out. But when he was in Florence none of that had mattered. He had mentioned these things to Leo as a joke, maybe to impress, but never dreaming what the outcome might be. What did it matter who drew what when or who first thought of what, anyway? If he had given Leo the benefit of his First Year Anatomy classes, who cared? The splayed out anatomy of the Vetruvian Man was an historical fact from hundreds of years before he, himself, had been born. There was nothing he could have done to stop it. All that was an irrelevance – being with Leonardo and being in love was everything.

PART ONE

'The farther backward you can look, the farther forward you are likely to see.'

Winston S. Churchill

1
The Committee

London
1977

'What do you mean – gone again? What the hell, Lewin?' Philip Carew sat bolt upright. 'How could he? How did he get in there – operate the machine?'

Lewin shrugged. 'He must have got into the building without anyone noticing, acquired a key to the room somehow, gone in and overridden the lock on the machine. How, I don't know but–'

'–may I suggest we find out?' Carew cut in. 'Someone is responsible for this cock-up! You've launched a thorough investigation, I assume?'

Lewin spoke slowly and deliberately. '*We* are the only people who can investigate, Carew, you know that. We six in this room are the only ones who know anything about it, the only people with keys.'

He watched as Carew stared round the small spartan room as if the walls might be to blame. Carew was a thin, nondescript man but today there was sheen of perspiration on his forehead and an angry flush on his cheeks. It had been raining all day and the room smelt of damp clothes. The rattle of rain on the windows threatened to drown conversation.

Carew folded his arms: 'Well, it was nothing to do with me. I've never used my key, let alone given it to a student...'

Joan Danes, a tall, elegant woman in her late sixties, spoke up on Lewin's behalf. 'The Professor's right. We're all in this together. We need to revise our security, that's clear – but playing this kind of blame game is unhelpful to say the least.'

Lewin nodded his appreciation for her support.

Dr Harrison seemed less impressed. She pushed a stray strand of hair back behind her ear deliberately as she spoke. 'Blame game or defining areas of responsibility? As our resident psychologist, Joan, you were the one who did the vetting, of course. Do you think *now* young Mark was a good choice? Or is there any room for improvement in that department?' Her voice, with its remnants of a Glasgow accent, held a note of hostility somehow at odds with her laid back, bohemian image and her, generally, ready smile. *Was this going to be a problem?* Lewin frowned momentarily.

'No. Perhaps not the best choice, as it turned out, Emmeline,' Joan was saying. 'He was psychologically stable, though, from a good, solid and close family and I am sure that he's in full possession of his faculties and knows exactly what he's doing. He's just young and he fell in love–'

'–fell in love! Totally unpredictable in a boy of his age, of course,' Carew said his voice heavy with sarcasm. 'Perhaps we should stick to more mature travellers in future.'

Julian Weatherspoon lounged back in his chair, hands in pockets, and raised his eyebrows, amused. 'On the grounds that we oldies are beyond the lure of love and the raging of hormones, I suppose? Really? Speak for yourself, Carew There's nothing wrong with my hormones, I can assure you!'

Lewin had had enough. 'Dr Harrison, Julian, Philip... please! As Chairman of the Committee, I do, of course, take full responsibility for everything.' He had spent the previous two days at the hospital trying to locate the missing medallion. He had neither slept properly nor washed and he knew he looked as crumpled and grubby as he felt. 'The question is, where do we go from here? Do we call a temporary halt to the Project while we investigate? Until we can sort out what went wrong and set up a better system for making sure it doesn't happen again?' He paused and looked round at the group, trying to read their faces before continuing with his next questions. 'Is it even possible to travel in time without leaving our footprints and a trail of anachronisms? Should we be taking 1978 technology to places it has no right to be, in the first place? This is what we need to be discussing.'

'Well, as far as I'm concerned,' Julian said quickly, 'I think it would be criminal to stop. Thanks to you, Professor Lewin, and our backers, the Janus Foundation,' he nodded in the direction of Anstruther, the Foundation's observer on the Committee, 'we have the opportunity to do what no-one has ever done before. We can go back to any time and, before long, forwards. I understand that's the plan, anyway. This was our first attempt and although it hasn't, admittedly, been a hundred per cent successful, it wasn't so bad. Da Vinci gets a possibly undeserved reputation – but only we know it was undeserved. No-one really cares. Nothing has changed the course of human history, has it?'

'Not so far, perhaps.' Carew was evidently still smarting from Julian's put-down. 'But what's the boy going to do now? He has, presumably, an indefinite length of time to do further damage. Or can we tell the extent of it from what we already know of Leonardo's work? That's what I want to be sure about.'

'That's a hard one to answer, I'm afraid,' said Lewin. 'If the world changed as a result of young Mark's further actions, would we actually know it had? What would be our point of reference?' He looked towards Anstruther as if expecting an answer.

9

None was forthcoming. John Anstruther was silent as always – merely acknowledging the question with a shrug. Not only did he represent the American charitable foundation which provided the funding for the time travel research, but, without Anstruther's technical input, Lewin would still have been shuffling laboratory animals and artefacts back and forth in time, never further than a couple of months in either direction.

Emmeline raised her head from her doodling. Lewin had noticed before that she tended to doodle at moments of stress – and she did seem quite upset by the reactions to Mark's departure. 'Actually, I think I can reassure you on that score,' she said, 'at least, if reassurance is the right word. Most of the anachronisms in Da Vinci's work can be accounted for by what Mark told us in his debriefing before he left again. Any others will be relatively minor, as far as I can see, and may well stem from seeds of ideas that Mark has already planted. What we can be fairly sure of is that he is reaching the end of his active influence with Leonardo.'

Carew looked at her intently. 'And how exactly do we know that?'

'Well, Philip, I did do some research on it all earlier. I managed to track down consistent references to a muse or a friend – someone mentioned in passing in Leonardo's sodomy trial in 1476. Not the male prostitute at the heart of the charges but somebody else. I also dug up an anonymous poem dedicated to one Marco Londinese. It's not an unreasonable supposition, I'm sure you will agree, that this might be our laddie. References to this friend stop around 1478 and there is no indication that he went with Leonardo to Milan in 1482.'

Silence fell as they all digested the significance of this revelation. Eventually, Lewin broke it. 'Erm…

thank you, Emmeline. That was a fine bit of research – and I suppose good news – in a way. I don't suppose we can have any idea of what might have happened to Mark?'

'No, not really. Cities in those days were constantly subject to plagues and epidemics of one sort or another and, of course, there were footpads galore who would cut your throat for your purse. Plus we know many, many a young man died in a drunken brawl. They were violent days and life expectancies weren't high, especially for those living on the fringes of society. And that's what artists were – men living on the edge, especially homosexual ones.'

'That's sad,' said Professor Danes. 'Poor boy!'

Emmeline nodded. 'I'm glad you see it that way, Joan.'

'Poor boy, nothing!' Philip Carew snorted. 'We're off the hook it seems in spite of his best efforts! And ours, I might add!'

'Can't something be sad, as well as letting us off the hook, as you put it?' Emmeline objected. 'It still begs the question of what we do now, though, doesn't it?' She looked around the room, her gaze lingering on Anstruther for a moment, her expression unreadable.

'Personally, I think a temporary break in our activities is called for – a space to re-group. Agreed, Anstruther?' Lewin was irritated by the man's silence. He knew Anstruther would have enough to say later.

Anstruther nodded. 'Shall we reconvene in six weeks?'

'And, if we go ahead,' said Carew, 'can we at least consider sending someone into my area of expertise? I have a student, Darren Blythe, who would be perfect.' He looked at the others anxiously. 'There is so much we have to learn about the pre-historic periods. We shouldn't just throw everything away because of one bad choice–'

'–and we won't,' Lewin re-assured him. 'We just need to take some time to re-consider our vetting and training procedures. It may be that we also need to work out how to make it harder for the travellers to lose their homing devices, whether deliberately or accidentally. Leave it with us. Six weeks.'

The Committee dispersed. No recordings were made, no minutes taken, but they would all be there.

2

Purple Ochre

Moravia
25,000 BC

The light faded and the air grew perceptibly colder; the old man was undoubtedly hungry, and it was doing nothing for his temper. Darren sympathised. Any spare flesh he himself had once possessed had fallen away within a couple of weeks of his arrival in this remote settlement. Hunger was now a way of life, a way of being. He had been here two months by the moon.

As the sun sank slowly towards the horizon, he sat slouched in the entrance of a deep cave, whittling away at a piece of mammoth tusk with his scraper. His pile of finished spear heads had grown no larger.

The cave was his home and his workplace. Turning up as a stranger, not speaking the language and wearing clothes that, in spite of weeks of research, looked pretty outlandish, he had, he reckoned, been lucky. The debate that had greeted his arrival had been alarming at the time. The people in the huts below didn't seem quite so suspicious now, it was true, but only once had he been invited to join them round their communal fire. He lived up on the hill with Old Hawk, a toothless hag who was presumably the old man's wife, and their daughter, Mouse.

The old man shouted at him again from the back of the cave. 'Hey, you! Look to the fire! And I don't suppose there's any food left.'

13

'No, master. I am sure there will be more when the men get back.'

'Well, just make sure I get some, this time,' muttered Old Hawk. 'You're a lazy good-for-nothing. What did I do wrong to get lumbered like this again? Youngsters! They live for their pricks and for hunting. A herd appears and everything else is forgotten!'

The old man could keep up the string of complaints and criticism indefinitely – but the fire was nearly out and it was true he hadn't eaten all day. If Old Hawk hadn't needed an assistant Darren knew he wouldn't have been taken in at all. He owed him. Times were too hard for the family to take in extra mouths that couldn't bring anything to the pot.

Old Hawk returned to his palette. The little piles of ochre – yellow, red, purple and brown – gradually picked up colour from the firelight. He made a paste of the red. The outline of a herd of mammoths, remembered from his youth, was already taking shape. His eyes were bright as he recalled the excitement and thrill as the men moved in, the smell of blood, the promise of meat. It was a rare event even then, although his grandfather had apparently talked of days when the plains were full of animals and birds, and you could stumble out of bed and your breakfast was waiting for you at the cave entrance. But now...

Old Hawk finally seemed to forget about his belly and the advancing night until darkness had long fallen and the pots of animal fat that he used for extra light spluttered out.

'Boy! Stir yourself and bring me a torch!'

The fire crackled as Darren poked a torch into the flames. He approached within reach of his master's stick cautiously. Then the strong, flickering light was playing over the cave wall. The herd of mammoths tumbled across the rock face trying to flee the charcoaled black spears that rained down on them.

14

His eyes widened.

'Master, will you teach me?'

But Old Hawk, too, was now staring – at the heavy-breasted ivory figurine still clasped in Darren's free hand. He took a deep breath.

'Yes, my son. I will. You are welcome to my hearth.'

It was a couple of nights later that Mouse came and sat by Darren in his allotted place set back from the fire, against the cold cave wall. She leaned into him and he felt her warmth permeate the rabbit skins he was wearing. He looked down into her angular, wind-chapped face and smiled. She responded with a broad grin. He sighed and hoped he hadn't given her the wrong idea. When the time came to sleep he turned his back on her and listened until he heard her go back to her mother's side by the fire.

The pattern was repeated over several nights. In the day, Mouse would sit with him sometimes and talk to him – an opportunity to learn that he could not pass up. He was under strict instructions from Carew to pay special attention to language, its vocabulary and structure. It was an unparalleled opportunity, he could see, to learn about a non-written language, a language in its infancy, and to observe its relationship with the development of thought and understanding. It was certainly an unparalleled opportunity for Carew to get one up on his peers and make his name, he thought somewhat cynically. But at what cost would this be to him, Darren Blythe? In the cold damp of the early hours he sometimes found himself wondering how he had ever agreed to the expedition. He certainly wasn't tempted to get more deeply involved with this family than he had to be.

He had reckoned without the cold, though, the insidious creeping cold that got worse and worse as the days got shorter. One evening, Mouse, who had been sitting beside him at the edge of the circle of light cast by the dying fire, did not leave him when Old Hawk started to snore. Instead she curled around his back and was soon snoring softly herself. He didn't wake her. The warmth gave him the best night's sleep he had had for days. A few nights after that he felt her arm going round him and her hand penetrating his furs and realised he was being seduced. He turned to her, welcoming the release from loneliness as much as the warmth she promised. From that night on, he became an accepted member of the family. Mouse cut meat for him when there was any and gave him the best of the berries and roots she collected on her long forays over the steppe. As time passed, he noticed that her haul was getting sparser and sparser and her absences longer. He began to wonder how the family would survive the winter.

In the following four months, before the subcutaneous transmitter in his arm alerted him to the fact that his stint was nearly up, he settled into the Family's way of life and began to acquire a sense of 'place' and belonging that he had never experienced before. Neighbours climbed up from the huts below and even from the settlement beyond the hill. They came to commission figurines and plaques, either to accompany the dead into the afterlife or to be cherished as talismans. Infertile women, in particular, seemed to believe his voluptuous figurines would help their bellies grow. Amazingly, he would frequently see a woman again a few weeks later when she came up to deposit a rabbit or a fox pelt shyly at the mouth of the cave. This was how the old man earned his keep, he realised, and since Darren's own arrival they had never done so well.

Maybe it was the number of figurines lying around the cave but it didn't take Mouse, herself, long to conceive. One day, not long before he got the tracker message, she came to him and laid his hand on her belly and said 'Baby, there is a baby in here.'

He told himself that, as he seldom saw anything of her but layers of fur, any bodily changes would have been well and truly hidden even if he had known what to look for. Nevertheless, he was shocked and amazed at his own stupid thoughtlessness – what price footprints now? He had no idea if there were any genetic differences between man in the 20th century and his ancestors in 25000 BC – there can't have been much or conception would not have been so easy. Or didn't it work like that? He really didn't know and wasn't sure he would ever be able to find out. He was an anthropologist but, strangely enough, the subject of inter-millennial miscegenation hadn't come up in lectures. He smiled and kissed Mouse's forehead.

'Extra rations for you now, Mouse,' he said in English with a sigh and patted her shoulder, smiling in what he hoped was a reassuring manner. He needed some space to digest the news more fully. He left the cave and walked rapidly to the top of the hill, from which point he could look down over the plain towards the river. It was a lonely and isolated part of the world and would only get worse as winter set in properly. The chances of Mouse coming to full term were probably slight; she would be hungry and tired, working harder and harder to find the dung-fuel and wood for the fire and roots for the pot. Without him, the supply of meat would dry up further. Even if the baby was born it would be unlikely to survive the winter. What had he done?

He realised that there had been a sadness in Mouse's face as well as pride – she didn't expect a successful outcome to this pregnancy, either. Still, it was a child – his child – a part of him; he couldn't just give up on him or her. He wouldn't be here to offer support or comfort to Mouse when the hard time

17

came, as it surely would, but he had to do something. He couldn't stay. It wasn't an option. All he could do was try to make life easier for the Family when he was gone. With this resolve he returned to the cave.

In the next two weeks he carved and chipped all day and most of the night in a frenzy of activity that bemused them all. He barely stopped to eat and at night he lay with Mouse until she slept and rose again to carry on at the back of the cave where the noise would not disturb them. By the time he came to go he was able to leave a substantial pile of tradeable goods in addition to the furs and ornaments he had already been given by grateful neighbours. He had no idea whether there would be any meat for trade when the time came but, if there was...

The night before his departure he slept by Mouse's side all night, holding her close, and rose at dawn. Without eating, and wearing the lightest of furs, he went to the doorway. He became conscious of being watched – and turned. Old Hawk was sitting bolt upright staring at him, a sadness in his eyes. He bowed forward in dignified acknowledgement of the occasion. Darren met his eye and nodded his own head. He held his right hand to his heart as he did so. Where that came from he had no idea but it seemed the right thing to do.

'Thank you, old man,' he said in English. 'You have taught me much.' The old man nodded. He understood. Darren left the silent cave and headed up the hill one last time. He did not look back.

3
Lewin

London
1978

Lewin smiled as he looked round at the four anxious faces around the table. It was a relief to have good news. 'You will be delighted to hear that we have debriefed our Ice Age explorer. The Xerox copies are in front of you but, to summarise, Darren Blythe came home on schedule, having found the transport location successfully via the chip in his arm – and has given no indication of wanting to go back!'

'Good news, indeed, Professor,' replied Joan Danes. 'Not that I understand exactly how a piece of fried potato would have helped him.'

'That's just what we – I call it,' he explained. 'It's the new homing device. We can activate it when we need to and the wearer will feel a tingling to alert him to the fact that he's being called back – and then he can tune it in to our signal to locate the exact spot to leave from. Gives us a chance to confirm arrival point coordinates. And, of course, the traveller can't just jettison the device. We'll always be able to keep tabs on him – or at least until we deactivate the thing here in the lab.'

'And the girl we have in the field now? She has one, too?' asked Joan.

Lewin nodded. 'Emmy Lou Dixon? Yes, of course. It wasn't such a big hop in her case – just a few years really – but I feel a lot happier with her having the chip in place.'

'Fingers crossed, eh?' said Emmeline, without raising her eyes from the elaborate drawing emerging on her notepad. She sighed heavily. 'Can we assume this Moravia trip was footprint free, at least? It is not my period, of course, but it's hard to see how Darren could have done anything too dramatic. Not unless he taught them how to rub two sticks together to make fire. Was he a boy scout?' Lewin got the impression she had wanted to change the subject. He wished he understood women.

'Oh dear, it really *isn't* your period, is it, Emmeline?' Carew seemed in a better frame of mind today. 'I don't think the Ice Ages would have left any survivors if they hadn't already had fire, do you? They had fire, weapons, tools and – it appears – used the long cold nights to develop art of some sophistication. Our man, Blythe, found himself living with an extended family unit who looked after him – an interesting development in itself. It's always been assumed that such units would have been intrinsically hostile to strangers. Not so, it would appear. We have learned something. I was there at the debriefing of this one at the end of December with Lewin, Professor Danes and Anstruther. Where *is* Anstruther?'

'Oh, he was called away somewhere.' Lewin waved his hand vaguely in the direction of the door as if illustrating Anstruther's exit. 'Urgent, I believe. Sent his apologies.'

'Well, I can't say I've ever noticed him contributing much anyway,' observed Weatherspoon. 'We'll survive. Tell us more, though, Philip. What *happened*?'

'No great dramas. Nothing for your next book, I fancy. It seems he turned up at a time when a herd had been sighted at some distance from the home caves and all the able-bodied men were preparing to go after it. That saved him, in a way, because they needed a dogsbody to stay around the camp and he was voted it. In particular, an old chap who earned his keep painting needed an assistant. So that's what Blythe became.'

'Another artist's assistant?' smiled Emmeline.

Carew nodded. 'It seems Blythe's a bit of an artist himself. Sculptor by inclination – but quite an expert on natural dyes and paints now. Planning on a change of career, sadly, since his trip.'

Julian snorted. 'I hope he can keep his mouth shut about his sources of information, then.'

'Well, he had the spiel from Professor Danes before he went, of course, about how he'd get himself locked in the looney bin if he started on that tack. And she repeated it at the de-briefing. He should be sound.' Carew sat back looking smug. Lewin groaned inwardly but Carew carried on, oblivious to the impact of his words on at least two of the Committee members. 'We make sure they all see One Flew Over the Cuckoo's Nest in training. Isn't that right, Professor Danes?'

The Professor shifted in her seat uncomfortably. 'Not my doing, Philip,' she said. 'Not my doing. It really goes against grain to scare people like that. And, I might add, I'm not wild about the expression *looney bin*. It's not one I'd use, myself. We do discuss the possibility of diagnoses of delusional states, though and if they ask about ECT, I can't deny that it would ever be used ...'

'A rather subtle distinction, I'd say,' challenged Emmeline.

'I think we all know the score,' said Weatherspoon. 'But it's worth considering, Philip, is it not, that the work of the Primitive Fauvists of the pre-war era, Henry Moore and so on, bears a marked resemblance to the kind of art work being discovered at that time in prehistoric sites? In Moravia, in particular, I understand? Or don't you think so?'

Carew shrugged. 'So what?'

'So *what?*' Julian sank his head in his hands in mock despair. 'Dear Carew! Listen to yourself! Did we learn nothing from the Da Vinci fiasco? I give up! Or, as some of us said then, do we decide that there's no real harm done?'

'I think we have to,' said Lewin with an air of finality. He wondered if he should have a word with Julian about the way he teased Carew – Philip Carew didn't seem to have much of a sense of humour. 'The decision we have to make now,' he continued, 'is *where to next?* Anstruther is thinking World War I...'

'*Really?*' Emmeline raised her eyebrows. 'Who here thinks that sending someone into a war zone is *remotely* responsible? What kind of idea is that? Would he like someone on the front line?'

'Alright. Alright. We'll discuss and vote,' said Lewin hurriedly. 'Let's get on.'

Roland Lewin sat for a long time after the others had left, lost in thought. The meeting had ended around 2.30, but the January evening was drawing in before he stood up with a sigh and reached for his coat. Committee days were always a write-off as far as his day job went. His day job, his pioneering research into machine diagnostics, magnetic resonance imaging processes and so on, had been what had led to his discovery of time displacement and, even more significantly, the survival potential of living cells throughout the process. He had been warned in no uncertain terms that any attempt to publish would cost him his job but word had got out in certain circles, as evidenced by Anstruther's arrival on the scene, representing the mysterious Janus Foundation.

Not much progress had been made with his MRI research since then but no-one at the hospital appeared to have noticed. He taught and kept up to date with developments and that seemed enough. He had commandeered a room in the basement for his time machine and meetings were held in his top floor office. These rambling old buildings had their uses. The Janus people had offered to fund a lab and offices elsewhere and even to pay him his full salary, but he wasn't ready for that leap yet.

The discussions of the meeting today, seldom completely amicable, had left his head buzzing. It was like being in charge of a particularly stroppy class of teenagers, he sometimes thought. Or being Speaker at Prime Minister's Question Time. He smiled at the analogy. Julian Weatherspoon couldn't resist teasing Carew, who never failed to rise to the bait. Emmeline seemed increasingly on edge and touchy. Joan Danes, his colleague at the hospital, kept her head down in general; her role being primarily to do with candidate selection and de-briefing. In theory, she represented the interests of the youngsters invited to join the programme but it would appear that she was not above compromise if necessary. Was it this that antagonised Emmeline so? Or something else?

They each had their roles. Emmeline was there as the historian of the group, a late arrival to the team, but already proving invaluable, as her contribution today showed. Carew was the anthropologist and Julian's role a bit of a mystery as yet. True, he was a high profile traveller and writer, but he had the most irritating habit of implying that he alone was capable of seeing the necessary bigger picture. Lewin was unconvinced. Larger pictures and lack of concern for individuals had been the justification for atrocities in the not too distant past; he could remember the post-war revelations all too vividly.

Lewin looked at his watch and stood up with a sigh, pressing one hand to his back to ease the stiffness. He

23

must do something about the ancient chairs that he had inherited with the room. He locked up and took the lift down to the main foyer and then, with a nod to the porter, went out into the damp, misty evening. He loved winter in London. People hunched up against the cold as they made their way home to warm fires and hot suppers. As always, he looked across at the Houses of Parliament and felt a stirring of affection for the city of his birth – it must be one of the most glorious urban views in the world and so many Londoners just walked right past without looking. After debating with himself for a moment he turned left. The walk to Vauxhall would clear his head. He cut down towards the river as soon as he could and stood for a moment listening to the lapping of the water in the mist.

It was seven o'clock before he reached the house with the blue door in Festing Road. He let himself in and felt the familiar silence wash over him. The house was the one he had grown up in and the furnishings were his mother's choice, heavy and dark as befitted a middle class family with aspirations to gentility. He always felt he was camping out there somehow or merely the lodger. One day he would get rid of all this stuff and spend a week or so organising new furniture and curtains to his own taste. The only problem with that was that he really didn't know what his taste was. He supposed taste was something that one nurtured and fed from an early age along with a sense of self. He had never had time for such things. First a student and then a junior doctor, determined to do well, work had taken up his whole life – and just when he might have found some space for a personal life, along had come the 'timeshift' discovery and Anstruther. Lewin had never met a woman he had much time for, anyway. They were either obsessed with appearances and salary cheques, in his experience, or they were as single-minded as he was himself and as obsessed with work. Still, the thought of coming home to a house with the lights already on and perhaps the smell of cooking had its appeal.

The meeting had got in the way of his usual substantial lunch and he was starving. He had bread, he had cheese, he had tomatoes – and he had a bottle of Hungarian red. Not bad. He turned on the gas fire and settled himself in front of it. With the new decor he would get central heating and maybe a fitted kitchen with a large freezer big enough for a stock of readymade meals.

'Of such dreams are middle-aged men's lives made,' he murmured. After the second glass of wine he put a Bob Dylan LP on the record player and took his plate out to the kitchen. At his time of life he felt he should be listening to Mahler or something more age-appropriate but Culture had passed him by, too. He returned to his armchair and closed his eyes as Dylan, at his nasal and nostalgic best, sang about a Girl from the North Country. Lewin sighed.

He was woken some time later by the jangle of the telephone. How long it had been ringing he had no idea. He dragged himself out to the cold hall and grabbed the receiver from its cradle on the narrow walnut table.

'Lewin.'

'Good evening, Lewin. Thought you must have gone out. About to hang up. Anstruther here.'

'Good evening, what can I do for you this foggy evening? Weren't you away somewhere?'

'I was. Just got back and thought I'd catch up on how things went at the meeting.'

'Really. Why not leave it till tomorrow? You must be tired tonight.'

'No, I'm fine, thank you. Rather get it over tonight

– that is, are you alone?'

Lewin sighed. Anstruther knew perfectly well he was alone. He felt cornered and irritated.

'I'm going to bed early tonight. It's been a long day.'

'Oh, that's OK, old chap. I can be with you in two ticks and we can keep it short and sweet. See you in a minute.'

Better than his word, Anstruther was knocking at his door in less than a minute. He must have been in the phone box at the end of the road. The confidence and arrogance of the man was astounding. Lewin stared at him resentfully. Anstruther was considerably younger than his host and well-turned out in a pale grey suit with a buttoned waistcoat and checked shirt. A veritable fashion plate of a man, thought Lewin.

'Glass of wine?' he said once his guest was seated, pointing at the nearly empty bottle on the table.

'Er, no. Thanks. I really won't detain you long. How was it? Were they pleased with the report from Blythe?'

'Yes, in general. The usual bickering and questions over footprints, you know. I'm not an art man but it looks as if he may have made his mark, after all. Carew wasn't bothered, though, this time. He was so delighted with the information Blythe brought back. Seems the lad found some quite sophisticated language development that changes something or other.'

'Really. Well I shall look forward to reading their analysis and report. Carew will be mortified he can't publish, of course, but the information will certainly give him an edge if used carefully.'

'I must admit,' said Lewin, 'I'm not sure how much this kind of academic research really benefits human kind. Interesting to do, of course, but, well, in a way it would be more meaningful if we *were* to influence events – but that's a no-no of course.'

'If you think about it, any interaction at all must inevitably have *some* effect on both parties, wouldn't you agree? We learn from other cultures in the present, after all, and don't regard that as so terrible. But I'm sure you're right. There are good reasons for the rules.' Anstruther sounded regretful.

Lewin looked at him, puzzled. As far as he was aware, they were Anstruther's own rules – always had been. What on earth was he saying now?

'Anyway,' continued the younger man blandly, 'what did they think of my idea of a trip to the Great War?'

'Not much, I have to say. The consensus was that sending young men into a war zone was tantamount to murder, to put it bluntly.'

'They don't have to go to the Front, do they? We could learn a lot from placing someone in London or Manchester–'

'–where they'd promptly be conscripted. That or tarred and feathered.'

'I think it was white feathers, but still, if that's how they feel... this is why we have a Committee, after all. But why did they assume it would it have to be a man anyway? We have a woman out in the field now.'

Lewin had no answer. He was somewhat taken aback at the thought of sending a woman to a wartime destination – but why not? They had none of them considered that possibility.

'It's a thought, certainly, but I still don't think there's any point pushing the war idea. The point was also made that that era is pretty well documented as it is. We weren't exactly sure what there's still to learn to justify the level of extra risk.'

'Fair enough; we'll leave that then. Did they come up with any preferences?'

'Weatherspoon came up with pushing on with the travel into the future.'

'You surprise me!'

'Well, yes. He's desperate to get on with it. I didn't comment on the feasibility of it yet. I didn't know what you'd think of the idea. It's a somewhat different ballgame, I feel. In a way, the past is familiar territory or, at least, *more* familiar. We knew which bits of the world in the Ice Ages supported life. We know when and where there might have been major conflicts going on... I don't know.' He rubbed his eyes and sighed. 'Launching someone into the future... I just don't know.'

Anstruther nodded thoughtfully. 'But perhaps we should start working towards it now, if that's what the Committee is thinking. We really would have something to learn from the future, it's true...' He glanced at his watch and stood up. 'Oh, my goodness, look at the time! You must be exhausted.'

Long after Anstruther had gone, Lewin sat back in his chair and went over the conversation in his head. Had he been putting the team's suggestions to Anstruther or was it Anstruther making the suggestions? And what was all that about interaction and influence? Communicating with the man was like walking on shifting sands whilst focussing on a mirage. He finished the bottle and went to bed.

4
Summer of Love

Nevada
1967

Emmy Lou slowed down and brought the Harley to a shuddering halt. The dope probably hadn't been the best of ideas. Neither was setting off on Jed's bike, with no map, little water and no clear idea of where she was heading. The stars were bright overhead. She couldn't remember ever having seen so many.

She shook her head but it didn't help. She blinked hard. Up ahead she could see the faint glow of a building – the tingling in her arm grew more insistent. *Beam me up, Scotty!* The phrase had been doing the rounds in San Francisco that summer. She had actually caught some of the first ever Star Trek episodes. Imagine that! Her cousin Al was a trekky – she could never tell him, of course. Frustrating. He would have been green with envy. Mind you, he was the only person she knew who would actually have believed her. Space travel, time travel – Al was there in spirit already. He would just nod sagely. 'They suppressed the series, you know, took it off the air, once they realised what it was about.' Paranoia was another of his *things*. How long had she been gone for? It seemed like a lifetime but what? Maybe four months? Four mind (and body) shattering months.

She had told them she was up for anything and, surprisingly, her degree in Scottish History had been considered an asset by these people rather than the total dead end everyone else had told her it would be. Not that you applied for a place on the programme exactly; you were sought out, recruited.

She'd met an American guy at the Picnic at Blackbushe Aerodrome in 1978. He'd been a bit older but they had similar tastes in music and they'd got off their heads together. They'd had a laugh and parted company a week later with no plans to meet again; but somehow he must have got hold of her address. She was sure she hadn't given it to him but there he was, a few months later, on her doorstep. He'd persuaded her to go to London for an interview for something 'way out' and that was it. She never saw him again. In fact, she hadn't seen anyone apart from the people involved in the project. It all still went on. Just like Burgess and McLean, she thought, vaguely struggling to remember exactly which was which. If her new friends had only known. She felt a twinge of guilt. It couldn't be called spying, really, could it? It was not as if she had landed up in Washington or NASA – and she hadn't been asked to inform on anybody. In fact she had been expressly forbidden from leaving 'footprints' of any description.

Feeling a bit better, she revved up and set off again – a bit more slowly now. She needed time to digest everything that had happened. It had been the Summer of Love and she had landed up in San Francisco – how jammy could you get? It'd been great – to start with, at least. Music, dancing, cool clothes and everyone stoned. Guys wearing sandals and looking like Jesus – she'd always loved that look. She'd got herself a prescription for the pill as soon as she got there and was away, in her element. Everybody wanted in on the San Francisco hippie scene but she was *there* – right in the thick of it.

There was always somewhere to crash and any food going was shared but before long she'd realised she needed an income and that had presented her with her first dilemma. Jobs were few and far between and tended to disqualify you from being one of the super cool guys: routine and office clothes didn't go with the hippie vibe. It was alright to be a waitress in a macrobiotic cafe or make clothes or jewellery to sell in the street markets, but there were too many people doing that already. Dealing was another source of income for some, but Emmy Lou eventually came to the conclusion that there must also be quite a few generous daddies around, prepared to fund a life style of which they could hardly have approved. She had a feeling that dealing wouldn't go down too well with the Prof and his mates, and her own Daddy was far, far away, thank God.

It was Jed who came up with the idea of turning her sketches of her friends to good account and she had ended up doing street life pictures and portraits-to-order, just as she had seen people doing in Montmartre on a school trip a lifetime ago. Haight Ashbury was already attracting tourists and she found a good market in them. Eat your heart out, Utrillo! Her position as a super chick was cemented. Having a bit of cash didn't detract from her popularity, either, she realised.

All in all, she had had a ball for a while but things had started to go sour towards the end of that summer of 1967 and she was happy when they all moved out from the city centre to try communal existence in the Mendocino countryside. They had even got hold of some chickens.

Why had it all gone sour? What had gone wrong? She was bound to be asked for her opinion when she got back to London. Drugs were central to it, she believed. The weed was nowhere near as strong as the stuff kids used at home but magic mushrooms and LSD were beginning to take their toll. She had steered clear of the real mindbenders herself, mostly, because of not being too sure how she might react. Always a

31

wee bit gabby when stoned, she just had to hope no-one had been paying too much attention to her ramblings as it was. If she had gone off on a real trip, who knows what she might have said or, indeed, experienced.

With the drugs had come the mega-dealers, the ones with the baseball bats and knives. Inevitable, really. Free-loaders had arrived, too, from all over the States. The circle of true believers had closed in on itself and some of the magic was lost. And then there was the sex. The sexual freedom and spontaneity had been fun. No ties, no commitments, which suited her fine, and the added bonus of freedom from fear. Lack of fear of AIDS, in the main. But free love was beginning to look threadbare in places. Some of her friends had, predictably, blossomed and swelled, producing cute little babies that they wrapped in tie-dye and beads and strapped to their bodies like the Indians did. They were expected to just get on with it, these women – it wasn't cool to complain or ask for help. The fathers glowed with pride and walked around with the tiny babies in their slings for a while – and then they would move on, leaving the mothers struggling to support themselves and their babies. Why had these women just accepted that?

Even more alarming was the age of some of the new arrivals. Younger and younger girls were finding their way to Haight Ashbury: thirteen and fourteen year old runaways were arriving at the bus station and being welcomed into the loose groups of people who were now crowding together in what could only be called ghettos. The kids took to dope like ducks to water and it'd become almost fashionable for a guy in his twenties to be seen hanging out with a juvenile hippie-chick. Emmy Lou, with her own memories of being fourteen all too fresh in her mind had tried a couple of times to talk to some of these girls, to tell them to go home, but they'd just look at her blankly through their grass-induced fug and said 'Hey, lady, be cool,' or some such bullshit.

She had learnt pretty quickly that hippie chicks were not expected to rebuff male advances at any age. But you couldn't fancy everyone could you? She had soon acquired a reputation in certain circles for being uptight – but she'd learned to fight her corner in a tough school and the old knee in the groin technique worked as well here as in Glasgow, she found. Becoming a couple with Jed had been a relief, in the end. He was a farm boy from Idaho. He had saved up his money, bought a Harley and headed west. He was a pacifist – a committed opponent of the war in South East Asia – and this was his last fling before embarking on some serious draft dodging. He'd thought of heading up to Vancouver and getting work there but, like many, was increasingly drawn to the thought of going over to Europe and making his way from there to India overland. He could make his money last a couple of years there, he thought.

'This time next year, I'll be in Afghanistan, baby,' he said dreamily one night. 'You coming? It'll be cool!'

She hadn't said goodbye to Jed. She had left the remains of her money in an envelope under his pillow. It would go a long way to replacing the bike but she still felt guilty.

Anyway, here she was drifting across the Mojave into Nevada by starlight. The lyrics of *Woodstock* were going round and round in her head. The guys at the commune had looked a bit confused when she'd first started singing about being starlight and golden and getting back to some garden or other, but were soon joining in. She hadn't been able to remember much more of the lyrics herself but began to suspect that she might have goofed. 'Still, what's a Joni Mitchell song compared to tanks and bicycles in 1400 and something?' she asked the night sky. She had genuinely believed the song would have been around in 1967 and Joni must have been have been hugely relieved when no-one turned up, however unfairly, to claim royalties. No harm done.

But there was that light. She'd arrived – although the set up wasn't at all what she'd been expecting. She'd been told she would find herself being guided to a quiet corner in the sticks where no-one would notice her glowing and vanishing into thin air – but this looked like some kind of military base. A high fence surrounded it, and the light she'd seen was from spotlights on watch towers. There was a barrier across the opening in front of her with a guard house beside it. Behind the barrier, she could see the black shadows of huts, some with lit windows and others in darkness.

Jed and the guys at the commune had been talking one night about somewhere they called Area 51. 'Everyone' knew it was some kind of top secret government place, something to do with UFOs. 'They keep all this shit quiet but there's evidence!' 'A man my sister knows met a guy who worked at this place in New Mexico. They got aliens in labs there, man!' 'Area 51 is where they land, though. People see the lights all the time.'

Could this place be the source of those stories? Area 51 was supposed to be in the Nevada Mojave, after all. Right here somewhere. Her heart started to race in a mixture of fear and anticipation. Wow! That could have some scary implications ... but the chip in her arm was telling her to go on and she didn't have enough gas to get back to civilisation, even if she wanted to.

She had slowed right down again but, taking a deep breath, she now pulled her shoulders back and made for the barrier at a steady pace...

5
Missing

London
1978

'Well, here we are...' said Lewin, striving for a jovial note whilst feeling far from jovial.

'Here we are indeed,' responded Carew drily. 'And where exactly is that? I don't know about the rest of you but as I haven't actually received our last intrepid traveller's report yet, I am asking myself – somewhat nervously – what delights are in store for us today.'

There was a murmur of assent as four of the six people in the room at the top of the hospital exchanged glances and shrugged. They had none of them heard what had happened to the delightfully named Emmy Lou.

'Well, erm...' Lewin looked at Anstruther but got no help there. The bastard just sat with his head lowered, scribbling something on a note pad. Lewin took a deep breath and carried on. 'You are, unfortunately, absolutely right to be concerned, Carew. We've had another glitch.'

'What, you've lost a young girl in San Francisco in the sixties? Quelle surprise!' said Weatherspoon, looking around the room with that irritating, superior smirk of his.

Lewin spoke slowly and deliberately. 'No, you will be glad to hear. In fact we haven't ever actually *lost* anyone, if you care to think about it. And neither did we let this one get access to the machine to go back to

San Francisco, even if she'd wanted to. As you know, it now takes two keys to get into the room and the code book is no longer kept next to the machine. What has happened is that Miss Dixon, having returned safe and sound and to schedule, has gone–'

'–gone? What do you mean by that, exactly, Roland?' Joan Danes was at her most icy – her voice the voice that had sunk a thousand students.

'Let me finish – she was due to come in for the debriefing last Monday. She said she was going to see her family for the weekend – and that was it. She went and we haven't seen her since.'

'You let her go *home* for the weekend – she's bloody Scottish!' Carew was going pink in the face with indignation. 'I sincerely hope you didn't pay her first!'

'No, we didn't pay her. Payment is on completion of the interview process and validation. And we are actually quite concerned that something may have happened to her. It is quite possible, you know, that she might–'

'–yes, precisely, Roland. Be quiet, Carew,' snapped Joan. 'We have to think of all possibilities. Have you contacted her family? Has she been in touch with them? It does seem pretty negligent, you know...'

'I know how it seems, Joan,' sighed Lewin, 'but she wasn't a prisoner – and she had just a couple more hoops to go through before picking up a considerable sum of money. Her parents haven't heard from her. Not even a phone call when she got back. They don't seem to have been particularly close. They showed no interest in what she'd been up to or when they might see her again. To be honest, I'm not at all sure she ever really intended going home.'

'Was there a boyfriend?' asked Weatherspoon. 'Surely she was asked about that sort of thing at her initial interview?' He looked across at Joan.

36

'We certainly did ask, Mr Weatherspoon,' she replied. 'Emmy Lou said she was unattached and we had no reason to doubt her. I felt, as her psychological assessor, if you like, that she was an exceptionally solid and resilient young lady, well able to withstand the demands of the assignment.'

'That's me told! But let's face it – the proof of the pudding and all that! What did *you* think, Emmeline? You were there as the history woman, presumably.'

'Do you know, I didn't actually get to meet her at her initial interview. I know I should've been sitting in but I, rather embarrassingly, had chicken pox at the time.' Emmeline gave a self-conscious little shrug. 'One rather hopes to have outgrown that kind of thing when one reaches a certain age but... there it was. Miss Dixon hadn't had chicken pox, it appeared, and we couldn't take the chance. I *was* looking forward to meeting her at the debriefing, though.' She paused for a moment staring intently first at Lewin and then at Anstruther before sighing: 'We *must* pull out all the stops to track her down, don't you think? If she was destabilised in any way following the expedition we need to be prepared to take some responsibility! She may be wandering around in a highly distressed state or – I don't know – she might have gone under a bus. It's possible that no-one else might be missing her and looking for her. They're encouraged to come up with a good story to cover prolonged absences, after all.'

'Hospitals? Morgues? What do you think, Anstruther?' asked Lewin, worried. 'We do need to take our responsibility towards this young lady further, don't we?' Anstruther had attended the initial interview with Emmy Lou, but was, as ever, showing no inclination to contribute to the discussion now.

Anstruther looked up. 'Me? Oh yes! Responsibility! Quite right, Dr Harrison... I'll look into that myself...'

'*Thank* you, Mr Anstruther. We can safely leave

that with you, then, can we?' said Emmeline.

'Don't you worry Dr Harrison. I will leave no stone unturned,' said Anstruther. 'I have to agree with Professor Danes that the girl did seem a good bet at the time. Still... exposure to drugs... we don't know what may have happened – we may never know.'

Weatherspoon interrupted impatiently. 'OK. We've agreed we have to try to find out – and we finally have a job for you to do, Anstruther. Let's face it, the likelihood is that the girl spent a couple of months stoned out of her mind and developed a taste for it but we are going to check out the alternative possibilities. But it does bring us to the *what next?* bit. What next?'

'Hold on, Julian. Do we learn something from her disappearance?' asked Emmeline. 'Are there any no-go areas? Any environments we should *not* be parachuting people into? Are we still considering a war, for example? Future travel?'

Anstruther answered this time. 'Professor Lewin told me you had all decided against a wartime, didn't you, Professor? At least for a young man. Far too hazardous. A woman might have been a better bet but you did also raise the question of the value of the research in such a well-documented era, anyway, I understand.'

'A woman, Mr Anstruther?' Emmeline looked up at him, eyebrows raised. 'You feel a woman would be a good idea? On the home front? In London perhaps? First hand reporting on the Blitz? Or in a war zone?'

'No. Of course not! Let's leave war zones alone for the time being, Dr Harrison. But I assume you're not eliminating women from future projects totally? On grounds of vulnerability, perhaps?' Anstruther queried with a smile.

'That'd be a statement,' muttered Weatherspoon, almost but not quite under his breath. 'Not but that you mightn't have a point.'

Lewin's heart sank.

'*What?*' Both women spoke in unison and turned to glare at Weatherspoon.

He raised his hands in mock surrender. 'Nothing. Nothing. We can't send them back with Tampax or diaphragms of course but ... far be it from me... let's move on, why don't we? How about my suggestion about future travel, Prof? Have you given that any thought?'

Lewin cleared his throat. 'Well, yes. I have. The technology is there, albeit untested. As I explained at our first meeting, we were able to explore the viability of historic travel to some extent by sending back artefacts to specific locations and checking the locations out in the present. And, as I explained then, we did also send back some living creatures and Dr Carew and Mr Anstruther helped us organise some tests on what survived of them to ascertain condition of health and so on. Not that accurate, of course, but enough to convince us that life could survive a short journey. Blythe, of course, knew this limitation to our research and went into his prehistoric trip eyes open.'

'More than the poor animals who were hobbled did,' commented Emmeline. Lewin liked the woman but she could be exasperating.

'Are you in favour of protecting our volunteers or not, Dr Harrison?' asked Carew. He had been uncharacteristically silent since his initial outburst. 'I'm not at all sure about the future side of things, myself, though. I mean *why?*'

'I'd have thought that was obvious,' said Weatherspoon leaning forward in his chair. 'Because it's there! How can we pass up this opportunity? To see what no-one has seen before? Perhaps to learn something? Where we are going? Man has never had this opportunity before.'

Carew shook his head in apparent disgust. 'And

39

what do we do if they're cocking it all up, eh? Sit here smugly? Maybe even gloating that all our predictions have come true? Is that a goal worth risking lives for? Do we really want to know?'

'Maybe if we did learn about something bad, Carew, we could do something about it... try to change it. If we had known what we know now about Russia, would we have allied ourselves with them so enthusiastically in the last war? If we had known about Thalidomide–'

'–oh, hold on. Hold on a minute,' Carew interrupted. 'Would the outcome of the war have been the same if we hadn't allied with Russia? That would be some footprint. And even the Thalidomide thing has had its impact on drug trials and so on – that's not going to happen if things don't ever go wrong, is it? What would've been the next scandal? The one that didn't happen?

'There may have been few real consequences in present time from our trips to the past,' Carew continued, 'just a few cultural anachronisms, maybe, but the economic and industrial prerequisites weren't there in the 15th century, for example, for anything to come of Da Vinci's borrowed ideas. And if something *was* invented before its time, who's to say what its time was supposed to be? Things get invented. People have cultural exchanges with other people.'

'This is a change of tune for you, Dr Carew, isn't it?' said Emmeline. 'Weren't you always the first to cry *footprints* at the drop of a hat?'

'We do need to drum it into our students to be careful, of course we do. But we haven't always succeeded in the past, have we?' responded Carew. 'I just think the consequences could be so much more severe in the case of forward footprints or whatever you call them, particularly if the results weren't those intended.'

'OK. I think we can take your point, Carew,' said Lewin. 'If I may summarise? Future travel may tempt us to make deliberate changes now, changes whose implications and ramifications we can't necessarily predict. Our track record with our travellers hasn't been a hundred per cent successful in the past, although their footprints may not have been catastrophic to date. That could have been just luck, for all we know.'

'We don't know what impact Emmy Lou might yet have, of course,' said Emmeline.

Weatherspoon shrugged. 'I don't know that anybody has suggested that her coming or going could have made much of a difference to anything. They were all probably too stoned to notice.'

Emmeline looked at him coldly. 'Possibly. So we'll just hope she doesn't decide to reveal all to the newspapers–'

'–something which, according to Professor Danes, wouldn't be believed anyway. Isn't that right, Prof ?' asked Weatherspoon.

Joan Danes nodded stiffly. Some people were 'Profs' and some were not – ever. She was one of the latter.

Emmeline was still glaring at Weatherspoon and looked about to speak again.

Lewin decided to get the conversation back on track – quickly. 'Be that as it may, we do have another potential problem with future travel, apart from a possible urge to make things better. I can think of circumstances where personal gain might be a temptation.' Anstruther had pointed this out to him; it wouldn't have occurred to Lewin on his own.

'We can't just throw away the opportunity because of a couple of slightly flaky choices in the past.' Weatherspoon urged. 'I do have a suggestion, though, if you will just hear me out. Promise not to shout me

41

down...'

Lewin sighed. 'You have the floor, Julian. Go ahead.'

'I know it was made clear right at the outset, when we joined this project that we're here in a supervisory capacity and to lend our professional skills.'

'Your *professional skills*?' snorted Carew.

'Yes. In my case, providing an overview of what might be achieved and to contribute ideas on directions for the project. To bring a larger vision, if you like.'

'I don't.'

'Carew!' snapped Lewin. 'For God's sake, let the man speak. You can interrupt later!'

'Yes, well, I might have put it differently but – thank you, Prof,' nodded Weatherspoon. 'What I'm suggesting is that we send someone we can trust totally – someone who can bring a measure of maturity to the task. I can't help feeling the use of youngsters may have been a weak link in the past – possibly a tad unethical to boot. I know physical fitness is very important – but I'm under fifty and I play tennis and squash. I had a routine medical for my insurance company only last month. I'd be more than happy to undergo any further tests you wanted. Even psych tests. You can try your best to pull me to bits, Professor Danes. If I turn out to be a nutter – well, so be it!'

There was silence for a full minute, broken only by the sound of Emmeline's pencil as she scratched out complex designs and patterns on her notepad, interspersing them with the odd cartoon character. Lewin recognised Bugs Bunny. He had always admired people who could draw.

Eventually, it was Carew who spoke: 'We did discuss this at some length at the time. There were good reasons we decided to stick to youngsters – more controllable for a start.'

'Has that really proved to be the case?' asked Weatherspoon. 'Is anyone controllable? At least I have the maturity to be fully conscious of the issues at stake and, I might add, a position of some substance to come back to, an incentive, if you like...'

'And how long before your adventures start appearing in print, I ask myself?'

Weatherspoon shrugged. 'Ask yourself away, Carew. Or, hey, why not ask me? I admit freely that I'd love to use my experiences – maybe in a futuristic novel. Much as you will no doubt use Blythe's in some roundabout way. Much as Dr Harrison will benefit from what we learned about the Medici court before our Marco went AWOL. But Science Fiction is, well, it's *fiction*. I've written half a dozen of 'em already. They've been bestsellers all over the world and, as far as I'm aware, they've not been taken as science *fact* by anyone. When I'm long gone people may commend me for my prescience but so what? They won't be acting on my speculations *now,* will they?'

'And what if there *is* a message that you feel is really important for people to hear?' asked Emmeline, frowning thoughtfully. 'Would you be able to resist trying to get that over? It would be a temptation.'

'It would, indeed. Maybe a temptation that we might all feel worth indulging. But how about if I guarantee to run anything I write past the Committee before sharing it with the world? You could take a vote on it. Lock it away in a time vault if you don't like it – or burn it ceremonially.'

'I don't think we'd go that far,' smiled Lewin, 'but, I must admit, if we *are* going to do this future travel, it might make more sense to have one of us going – at least for the first time. Just to see what the problems might be...'

'And having, arguably, contributed to the deaths of

one, possibly two, of our three volunteers to date – perhaps it *is* time we took some of the risks ourselves.'

All eyes turned to Emmeline. There was an immediate, indignant response from Carew. Weatherspoon, however, nodded approvingly at her. Anstruther stared at her, his face devoid of expression.

Lewin nodded. 'You and Julian both have points there, Emmeline,' he said. 'My mind is boggling at what you are planning for yourself, or me! But we can leave that for another day. I don't think anyone will be making this compulsory, Carew, so I think you can relax, too. What do you reckon, Anstruther?'

'I'm not sure about the validity of Dr Harrison's argument,' Anstruther replied stiffly, 'but Mr Weatherspoon is probably right in that nothing he says on his return would be believed, anyway. We have no need to *control* him, as Dr Carew puts it.'

'Well, we appear to have a decision, Weatherspoon. Man's first expedition into the future! Congratulations!' Lewin leant forward and shook Weatherspoon's hand. 'We'll have to have the normal physical and psych assessments, of course, and the standard pre-op training drill. And we need to do a bit of research into the whens and wheres of the trip. I'm not even sure how accurate we *can* be in future travel. We have no idea what'll be going on in any given location, so we'll have to build in some flexibility. Give you the ability to *hop* if you end up heading for the centre of an erupting volcano or something. Should be doable, shouldn't it, Anstruther? What do you think?'

Anstruther nodded. 'Yes, good thinking. I'm sure you'll be able to do that Professor Lewin. It'd just be matter of making the chip more accessible, wouldn't it? More like the original one? It's already programmed not to land the wearer in water or solid objects. You'd have to make it re-programmable by the wearer, too, so they don't have to wait for us to call them back here.'

'Yes. Maybe,' said Lewin. 'Leave that with us anyway, Weatherspoon. Any more comments or questions?'

The group was unusually subdued as the participants stood, one by one, thanked Lewin and headed for the door. Weatherspoon was the last to go.

'Really grateful, old chap. I won't let you down, you know,' he said. And then he, too, left.

6
Julian

His eyes stung and his first breath scorched his windpipe, producing a gasping cough and a convulsive pain in his chest. He blinked rapidly and looked around. He could see nothing, nothing at all. It wasn't night time, of that he was sure, but there was an opaque, grey-yellow thickness all around him. He took a step and stumbled on a brick or a rock. He couldn't see. His lungs were bursting. He was unprepared for the blind panic that threatened to overwhelm him. This is what it must be like to drown. He squeezed his eyes together to produce some lubrication: he knew what he had to do, if this was not to be the end. Feeling his chest spasm again, he reached into his clothes for the medallion round his neck and felt for the carved symbols on it. Each one represented a number. He needed to displace himself. He'd always assumed he'd be able to see the medallion if he needed to re-programme it but he couldn't, and must do it by touch alone. He tried to calm himself and steady his shaking hands. The wait seemed interminable and the tingling sensation, when it finally came, coincided with a desperate gulp for air. As a result, he was still spluttering and choking when he arrived at his destination.

He found himself alone, lying on hard, dusty ground

littered with small rocks. He sat up and willed himself to stop coughing; he needed water.

He looked around. The contrast with his previous location could not have been greater; a brown, rolling expanse, broken by occasional scrubby bushes and clumps of dry grass, stretched as far as he could see. In one direction there were low hills in the distance, in all the others more desert. The terrain was criss-crossed with narrow tracks, but what struck him most was the sky. He had never seen such a vast sky, or one so blue. It was the perfect, pure, cloudless azure of a child's painting; the sun was some degrees off its zenith and he sensed it was early afternoon. The air was clear – the clearest and cleanest he had ever experienced. It was like balm to his scalded airways – but he did still need water. Thankfully, it was not hot. If it had been, his chances of survival here would have been minimal as there was no shade to be seen in any direction. This was not Manchester: he knew that for sure. It was even more of an adventure than he had anticipated and a wave of excitement stirred within him. The chains of responsibility and habit fell away. He was free. He laughed out loud – the sound small in the vast silence about him. There was no sign of water or the vegetation that would indicate it, and no sign of habitation. The only thing to do was to pick a direction and walk, using the sun as a compass. He decided to head in the direction of the hills.

As he started walking, he recalled a trip to Egypt in the early sixties, before the dam was built. They had gone up the Nile in a felucca and journeyed for some days into the increasingly arid desert. They had had a jeep then, of course, and crates of soft drinks and containers full of water. He had been fascinated by the desert culture and on his return had planned to write a novel but he'd made the mistake of discussing his ideas with an American writer he met, only to see the fellow get into print first, having purloined all his ideas. He never made that mistake again. He'd kept his ideas close to his chest since then and was extremely wary of other writers. He had been young and naive but, as he eventually admitted to himself, probably not up to the job himself at that point. The American had, arguably, done the world a favour.

His own success had come easily enough when the time was right. Book after book seemed to hit the mood of the moment, whether a spy novel, a travel book or a futuristic fantasy. His agent and publisher loved him and the money flowed in. With that came the penthouse flat, the stunning girlfriends, the Aston Martin and, ultimately, frustration. There had to be something else, something more. When offered the chance to get involved with the Time project he had leapt at the opportunity – only to find his frustration increasing as he watched others having the adventures he wanted for himself.

Distance here was deceptive. He reached the hills sooner than he thought and quickly lost sight of the plain behind him. He started to follow the tracks in the sand, thinking they might lead to a larger trail and to – somewhere. After a while he began to suspect he was going round in circles, a suspicion borne out by the angle of the sun. He decided to abandon the paths, which were probably just goat tracks, and head for the highest point he could see. On cresting the first rise he saw another hill ahead of him, a slightly higher one with what looked like a cairn of pebbles on top.

Something bright and blue fluttered in the stones. He ran down the slope and up the other side, finishing with an awkward scramble over the last scree. It was indeed a man-made cairn. In and around it were tiny scraps of loose woven blue cloth and leather. There was something familiar about it and it took him a moment to place the memory: McLeod Ganj. He had once had the opportunity to meet the Dalai Lama, in the mountainous part of India where the Tibetans had settled. Flags had fluttered in trees – prayers to be carried by the wind. But he knew this was most definitely not the Himalayas. He circled the cairn following a well-trodden path and crossed to the far edge of the hill. Another huge expanse of scrubby desert lay ahead of him. Here, at last, he saw signs of life; he could see a herd of large animals in the distance, some lying down and some moving. Beyond them a bright white structure nestled in a sheltered corner. His thirst was extreme now but where there were herds there would be farmers and where there were man-made structures there would be people – and where there were people there would be water.

He set off down the hill. His progress developed a dream-like quality as he wandered through a landscape without focus or perspective. How long it was before he reached the herd he had no idea but the sun was significantly lower in the sky. The animals were camels – not the kind he had got to know, only too painfully, on his Egyptian trip but the smaller, two-humped variety of central Asia. He tried to remember which sort Australia had but couldn't. The camels' coats were ragged and patchy which led him to deduce that it must be spring-time wherever he was now. He would know more once he saw the human inhabitants of the region.

He didn't have long to wait. A dust ball in the distance, from the direction of the white structure, materialised into a horse and rider hurtling towards him at breakneck speed. He stopped in his tracks and raised his hands above his head. Why, he wasn't sure. To show he had no weapons? The horse and rider skidded past him and turned in a tight circle to face him once again. It was a young boy of about fourteen carrying a bow and arrow in one hand, his long, black

49

hair streaming behind him as he turned; he was wearing a brown coat of some woollen material and boots of felt. His face was round and flat-nosed – not quite Chinese but not European either. The boy had his lips pulled back in a snarl as he fitted the arrow onto the bowstring.

'Please, please,' said Julian quickly and, grasping at words in every language he knew, 'I'm a friend, amigo, drug, pengyou.'

Something appeared to work – either the Chinese or the Russian, he guessed.

The boy lowered the bow. 'Oros?' he asked pointing at Julian.

That was Russian. 'English... Angliski,' tried Julian.

'Ah, Angliski.' The boy nodded sagely and wheeled his horse about, racing back the way he had come.

Julian sat down and thought. Central Asia, desert, two-humped camels – could only be the Gobi. Russian language? This must be Mongolia, Outer Mongolia. Hard-line communists nowadays – but was it nowadays? It wasn't enough to know *where*. Not in the future, but not in the Stone Age either, he guessed. Was he going to meet Genghis Khan? A great opportunity for a writer – but possibly not one he would survive to exploit. He remembered the cairn. Where did that fit in? Was Ghengis Khan a Buddhist? He relaxed. Speculation was pointless, so he sat and waited.

A second, larger dust cloud turned out to be a group of three men and the same young boy. They had brought a spare horse on a rope. That was promising, he thought, as he stood to greet them. He nodded his head and repeated, pointing at his chest, 'Drug... Angliski ... Hi ... Hello ...'

The leader of the four grinned at him and turned to repeat his words to the others – evidently finding his halting speech entertaining – before indicating that he

50

get on the spare horse. He did so with some trepidation but the ride to the yurt, which he now saw was what the white structure was, was slow and the horse relatively calm. There were a few jokes at his expense, but he didn't disgrace himself by falling off.

The yurt he'd seen in the distance turned out to be one of two, squat and low against the hillside. The low, wooden door of the large one was red and painted with an elaborate design; the other, smaller, tent had a plain door with no embellishments. It was into this second one that he was ushered. Even at this time of day, there was a surprising amount of light spilling down from the hole in the apex. Around the walls was a wooden lattice upon which were suspended cooking implements, clothes and an assortment of rags and towels. Crouching by a large shallow pot on a stove in the centre was a young woman stirring a brown concoction with a large lump of fat in it.

'Chai,' said the man who had led the way. He gestured to his own mouth and then to Julian's in an obvious invitation.

'Yes, yes, please! Da!' Julian nodded enthusiastically. The woman fetched a metal bowl which she filled with the soupy mixture from a scoop. He drank it quickly and the refill which followed. Finally she brought him a glass of water. He hesitated for a fraction of a moment and then took that, too. It was sweet and cold.

Two children entered the yurt and came forward shyly. The older one pointed at herself and then the little one and said 'Engke ... Turuu.'

It seemed less and less likely that he was about to be skewered by a Mongol arrow or handed over to the secret police. It had occurred to him rather belatedly that, if he was indeed in contemporary Mongolia, it may have been unwise to declare himself as English.

Engke and her little brother crowded close now,

51

touching his clothes and grinning. The adults, including their mother, had disappeared outside. There was a lot of bleating and shouting going on. If only he could ask the children exactly *where* and *when* they were. Surely, if it was modern times there would be some signs of the 20th century. Or were there really still people living like this now without any obvious 20th century amenities? If not, how long back would he have had to go to find them? His own ignorance frustrated him.

Before long, Temulun, as the woman was called, came back and started preparing the evening meal. At a word from their mother the children took him out and showed him the hole in the ground that was the toilet and the pile of dried dung that was the fuel for the stove. He helped them gather up the dung and took it back inside. The fenced areas around the camp were now full of long-haired goats.

After their meal of stew and pasta, they all moved over into the larger yurt and sat on iron bedsteads around the walls. One of the younger men produced a square-shaped guitar and began to strum. The older man passed round a small cup containing a clear fiery liquid. As the light faded, tallow candles were lit and the singing and drinking continued. Julian felt warm and drowsy. The hangings and religious pictures lining the tent lost their tawdriness in the candle light. That night he slept on the floor near the fire, wrapped in a felt blanket, and felt more content than he had for a long time: a contentment which would be challenged all too soon.

When he awoke in the morning, it was to find himself alone. He got up and wandered around looking more closely at the pictures and artefacts. The first thing he registered was that the bits of writing on the hangings were not in Chinese script or Cyrillic but in a script totally unfamiliar to him. The next thing he noticed was that the pictures were printed and some were behind glass. There was a shrine facing the door with small ornaments, some of brass and some ceramic. Everything looked old and worn. The beds themselves were iron: the significance of this had escaped him in his exhausted, alcoholic befuddlement the previous night but he felt he was beginning to answer some of his own questions now. He was definitely in Mongolia and 20th century Mongolia at that. These people were living the life their ancestors must have lived for centuries; a few traded and handed down items and everything else from their animals. Right up Carew's street, he thought. The thought of Carew and St Jude's had a dream like quality to it already.

Over the next few days life settled into a routine of eating, sleeping and helping with the goats and camels. They all needed milking in the morning before they were let loose and then rounding up in the evening and brought back to be milked again and locked away behind the wooden fences. The newest offspring occasionally need reuniting with their dams and that was a challenge in itself. Being a man, Julian was exempt from the milking – the one attempt he'd made reducing everyone to hysterical laughter. He was soon trusted with a horse to ride, though, and joined the men as they trotted around the countryside checking on the herds and making sure that the females were looking after their young. In the afternoons he wandered off with the children naming animals and objects in Mongolian and, in turn, teaching them the English words.

It was on one such foray that he received the next jolt to his perception of reality. He had asked where the water came from. It was obviously a precious commodity and there was no sign of a well. Engke and Turuu took him by the hand and dragged him off on a much longer walk than usual, along a dried riverbed, gradually climbing.

Finally they looked down over another plain as bleak as the one in which he had first arrived. In the middle distance he could see a metal structure standing alone amongst rocks. Twenty minutes or so later he arrived at an old, rusted winch over a well. The children had brought leather buckets and bottles and he was set to work operating the winch. Up close he could see that many of the 'rocks' were in fact lumps of concrete and he could recognise the remains of buildings. When the containers were full, he wandered around fascinated while the children chattered. There was a school, a clinic and a market, they told him; the words were similar to the English ones. They said the place was called Bayan. What had happened to it? Why had it been abandoned? He couldn't ask and they couldn't answer. In one place concrete lumps had been piled up to make a high wall and the children pulled him over to look behind it. There, in a pile, were half a dozen large rectangular frames about a three foot high and six foot long; beside them lay bundles of metal rods that looked liked supports. The frames were made of white, hard plastic and some contained multilayered, opaque panels: they looked for all the world like the solar energy collectors that were used in space programmes and exhibited around the world. Expensive stuff, if that's what they were. Why on earth would they have been dumped in the middle of the Gobi desert? He was thoughtful and abstracted on the way home.

That evening, when they went to the larger yurt (or ger, as the family called it) he scratched out a picture of the panels on a piece of sandstone and showed it to the grownups gathered round the fire. Altan, the eldest of the men, chuckled and pointed up to the roof. He mimed rain or rays falling down. Seeing the

54

puzzled expression on Julian's face he then got up, went over to one of the beds and pulled out a large box from under it. He beckoned Julian over. In the box was a battery, not an enormous car battery, but definitely a battery. Beside it lay two long tubes that looked like lights. He then pulled out a slim leather-bound notebook. Inside, instead of pages, was a flat black screen: no buttons, no obvious function. Julian picked up the screen and turned it over curiously. After much scuffling under one of the other the beds, Temulun produced another box of precious objects, all wrapped in felt; more of the screens of varying sizes and small cards made of plastic. Bank cards, he realised with a jolt. But bank cards with a difference – each had a small hologram picture on it of the kind you could find on key rings and novelty jewellery. Temulun stroked everything reverently before replacing it in its wrapping and, finally, producing what she had been looking for. It was a booklet, the first paper item Julian had seen, and on it was a picture of one of the screens. He opened the booklet carefully and looked through it until he found the section in English. The smallest screen was a telephone – a tiny flat telephone with no wires. He looked up to find everyone grinning at him.

Altan shrugged and waved his arms in the air 'Pwoof! Finish!' he said.

Temulun joined in the mime, putting her hands over her face and coughing and spluttering. The others all cheered and clapped; the music and chat began again, leaving Julian to pore over the instruction manual. By the time he found the publication date, 2080, he was already facing up to the fact that he might, actually, be in the future as originally planned. What had happened to the world in a mere century?

These people had had access to advanced

technology or at least technology more advanced than he was used to in 1978, but here they were living as herding families, carrying their water from a well a good mile away and cooking on dung stoves! Was the *Phwoom!* an explosion or a bomb? What had caused the choking Temulun had described? Could it be the same fog as the one he had experienced in Manchester? If, indeed, it had been Manchester.

It was a week later that Julian awoke to find the gers bustling with activity. Bedrolls were being packed up, harnesses checked and bottles filled with water. In the small ger Temulun was stuffing and cooking pasta dumplings and apportioning lumps of hard cheese between the men of the family. Each had a ration of dried meat. To his surprise, he found that he too was being included in the share out. Engke and Turuu were complaining bitterly and vociferously and he smiled at them in sympathy. What child would want to be left behind? The final items to be packed came from another of the under-bed boxes and consisted of rectangles of fine felt fabric and twine. Filters.

An hour later the camels were loaded, the horses saddled and they were off. There were the five of them and another three men he hadn't seen before. The journey took a full week. The nights were cold once the small fires they lit had died down, but in the day the sun beat down relentlessly. One day the wind, always present, began to build up and a distant cloud of dust on the horizon came whirling and spiralling towards them. The sandstorm was like flying razors and they quickly hunkered down in a small depression and covered themselves with their bedding. The animals, with their eyes protected by the felt blindfolds, seemed content to stand with their backs to the onslaught. The next day it was as if nothing had happened and they carried on with their journey.

Towards the end of the fourth day Altan pointed

out hills on the horizon, taller than any Julian had yet seen. That day they stopped by a well and replenished their now-empty bottles. It was fortunate that somebody knew their way around this seemingly featureless desert.

Gradually the air lost its clarity and they found themselves travelling into a haze that thickened as the days progressed. They lost sight of the hills ahead. They wrapped their faces in the felt and accustomed themselves to breathing through it. At night they camped with no moon or stars to brighten the sky. Julian found himself thinking of Frodo's journey and was therefore prepared for the Mordor that greeted them when they finally rode through a gap in the hills and saw the remains of the city beyond. Through the dark smog he could see ragged buildings towering over their heads. They joined a surfaced road several lanes wide, keeping close to one another, the men constantly looking about them. Sometimes Julian thought he saw shadows of movement in the soot-blackened buildings on either side. They would not be alone here, of course. He noticed that the men had drawn their bows and arrows. The incongruity of it made him shake his head.

The purpose of the trip was, it appeared, to salvage metal and wood from the buildings – and anything else that looked as if it might be useful. They passed shop fronts where he saw more of the large flat screens, some of them evidently televisions; washing machines, dishwashers and tiny electronic ovens – luxuries in London still – were being pulled apart by men carrying bows and arrows.

Over the following week, the party made several trips into the city to load up the camels, harnessing some to drag the larger lengths of wood. When Julian asked his well-practised question *Why?* he got the doubled-up coughing response. Finally, they ventured into a big store which had been taken over as a market. Shrouded men and women sat in the gloom behind piles of crockery and cooking items and Altan produced dried meat and cheese to trade.

On their last day, leaving the others to guard what could only be called the loot, Altan took Julian to the outskirts of the city. There stood an enormous, squat, windowless building. They rode up close to it until they could clearly see a long vertical crack in the wall. Altan got down and drew a circle in the dust with a smaller circle in the middle, then a similar circle with an inner one cleft by a lightning bolt. *Phwoom!*

Nuclear fission? A nuclear power station, of course! Why, then, the sooty, choking fog? What had happened?

As if in answer to his thoughts Altan repeated the *Phwoom!* and mimed digging into the ground, hauling up a heavy sack and lighting a fire. Then, to Julian's puzzlement, he kicked his horse forward moving his hands as if on a steering wheel. Turning he waved his hands as if brushing away a fart and then, of course, nearly fell off his horse laughing as he realised what he had done. *Coal for heating and exhaust fumes,* thought Julian.

The journey home, fully laden, took even longer and they were tired, dirty and hungry when they finally got back to the gers – to a riotous welcome. It was like Christmas as the loot was unwrapped and inspected. Julian had found a small corner of a mirror in one of the deserted houses and had managed to extract some ball-bearings from a tumble drier. These were greeted by Engke and Turuu in much the same way as his own niece and nephew would have welcomed the gift of horses and bows and arrows. He knew his time here must be drawing to a close and he was saddened by the prospect. Thinking of London, and his family, depressed him beyond measure. Not to mention the thought of nuclear power stations and nuclear bombs. He'd never been one for demonstrations, regarding them mainly as hindrances to traffic, but maybe the demonstrators had a point. There was much to think about, much to report. He wished he knew how much of the world had been affected. Europe and Central Asia, evidently, but what about the USA? Canada? South America or Australia? Was everyone in the same boat or had the affected people migrated safely to these other countries? Surely, they could not all be living like the herders of the Gobi! Altan and his family may have been the lucky ones – they had had a memory, a tradition that had survived and provided a life that they could fall back into as if the previous centuries had not existed. At least Engke and Turuu would have a good future here. Julian wished he could say as much for children in other parts of the world. It didn't look very promising so far.

He knew he had to get back to London as a matter of some urgency but he realised as he looked at the family around him that he was not looking forward to it. The children, in particular, had taken him into their hearts and found their way into his. Still, if he could do little for this family now he must at least go home and help the people he could.

7
Reactions

London
1979

In the normal way debriefing was done by Lewin, Anstruther and just one of the others, but on this occasion everyone turned up in the office in St Jude's promptly at 11 a.m. It was a cold Monday in early February, the day after Weatherspoon got back to London.

'Dear me! The biscuits will have to be rationed.' Lewin looked around the room, checking that everyone had finally got a chair.

'It might be warmer, at any rate, with more of us,' grumbled Carew. 'It's bitter out there and this room is draughty as hell. Can't you do something about it? Get somewhere better?'

'But this is ideal!' Lewin protested. 'No-one notices what I do or what meetings I have up here... and no-one else is after the room for themselves, for the very reasons you mention. I agree, though, that the heater isn't man enough for the job in weather like this. I'll put the kettle on, that might help.'

'What's with all the demonstrators and yelling outside?' asked Julian. 'I felt I was taking my life in my hands. No-one recognised me, fortunately, and I told the policeman by the door I was an electrician come to repair something.'

'Oh yes... you've been out of the loop, as they say, haven't you?' said Lewin. 'Strikes everywhere for months. We've had to cut down on our non-urgent admissions and cross our fingers that no-one dies of some rat-borne infection. It's all those little people we so rely on (and generally ignore) who are refusing to play ball with the government, and they're making themselves felt. The mice that roared.'

'Well, it'll be the end of the Labour government anyway. Then they'll have something to complain about.' Carew seemed to view this outcome with some satisfaction. 'Welcome to 1979, Weatherspoon! How was the trip?'

'Perhaps if you just give us all an overview and answer some questions we can have a formal report later?' suggested Lewin. 'I must say, I would hardly have recognised you. Lost weight?'

'Yes I have – a bit of clothes shopping coming up this week. But, well, what to say? Where to begin?' Julian took a deep breath before launching into his account. 'The first thing is that I didn't end up where I was supposed to be. I was meant to go to an urban area away from London a hundred years hence, if you remember. Far enough ahead to learn something and not meet myself, but not so far that Armageddon would have come and gone and we would all have antennae.'

Lewin nodded. 'A slight simplification of the decision making process but yes, more or less that. We set Julian up with the option to re-programme,' he explained to the others, 'because we couldn't know exactly what hazards there might be. I believe you did have to do a last minute dodge, didn't you?'

'I did indeed, quite a dodge! A leap into the dark would be more accurate. I arrived originally at what was supposed to be somewhere in the region of Manchester and probably was Manchester, in fact. But it wasn't Manchester or even Britain as we know it.' He had their attention. 'It was dark and the air was so

61

thick... I took one breath on landing and that was it. I had to get out before I could let myself take another. I jumped blindly because I couldn't see my hand in front of my face, let alone the detail on the medallion. I believe I kept the time dimension but I travelled to the other side of the world.'

'That's ridiculous,' interrupted Carew. 'That can't have been Manchester, what on earth made you think it was?'

'I didn't think it was Manchester, either, to start with. I thought the machine had made a mistake. Neither did I believe I was in the same *time* when I got to ... to where I ended up. I'm giving you my ultimate conclusions first. Listen.'

Slowly and carefully, Julian went through his arrival in the desert under that incredible blue, blue sky, his initial fears and assumptions and his gradual realisation that he had, in fact arrived in 2080. He rounded off his story with an account of his visit to the abandoned skyscraper city. The silence that greeted the end of his tale lasted for a full minute.

'That's some story, Julian,' said Emmeline eventually. 'How are you? How are you now?'

'I'm OK,' he answered. 'I made friends who looked after me. I saw, I believe, where we're heading. That's the main thing. I know we discussed this before I left and there was a good case for leaving the future alone, but we can't! If I'm right, this is not a future we can bequeath to our children. We have really got to be looking at all this nuclear power stuff.'

'Didn't know any of us had any children,' said Carew with a sniff. 'You've drawn an awful lot of conclusions from flimsy evidence, I'd say. Was it a bomb? A power station failure? Or just plain old smog? If it was the smog we need more nuclear power stations. If it was power stations, we need better ones but, anyway, if it *was* the power stations, it wouldn't necessarily affect the whole world or even a whole country at the same time. If it was a war it might but then we need to avoid having a war, which is what we try to do anyway. The Bomb's our best way of protecting ourselves from that one. In short, if you're heading where I suspect you are, think on this: if we all start going Luddite over nuclear energy, we're more likely to bring on either the war scenario or the pollution one. If we start jumping up and down about all that now, aren't we likely to actually *bring on* whatever it is you think you saw?'

'Carew may have a point there, Julian,' broke in Lewin. 'If, as you suspect, power stations failed at more or less the same time as far apart as Mongolia and Manchester, wouldn't that be a bit odd? Each country would presumably have built its own to the best design they could come up with and even if one country cut corners or failed to maintain them properly, not *all* of them would fail at the same time, surely?'

Julian had evidently given this some thought. 'I take that point but I saw what I saw. The damage was localised, in Mongolia at least. No obvious signs of widespread destruction like we saw in Japan after the war. The thing hadn't blown up, true, but I *saw* the crack. Do they actually blow up or just leak?'

'There have been quite a few leaks,' said Lewin, 'mostly in the Soviet bloc. Probably more than we've ever found out about. There've also been plenty in experimental plants in the US and Canada. Our own Chapel Cross in Scotland was another but, fortunately, no harm done. No explosions as such.'

'Might they have closed the reactors because of cracks and leaks and then had to go back to coal and oil and so on? That would account for the smog. If the reactors were built around the same time, maybe by the same international companies, mightn't they have failed at around the same time? Wouldn't that make sense?'

'London is a hell of a sight better since the Smoke Control Act.' Emmeline was looking thoughtful. 'Don't you think that kind of legislation would have been extended everywhere by 2080?'

'Maybe, but what if we didn't bother because we thought we didn't need that kind of fuel any more anyway? And the new alternatives failed? And what about the cars? I tell you, when I was walking here this morning through the traffic jam on the bridge, the air was barely breathable especially after the clear atmosphere I've been used to. We'd have had to find some way of controlling traffic fumes, too, and, if we were all driving nuclear-powered or electric cars – why would we have bothered?'

'It's a theory, I suppose.' Lewin wasn't convinced. 'But if we assume that we get over-reliant on nuclear power and go back to having smogs when it fails, it still all seems a bit – *cataclysmic*. Like a catastrophe hitting overnight when, surely, we would've had some time to prepare either by sorting out alternative cleaner fuels or by protecting ourselves some other way. The abandonment of cities takes generations, however bad they are.'

'We *have* generations, or at least a couple. And what if the failure of the power stations was a targeted act of aggression? We don't know what technology there will be in a hundred years to sabotage these places from within, even assuming they were not somehow built to fail.'

'Well, I think this is all a bit paranoid, Weatherspoon.' Carew slapped his palm on the table with the air of one bringing the discussion to a conclusion. 'We none of us can be sure you saw what you think you saw or that you've interpreted it correctly. If you provide these *theories* as weapons for

64

the anti-nuclear mob, then you, yourself, might be the one responsible for whatever happens. Keep plugging away for clean air if you must but I think you'll find that the nuclear scientists are your best bet. I certainly won't be endorsing any action on this.'

'Why does that not surprise me?' Weatherspoon sighed.

'Don't be so touchy, Julian,' said Emmeline. 'It seems a valid point of view. I think we'd all benefit from reading your report in full, though. For myself, I must admit I'm more nervous about creating these footprints into the future than I was about the other way round. The implications seem, potentially, so much more drastic.' She closed her notebook decisively and put it in her handbag. 'Is there anything else for now? I have to get home to Canterbury this evening and heaven knows what the trains will be doing. How they manage in places like Russia and Canada I can't imagine. Or Mongolia.' She smiled at Julian.

'I wasn't there for the winter, happily, but I expect camels will be the order of the day. That and not trying to go anywhere.'

The group disbanded and each member made his or her way home through the rush hour, each huddled and swathed against the cold and all too aware of the stench of traffic fumes.

It took Emmeline four hours to get home to her attic flat in Canterbury. She and her cat, Whimsey, had lived in the old, ramshackle house on the Whitstable Road ever since she had got her current job at the University of Kent. It was dark and shabbily furnished. It would take at least an hour to get rid of the damp chill that greeted her but she sighed with relief as she kicked off her shoes and shoved her feet into her slippers by the door. What first? A cup of tea?

She went into the kitchen and retrieved a bottle of red wine from the cupboard. Next stop was the stereo in the sitting room. Before long the sonorous notes of Mozart's Requiem were filling the room and she felt the tensions of the journey and of the meeting slip away.

She was just dropping off to sleep in the chair when there was a knock at the door. It was Jim Hexham from the bottom flat – a policeman, if she remembered rightly. He was holding a protesting Whimsey under one arm and a large cardboard box under the other.

'I found the cat on the landing,' said Constable Hexham. 'And I've got some papers and stuff here that you might be interested in. There's a bit of a strange story as to how I came by them, if you have a few minutes ...'

8
Sand Martins

Kent
1979

Derek Pratt worked in Accounts at a large department store. It was the first day of his annual holidays. His neighbour, Mrs Carter (a curtain twitcher if ever Constable Hexham had seen one) had heard the alarm go off at 7.30 am. Derek had evidently got up and made himself a cup of tea and a plate of eggs and bacon. By nine o'clock the bed was made, breakfast washed up and the dishes stacked neatly on the draining board. Mrs Carter had seen him leave the house all kitted out with a knapsack and heavy duty binoculars.

The trip to see the nesting sand martins in the cliffs at Reculver was what he always did on the first day of his annual holidays, it seemed. The heavy rain of the previous week had been a bit of a worry, he told Mrs Carter, but that morning had had all the fresh-washed brightness of a perfect summer day in the making.

His car had started first time in spite of not having been used for a month or more – he had always said there was nothing like a Japanese car for reliability and his little blue Civic had served him well for many a year. This, Constable Hexham told Emmeline, was to be the best part of Derek's day.

He had parked his car by the pub and walked down to the sea. The tide was high but had turned so he had set off along the narrow, boulder-strewn stretch of exposed beach to where he could see the pocked-marked cliff looming above him, each little dark hole home to a family of immigrants from the African Sahel, possibly (he liked to tell Mrs Carter) all the way from Timbuktu!

He must have been so absorbed in his study that he failed to hear the panicked shouts from above and by the time he'd realised that the cliff face was crumbling and moving towards him, he had left it too late. He had started to run towards the waves, slipping and sliding on the treacherous rocks and almost made it to the water. But it was not to be the stones or the mudslide that killed him, anyway, but the carved marble chest that hurtled down from the cliff with them.

Karen Gillespie and her friend Cindy had only just managed to rescue little Jason from the cliff edge in time. It was his shout of 'Hey there's a man down there, Mum!' that had alerted them to just how close to the edge he'd got. He was, in fact, lying on his tummy hanging over the rim of the cliff. 'And there's all birds down there. Come'n look, Mum!'

Karen had shrieked and dashed forward grabbing him by his heels, while Cindy stood open mouthed. 'Cindy never did have the sense she was born with – how she expects to bring up a live child is a mystery,' Karen had told the Constable. As the women dragged Jason back to the path they saw the ground cracking around them, there was a sound like the rumbling of thunder and they ran across the field as fast as they could, screaming and yelling all the way.

'What the hell did you think you were doing?' Cindy had demanded from Jason when she got her breath back.

'It was the man!' shouted Jason indignantly 'He was down there spying on us with binoculars!'

Cindy and Karen had looked at each other, aghast.

'Are you sure, Jason?' asked Karen. 'This is really, really important, love! You're sure there was a man down there?'

'Course,' he had responded sullenly. 'That's why I was looking, wasn't it?'

'We better get the coastguard, the police – I don't know – both!' Karen was tightening her shoe laces as she spoke. 'You wait here!' She shot off down the hill back towards the pub at the bottom of the hill. It had never seemed so far. The landlord and pot-boy were out at the front when she eventually got there, with a woman who looked like she might be the cleaner. They were comparing notes about previous landslides and reiterating again and again exactly what they had been doing when they'd heard the noise. A couple of youths were heading for the beach to get a better look.

'There's a man, there's a man,' she had spluttered. 'Jason saw him ... call the police, the coastguard ... it must have got him!'

The landlord ran indoors, leaving her on the outside bench seat in tears.

By the time Constable Hexham had got to the scene of the landslide a small crowd had gathered on the beach. From the caravan park, he guessed. The coastguards, led by his old friend Geoff Welch, had got there just before him and were standing back watching a man who had declared himself a first aider. He was standing over the muddied broken remains of Derek Pratt telling everyone to 'Stand clear, ladies and gentlemen, *please!*'

'What a wally!' muttered Geoff Welch 'There's always one. The poor chap is as dead as a door nail. Look at the side of his head? Right mess – don't need to be a brain surgeon to know what happened to him. You break it to that prat, Jim.'

The constable took control. 'Move along, move along! This is an accident scene and you're none of you helping. You, too, sir. I suggest you all go back to the pub and give your names and addresses and phone numbers to the landlord. If you saw anything you can wait for me to finish here and give me a statement or just go home and we'll be in touch.' The Dixon of Dock Green approach had seemed to work and the group drifted away. Hexham had got out his notebook and looked around. The beach was waist high in mud by the cliffs and the mud extended down towards the still-retreating sea.

'How long have we got before all this is covered again?' he had asked Geoff.

'It'll be on the turn around four. We need to get him away well before that and the area checked. Shall me and the lads take him up to the top?'

'Right. Thanks. Just let me check his pockets first and log it all in my book. Was anyone down here when you arrived?'

'Yep, a couple of lads. They were up in the pub. Said they work there but more likely a bit of before-hours boozing. We had a look to see if there was anyone else here but who knows who's under that lot! The witness, the little boy whose mum called us, says no. I told his ma and her friend to wait for you.'

'Thanks, mate. Let's have you and your men spread out that way when you get back, and I'll go along towards the slipway and well, we just look for anything we can see. Should get some extra manpower from the Bay soon.'

Constable Hexham had quickly ascertained the victim's name and address, that he was a birdwatcher, had a car and that he still had five pounds in his wallet.

The search through the mud had been a hot and exhausting business. They found a pair of binoculars, a boot that must have been wrenched off in Derek Pratt's final fall and a cap, some distance away. What

Hexham could not find was the rock or boulder that had done for poor old Derek. There must have been blood, hair and brains on it and it couldn't have gone far, but even after enlisting Geoff's help to turn over all the rocks in a two yard radius he could find no sign of it. This would all have to go in the book. It was only on walking over to the other side of the groins extending down from the slipway that he had seen the tell-tale signs of a heavy object having been dragged across the sand and mud. He had cursed roundly. Whatever it was had gone. It must have been removed while they were all concentrating on the beach around the body, or before they had even got there. As he turned back, his eye was caught by some pieces of wood; driftwood, he thought at first, and caught under them several rolls of some fabric. Closer inspection had shown that the wood had writing on it and the fabric, also with writing on it, was fine leather – not the kind of thing that normally got washed up. Perhaps it was a clue to the missing whatever it was that might have killed his birdwatcher. The writing was barely legible but reminded him of old gravestones. Latin, maybe? At the last minute he decided to slip the pieces of wood and the scrolls of writing under his jacket. With a shout and a wave to the others he climbed back up to his car and put the objects in the boot.

Some weeks later the coroner had declared that Derek Pratt had died from accidental causes. If the lads from the pub had been a bit light-fingered, the sergeant had said, it would be impossible to prove and there was no reason to suppose they had had anything to do with Pratt's death. There were enough witness statements to the contrary and no motive. So that was that.

Once the case had been definitely closed, Constable Hexham had dug out the pieces of wood and bound scrolls from the back of his cupboard at home and, remembering the lady upstairs who worked at the university, climbed the stairs to Emmeline's flat, grabbing her cat on the way, and here he was. 'I thought you might know what to do with them, seeing as how you teach history and that. If I know our lot at the station, it would all have been used for firelighters by now if I'd handed them in.'

As soon as he left, Emmeline settled down with a cup of coffee and her large Latin dictionary and carefully unrolled the first scroll.

9
Roman relicts

Reculver
479 AD

Maybe the messenger got it wrong or maybe Publius wasn't listening properly. No-one ever knew. Whatever the cause, the outcome was that the platoon marched out of Reculver on 3rd March 479 AD, just before dawn, and never came back. After a few weeks without any news, Publius' wife, Flavia, took charge. Whilst there may have been plenty of speculation about their relationship in the bedroom (slaves do talk) no-one doubted that Flavia had long been the controlling hand in the administration of the camp. The women would turn to her in cases of financial difficulties, straying husbands or problems back home. She mightn't always be able to make the problem go away but she was a good listener and many a husband returned chastened from an interview with the boss's wife. Damp buildings were fixed quickly and letters were written. This much Emmeline learned from the diaries and unsent letters of one Aquilia Severa – who also gave Flavia the credit for the formal agreements that kept life in their corner of Kent so peaceful. Publius may have led the glittering columns away to tackle the odd minor rebellion, in a flurry of stamping feet and burnished brass, but it was Flavia who saw to it that Roman gold passed to rebel leaders and their eldest sons became semi-permanent 'guests' in the Roman camp, learning Latin and making friends with their Roman

73

contemporaries.

From a letter Flavia herself wrote to her cousin Juliana in Gaul – a letter cached away to await a Gaul-bound messenger who never came – Emmeline learned about what happened next. After her husband had been gone a couple of months, she sent out her major domo, Antonius, to see what he could find out about how the campaign was going, the whereabouts of the camp's menfolk and when they were likely to be back. She said she would have trusted no-one but Antonius. He was a freed slave, a Nubian, whom they had found during their tour in Gaul. He had shown himself to be brave, resourceful and intelligent. He was never going to fit in well with the common soldiers and was obviously not officer material, but the niche Flavia had found for him in their household suited them both.

When, several weeks later, Antonius returned at dead of night and demanded entrance to her chamber Flavia dismissed her maid, poured her major domo a glass of wine and listened in silence to what he had to say. When he had finished, she swore him to secrecy and dismissed him. She sat alone in the flickering light of her oil lamp until the sky in the East began to lighten.

Nobody seemed to miss the soldiers, at least not until Midwinter when the Saturnalia parties and ceremonies seemed a bit flat without them. The men who were there, civilians, slaves, lads too young to fight and old men, were no substitute. That winter was a long, harsh one. The fort was on a headland and the wind whistled in from the frozen lands across the sea. The local fishermen braved the waves and storms and there was a steady supply of fish to supplement what was in the store houses but life was hard and grain levels were getting low.

Come the spring it was time to plant again and without the men, the wives had to enlist the help of children and the handful of local people who could be spared from their own meagre farms inland. It was a good year and by August there was an abundant crop to be harvested. Flavia sent Antonius out to the villages with a purse full of gold and he returned with a dozen lusty lads raring to finish quickly and claim their bonuses in time to get back and help their own families. Antonius had chosen some prime specimens: Flavia herself observed this as she watched them wielding their scythes, stripped to the waist and gleaming sweatily in the dying light of the sun as it set in an explosion of colour over the sea to the west. Her observations were recorded in another letter to Juliana, a letter that was stored away with the other documents.

Flavia was not the only woman to have been impressed by Antonius's choice of hired help; this became apparent over the next winter as more than one young wife blossomed in a way that would have shocked her soldier husband, now absent for over eighteen months.

Worried and not sure what she should do next, Flavia summoned Antonius to her rooms. She had grown to rely on his advice and he, of course, was the only person in the settlement who could fully appreciate the situation they found themselves in. She had sent him out on regular expeditions since that first one and although each trip brought more information, there was never any good news.

She told Juliana that, to start with, she was none too happy about being told what to do by a servant but had to confess that Antonius's willingness to share the burden of responsibility was a huge comfort. Sometimes, she looked up at him and caught a twinkle in his eyes. It had been many, many years since a man had looked at her like that, and then she had had to leave him behind to marry Publius, as Juliana would remember.

After a while, finally convinced by Antonius that the men were not coming back, Flavia called a meeting of all the free citizens and women of the camp. There was a bustle of excited chatter and speculation and a few worried glances were exchanged between the young mothers-to-be. Flavia called order and invited Antonius to speak. There was a shocked silence but by the time anyone thought to object to the idea of an ex-slave addressing an assembly of free men and women, Antonius had launched into his account of his travels over the previous year.

He had found the forts at Canterbury, Dover and Richborough empty and deserted – other farming settlements had also been abandoned. Not only, it seemed, had all their soldiers marched forth, as they had from Reculver, but their families had been loaded onto wagons at the same time and had made their way to Dover behind the platoons. They, with the soldiers, had been put on boats and launched over the sea to Gaul. He had found some local people who had witnessed this epic exodus but many had been loath to talk to him, possibly because of the Roman tiles, ornaments and even bricks that had found their way into the local mud-walled villages. Antonius had heard rumours of some Romans who had stayed behind and gone native and had finally caught up with one on a shebeen on the Isle of Sheppey. The man had needed some persuading to talk (Antonius didn't go into details) but was absolutely convinced that the Romans had left Britain for good.

No-one spoke in the small hall for some moments and then there was a babble of voices and, finally, the question. 'What do we do now?'

As any tactician knows, the time to attack is when

the enemy is in disarray. Flavia was nothing if not a tactician and she had drafted her plan with the help of a man who was fully her equal in this. If it ever occurred to her to wonder where Antonius acquired his skills, she must have quickly abandoned the thought as one to which she was not sure she wanted to know the answer.

Once the full import of the situation had sunk in she made her famous 'Duty of Women' speech, carefully recorded on what looked to Emmeline like a papyrus scroll.

Firstly, it was to be assumed that they would continue to live in Reculver and would have to do whatever was necessary to survive. Absorption into the barbarian community could not be considered: after all, as Romans, they were people of culture and tradition and that alternative did not bear thinking about. The women would have become trophy wives of barbarians, little better than concubines, and for the boys and old men the prospect was even worse.

Secondly, and following on this, they had, however reluctantly, to face up to the fact that some women had already fallen victim to the savages and the community was going to have to face the arrival of children with roots both in the Roman tradition and in the local tribal structure. (To what extent the women had 'fallen victim' was obviously a moot point but, as Antonius had previously pointed out to Flavia, giving them the opportunity to save face could only help to bring them fully on board.) These children, Flavia proposed, would either be returned to the local tribes, to have no further claim on the Reculver community, or would be brought up as free Romans without further contact with their fathers. There would be a need for more young people if the Romans were to survive with any degree of independence so, far from those mothers being censored in any way, *all* women would have to do their patriotic duty and have as many children as they could.

This led to the third point. As the number of women was considerably more than the number of men and most of them were now husbandless or unwed, it would now be necessary for them to find partners amongst whatever Roman men were available and for the men to spread their seed as widely as possible. Fortunately the gods had decreed that men continued fertile much longer than women did – no doubt just for this kind of eventuality. Any woman who had been left well-provided for by her husband need not hold back for fear of jeopardising her wealth and security, but would be legally entitled to retain all her property: no man would have any claim on her wealth just by virtue of having fathered a child. The financial support of the children would have to be shared by the community as these couples would be doing a public service in producing them.

The fourth and final part concerned the governance of the camp. There would be three proconsuls and every year all free men and women would have a chance to vote to replace one of them. The proconsuls could be men or women and, so long as they were free, did not have to be actual Roman citizens. This was indeed a dramatic break with tradition although not, Flavia pointed out, without precedence even in these benighted islands.

These dictats formed the basis of what became known, originally ironically, as the Flavian Code. Some of the men objected, of course, when the significance sank in but Antonius managed to 'talk them round' according to Aquilia. And, of course, the men were substantially out-numbered by the women and therefore had little choice. In the end the main objections came from the Christian priest, who had not been at the meeting, and his small but vociferous flock. This was solved by bricking up the door of his church in the camp and inviting him and his acolytes to go and join the fishermen in the bay. Most of the Romans were only too happy to return to the fold of the true gods. The Empire in Rome might favour the Christians but the Empire in Rome had abandoned the people of Reculver. The reputation of the priests for hoarding valuable relics and gold and silver in their churches would only attract the northern raiders who targeted all coastal communities, anyway.

The increasing boldness of these raiders was a major concern for everyone and Antonius came up with the idea that the remaining valuables and important documents should be stored in special tunnels in the sandstone cliffs and that the tunnels should be big enough and safe enough for people to hide in if necessary. He had plenty of other suggestions for defence, too, based on how things were done in Nubia. The Nubians, it seemed, were fierce archers and had a special way of making bows that could be adapted to the trees found locally in Kent. Archery was a skill that women could be taught and if they loosed their arrows from specially constructed holes in the walls, it was a relatively safe way of repelling the invaders before they could land.

Most significantly of all, from Emmeline's point of view, Antonius told Flavia about a special kind of fire commonly used by Nubians in warfare. He spent much time over those next years locked away in the old church experimenting with coal and peat and the dung from the few horses the Romans had left to them. Eventually he managed to replicate the flash and cracking of Nubian fire, but never, sadly, the destructive potential he had promised her. It was work done by special priests in his country, he told her, and this was the best he could do. However, it was enough to give the women of Reculver a reputation for witchcraft and magic and that, as much as anything, discouraged visitors.

He drew designs for a tall brick building much, much higher than any that had been seen locally. 'Just like in Rome,' he said. But this one, rather than being a Roman-style tenement, would be to protect people and give added height to the defences. There wasn't the manpower within the community to get started with the project straightaway and men from the surrounding villages were understandably reluctant to work in the camp once they had seen and heard the Nubian fire, but Antonius was determined it would be built eventually.

Safe from invasion, the men and women of Reculver put the Flavian Code into practice and found it broadly worked as intended. There were still far too few men but many, many children came along in the first ten years. Flavia herself led the way, producing, after eighteen years of fruitless marriage to Publius, no fewer than four sons. Aquilia Severa commented in her journal that the boys were noted for their good looks, height and black curly hair.

It was four o'clock in the morning, after three days shut away from the world, when Emmeline finally closed her dictionary, stood up, stretched to ease her stiff, aching joints and made her way to bed. She lay for a long time staring at the ceiling before finally falling asleep. She was going to have to trust someone at some point. But whom? Constable Hexham had no idea of what a Pandora's Box he had inadvertently opened.

10
Emmeline

London
1979

The next meeting of the Committee wasn't until July. It had been called to discuss the possibility of Julian Weatherspoon returning to the future on a second trip, a few years later than his Mongolian one. This time he wanted to go to Australia with a view to finding out exactly what had happened (or was going to happen). Feelings had run high with Carew accusing him of chasing a political agenda that was totally unacceptable and 'turning into a raging Leftie'. Emmeline had finally weighed in heavily in support of Weatherspoon. If the suspicions he had were founded in any truth, surely the sooner that was confirmed the better for Britain and the world. If they were not confirmed well, at least they would know. Lewin was inclined to agree with her and had said so but he knew he needed to wait until he had had a chance to talk privately with Anstruther before committing himself. He didn't share that with the group, of course. They agreed to re-convene in two weeks when Julian would present them with a more detailed plan, including a cover story for himself.

Emmeline was still packing her capacious handbag when the others had left the room.

'You need a smaller bag, Emmeline,' smiled Lewin. 'It is a well-known scientific fact that load carried is a function of available space.'

'Is it.' Her tone was acerbic. 'Professor, I really need to talk to you about something. I've been thinking about it for some time... but, well, I couldn't make up my mind, and now more has happened.'

'Sounds complicated! Is it something we can discuss over a drink and a sandwich? Or would you like to stay here? I haven't got any biscuits left.'

'No, a drink would be great. It'd help, in fact, if there's somewhere we can be really private?'

'Or how about we go to Putney? Once we get to Waterloo, my house is just ten minutes away and we can pick up something to eat en route. Waterloo is your station for Canterbury isn't it?' He was quite taken aback by his own temerity and hoped she wouldn't reject the offer. He wasn't the kind of man who invited people over to his house as a rule, but he'd been feeling for a while that he would like to get to know Emmeline better, and he was intrigued. She agreed cheerfully and he felt himself relax.

Once back in his living room he swept a pile of newspapers to one side and picked up a stray sock and his plate from the previous night. Emmeline didn't appear to notice but busied herself sorting through a folder of papers that she had rescued from her bag. He put a glass of beer in her hand. 'Hope this is OK to wash down a kebab.'

She nodded. 'Professor Lewin, Roland, what I am about to share with you is in confidence, at least for now. It may be nothing but if it *is* something... well, we would need to think carefully about whom we shared it with. Do you think you can agree to that?'

'Yes, yes, of course! All a bit mysterious but I think I can be discreet. What is it? You're not leaving us, I hope.'

'No. Far from it. Unless you think, that is...' She took a swig of her beer and a deep breath simultaneously. When she had stopped spluttering she got to the point. 'Have you ever wondered if our project is the only one of its kind? You invented the machine and I don't want to know the details – wouldn't understand if you told me – but could anyone else have arrived at something similar?'

'Hmm. What a thought! I really don't think so. Anstruther and I worked at this for two years before we even got it to the trial stage and I don't know of anyone else working in the same field – not at the moment. It's quite a small world, the scientific community, you know.'

'Does that mean that others couldn't have worked out about our machine's existence? Why wouldn't they, in such a small world? And then, if they knew what they were looking for–'

'–Emmeline, I think I do need to know what this is about. It might help me answer your question.'

She spread the papers on the floor in front of her and sat back again. 'A few weeks ago my neighbour, a police constable, gave me some tablets and scrolls and these are my attempts at translating them. He found them and he knew I was a historian at the University. Not my era, of course, but one historian is the same as another to most people. My thing is modern history. But he gave them to me and, having studied Latin to Special level at university myself, I decided to have a look at them before passing them on. I haven't passed them on, Professor.'

'Roland,' he said absently, his interest aroused by the earnest expression in her face.

'Roland. These papers are the records of a community of Romans who survived in our corner of Kent long after Honorius pulled the plug on the occupation and called all his soldiers home. The records were found after a landslide in the cliffs – a landslide which also exposed a network of ancient tunnels. There's reason to suppose they were originally in a box of some description but we think that was removed before the police got to the scene. Anyway, this community which appears to have lasted two or three hundred years after the Roman withdrawal shouldn't have been there. On top of that, it was led by women. Unheard of at that time – for Romans, at least. But the main thing is, they should none of them have been there at all. And certainly not without there having been any outside contemporary reference to them.'

'And there wasn't? No, of course there wasn't... but what makes you think–'

'–think it's odd? Apart from that? Well, they should by rights have been wiped out by the Anglo-Saxons and Jutes – Hengist and Horsa, remember them? They were rampaging about the whole area within less than forty years. We have records existing from that time – not many but some. No mention of this settlement at all. *That* as much as anything is what made me think... Haven't you noticed that our travellers and their achievements seldom make it into contemporary records in any identifiable form and yet they must have made an impact at the time.'

'True, but that can't be enough to assume a traveller was involved in this instance, surely.'

'No. But that isn't all. The Romans built nothing like those tunnels anywhere else. They made tunnels, of course, but these ones were made specifically to *hide* in. The people defended themselves with bows – using arrow slits in the walls. Romans weren't bowmen really, apart from the Thracian corps perhaps, but there's no evidence of *them* in Kent at this time. These people weren't Thracians.'

'I see where you're heading, Emmeline, but it's a big jump. Is there any record at all of a stranger there? Someone who didn't fit in?'

'Yes. That's it. There is. There was a so-called Nubian who appears to have been a servant and, coincidentally, the lover of Flavia, the woman who took control when the soldiers left. He was in charge of the defences and – wait for it – he appears to have scared off the Anglo-Saxons with gunpowder! He made some powder from coal and horse dung, powder that went off flashing and banging when lit and terrified the daylights out of everyone. I've looked up the recipe. A chemist could do it with materials from this country. Not in a spectacular way or in particularly destructive quantities, but he could do it. The Romans couldn't, and the local Celts certainly couldn't.'

'This Nubian. What happened to him? Do we know any more about him?'

'Only that he fathered four children on the woman who was in charge and was a good-looking chap! Black. And that one day after about fifteen years he went off on an expedition to get more coal for the gunpowder and disappeared. Flavia was devastated. Multae lacrimae.'

Lewin sat and stared out of the window. 'Gunpowder... what are you suggesting we do here, then?' The implications of there being an unknown person, time-shifting independently of their own group, were mind-boggling. Where would he be from? When would he be from?

'I think we have to go, or send someone, back to track down this Nubian and find out if I am right and who he is... was.'

Lewin sighed and looked down at his glass – empty. 'But who do we send? One of us? Weatherspoon? I don't think we can send a young volunteer on a trip like that and I'll tell you now that my foraging skills aren't up to much – and as for my Latin!' His little attempt at humour was ignored.

'I have someone in mind, as it happens. Does this mean you're with me? You think we can do it?'

'Well, we have the technology, don't we? I would have to run it by Anstruther, of course. He and I always set the trips up together so that we can double check each other's work and there's less chance of mistakes. And I can't see why the other members of our committee shouldn't be involved. I'm sure they would agree.'

'No!' Emmeline looked up sharply. 'Not Anstruther! You promised! And even the others – I'm not sure. You know I lie in bed at night and wonder if anything is how it looks – if anyone is who they seem to be...'

'All right, all right. Not Anstruther, not anyone – for the time being anyway. I still don't understand why you dislike him so much, though. Anstruther is my research assistant, more of a partner really. It would feel quite odd to do something like this without him.'

Emmeline frowned and stared at him for a moment. 'Really? Which is he? Assistant or partner? Sounds a bit vague to me. Are you sure he is either?'

It was quite unsettling; the woman was a bit too observant sometimes. Obviously, Anstruther was neither of these things but Lewin was not sure he could or should explain. The two men had had an understanding from the start that Anstruther would take a back seat in the Committee discussions and would be presented as a technical assistant and observer on behalf of Janus, rather than one of the decision makers. Indeed, it had been at Anstruther's insistence that Lewin chaired the meetings. Even that agreement was something that had been arrived at without him really knowing how or why. Why should Anstruther be perceived as little more than a lab assistant when he had contributed several key ideas

86

that had led to the development of an effective machine? Would Lewin ever have gone down those particular research paths without Anstruther's influence and prompting? Most of the major leaps in understanding had evolved from conversations between the two of them and for the life of him he could not recall exactly who had said what. If ever he got the chance to publish, he had long resolved that they would get equal billing. But again? Why had they been so determined on secrecy? There were arguments for both approaches and he really couldn't remember why this had seemed the only way.

Lewin looked up at Emmeline who was now regarding him with amusement in her grey eyes. 'Have you got any wine in the house? There is more. Much more. And you may need a nerve-steadier.'

'Would whisky do?'

'Am I a Scot?' Her accent broadened and he laughed.

'I'll be with you in a minute. Will you be taking water with that or lemonade?'

'How well you know my countrymen, Roland! But I do stick to water myself. If anything.'

'Where exactly are you from, Emmeline?' he called through from the kitchen. 'You were at Glasgow, weren't you?'

'Yes, I was, for my first degree. I grew up in Kilmarnock. Didn't have to travel far. Came down to Cambridge for the second one and the PhD and never went back. You?'

'London, born and bred. I qualified here at St Jude's and then went over to New York for the MRI research. Full circle now.'

He handed her a tumbler of whisky and the water jug and sat down. 'Well?' he continued, 'Fire away... there is more to Anstruther than he lets on, it's true, but why so anti getting him in on this? He could help.'

'It's a long story; I've not really known who to trust with it myself but then this business at Reculver came up and, well, you'll see the problem... do you remember Emmy Lou Dixon?'

'Yes, of course.' Lewin was surprised. 'The girl who buggered off before she could be debriefed.'

'Yes and no. That's the one, but she didn't bugger off as you put it. And she was debriefed.'

Lewin was not sure he liked where this might be heading but he nodded. 'Carry on,' he said.

'I got hold of a recording of her debriefing interview from the Sunday, the day before you thought it was going to be. Just listen and bear with me. There'll be time for questions later, as they say.'

Lewin sat back in his chair with a shrug as Emmeline fished out a small voice recorder from her bag. 'It's here, one of those mini-cassette tapes. You can have this and listen to the whole thing later but I've done a transcript of it, too. Basically, Emmy Lou did what she was supposed to do in San Francisco. She observed the cultural and social changes, made friends with the movers and shakers, the artists and so on. Probably enjoyed herself a bit too much, it's true, and then, when the chip in her arm told her to get moving, she did. She borrowed a motorbike and headed into the desert towards Nevada. It took her a while. She ended up miles and miles away from anywhere–'

'–so far, so normal but, Emmeline, how did you–'

'Wait. Please. Just bear with me. Emmy Lou landed up at some kind of military installation in the middle of the desert. I've forwarded the tape to the point where she describes what happened next. Here... this is it, in her own words, at her debriefing. Listen to this.' She pressed the play button on the small Dictaphone and placed it between them on the coffee table.

11
Debrief

London
1978

Emmy Lou: Milk, one sugar, please. Oh, you've no idea how good it is to have a proper cup of tea! There is only so much herbal tea, you know...
(sound of tea being poured, cup chinking)

Anstruther: I'm sure. But let's get on, Emmy Lou. Professor Lewin has sent his apologies and Dr Harrison has got flu this time. So it's just us. You've got as far as the gate to this 'place' in the desert.

Emmy Lou: Yes, well. It was really weird. I rode up to the barrier and this man comes out of a sort of concrete room to the side. I was expecting a soldier or something but he was wearing a white boiler suit and had a white scarf round the lower part of his head so all I could see was his eyes. Mind you I had a bit of tie dye wrapped round my head against the dust, so it was the same for him, I guess. It was blowy and the grit got in your eyes and mouth all the time if you weren't careful. It tasted of salt – horrible. Anyway, he has a big gun over his shoulder and a little one in a holster. I'm thinking, there's no way I'm getting in here! What now? But, he says 'Name, please.' and I say 'Emmy Lou Dixon' as if I've every right to be there. As per training, you know.

Anstruther: And?

Emmy Lou: And guess what? He lets me in! Up goes the barrier and he lets me in! 'You'll have to leave the bike here, ma'am. The reception area is straight ahead.' He did give me an odd look, mind. The tie dye

89

and the beads and so on, I expect. I threw him the keys and walked across to the reception building slowly as if I was used to this kind of thing every day. I didn't know what to expect, honestly. I could've been anyone and they'd let me in just like that. It was a bit worrying when I'd spent the last couple of months being looked at like I was a piece of dirt or a tart by every policeman I saw... Anyway, it got weirder. I walked in and there was a woman at the desk. She had hair that was so lacquered it could have been a wig, and a label saying 'Celine Andrews, Manager'. She says: 'Good afternoon, Ms Dixon' as if there was a smell under her nose, 'I hope you had a good trip here. You came by bike, I see. Well done!' And she gives me this smile that made me want to kick her or burp in her face or something! Dr Ely is waiting for you in C block. He'll check you over and take you on to the next stage of your repatriation. Something struck me as odd, but I didn't twig till later–

Anstruther: Interesting. You didn't need help to leave, did you? Was this Dr Ely just providing you with a quiet place in the complex to leave from, do you think? Maybe the woman didn't know what kind of repatriation you were there for... I wonder. Another biscuit?

Emmy Lou: Thanks. I don't know what was going on but they must have been expecting me. Wouldn't the guards have noticed if I just vanished into thin air? Never left the building? Anyway, if Ely knew what it was all about, why shouldn't they? I must admit, it never occurred to me at the time that they might *not* know what I was there for and, as it turned out, it was clear that they *did*.

Anstruther: As it turned out?

Emmy Lou: Yes. But anyway, the silly cow just waved me out the room. I hope she got the sack.

Anstruther: Why? Why do you say that, Emmy

Lou?

Emmy Lou: I was supposed to be finding stuff out, wasn't I? I wasn't going to just go along and do as she told me without having a look around, was I? There was no-one there to see me, so I went over to the first of the buildings and opened the door and slipped in quietly. It was like a workshop but no-one was there either. There was loads of machinery and stuff on the benches obviously being worked on.

Anstruther: What kind of machinery?

Emmy Lou: They looked like *our* machine. They really did. But several of them were in different stages of being built or repaired. There was a door at the back connecting through to another room so I went to have a look. Fortunately, the door was a bit open and I could look through first, and there they were having a coffee break. 'Got a limey going back this afternoon,' one was saying. 'Pretty, too, Earl said. Do you think I could hitch a ride? Get a peek at the Major League results – she's not going far.' Another one says: 'Not in London, pal.' And then they start talking about baseball and soccer and cricket. *They* all knew. No doubt about it.

Anstruther: I see. Go on.

Emmy Lou: I came out again and went round the back of the next building, B Block, to look in the windows. And that was like a classroom. There was stuff on the board about Chile and big photos from newspapers on the walls – and everything was in Spanish. It was really strange. What do you think was going on? It was old stuff, I could tell that. I'm sure one of the pictures was of Allende but he was looking much younger. I had a Chilean mate in San Francisco who had an up-to-date picture on his wall so I'm sure I'm right about that. Anyway, the door opens and three fellers came in. Young guys in their twenties, I'd say. Dark looking, like they might be Spanish. I couldn't hear what they were saying so I ducked out of the way and moved on.

Anstruther: And then?

Emmy Lou: And then there was a sports hall with gym stuff in it and basket ball hoops – nothing interesting really. Deserted. And then I got to C Block.

Anstruther: And there was someone there?

Emmy Lou: Yes. There was a guy there; an older guy, white coat and specs. He had a label saying 'Dr Ely' and he was waiting for me, just as the bitch on the desk said he would be.

Anstruther: Did he see you?

Emmy Lou: Yeah. I went in and introduced myself and he seemed to know who I was. He started to chat to me, asked me how I'd got on in San Francisco. Had I met anyone interesting? What people were into. Did we all go on sit-ins and demonstrations and so on or was it all pot and flowers. He said he had a daughter my age who wanted to go and he was worried about it. That's why he was asking.

Anstruther: Understandable, I suppose.

Emmy Lou: Pish! He was digging! And not very subtly either. Anyway, after ten or fifteen minutes of this, he says: 'I'll be off now, Miss Dixon, and leave you to it. Make yourself a cup of coffee, if you want. Bathroom through that door if you want to brush up.' And he then left. So I activated the chip and came home.

Anstruther: OK, OK, Emmy Lou. This is all very strange. I need to give it some thought – discuss it with the professor. He's going to want to go over all this with you himself, I'm sure, but he just couldn't make it today. Let's leave it for now. You look tired. We'll have another meeting later in the week, with Professor Lewin, and see if we can work out what was going on. D'you fancy a beer? It's the least I can do after taking up half your Sunday on your first weekend home. Or is there someone waiting for you?

Emmy Lou: No. I don't really know anyone down here. The bedsit you got for me is fine but I'd love a beer! It's too early to go back and go to bed. My head's still buzzing with everything. I'll ring the people back home later on and tell them I'll be in Scotland next week. That'll be time to sort out everything here, won't it? No-one'll be expecting me home from my backpacking trip yet but I feel I've been away a life time. You know, I didn't catch your name?

Emmeline pressed the stop button. 'He tells her. They leave the room and that's where the tape ends.' She sat back and looked at Lewin, eyebrows raised expectantly.

Lewin picked up the bottle and held it to the light. It was nearly empty. He doled out what was left carefully and added the water. He stared at the amber liquid as if unsure of what was in his glass. He could feel his world imploding. Then he put the glass down and sank his head in his hands. 'Anstruther! Anstruther! What the hell is it about, Emmeline? Why on earth didn't you tell us about this earlier, tell me at any rate? Have you really been sitting on this for *two years?* Were you actually going to tell me today, even?'

Emmeline looked defensive but had the grace to blush.

'No. Yes. I don't know. But, you see, I didn't get the tape straightaway. By then I had sat and listened to you all saying that the girl had disappeared before she could be debriefed. I didn't know who to trust! I had only yours and Anstruther's word for it that you waited for her on the Monday. And I knew *he* was lying.'

'*I* wasn't.' Lewin felt affronted. 'Let's look at this logically. I'm pretty sure that was the girl we prepped

93

for the trip and it was most definitely Anstruther. Ergo they met. Anstruther and I waited for her to turn up for her debrief on the Monday and she didn't. Ergo, Anstruther has been lying to all of us.'

'Who made that arrangement with her?' interrupted Emmeline.

'I can't remember. Oh, I know. The secretary did. She told Anstruther before she went home on the Friday. Emmy Lou had arrived early Friday morning and made contact with the department.'

'So, you heard it from Anstruther,' Emmeline nodded.

'Yes, I suppose I did. He must have brought the debrief forward to the Sunday or maybe he picked up the girl's call and it never did go through the desk. I can ask Janice if she can remember after all this time but it doesn't actually matter. Anstruther did the debrief all on his own and then chose to keep quiet about it. Why? Because she disappeared? Because he had been the last person to see her? It really doesn't make a lot of sense.'

'You're a nice man, Roland. But you may be a bit naive?'

'What? Why? Oh, you mean maybe he didn't want us to hear what she had to say? Why not? And I'm still confused, Emmeline, there are some other questions—'

'—that need asking. I know. But Anstruther *planned* to be the only one to hear her story! Surely you get the significance of that... *He knew in advance what she was going to say!* Or at least enough of it not to want you to hear it. Think! What was to stop Emmy Lou contacting you later in the week?'

'You mean he persuaded her to disappear? Bribed her? But she did contact you, didn't she? She sent you the tape! And, come to think of it, what was she doing taping her own interview? What was she playing at? I think you have to come clean with me, Emmeline.

94

She'd never met you and yet she sends the thing to you not me... don't you think that's odd? How did she even know your name, let alone your address?'

'Why me? Maybe she felt she didn't know whom to trust; you had been involved from the beginning, remember. How she found out about me – you'd have to ask her that.'

'Too easy, Emmeline! I'm disappointed in you... I'd guess she knew you before she left. Where was she from again?'

'She was from Paisley, I believe.'

'You believe? You *know*, don't you? I thought that there was something familiar in that accent on the tape. Who is she or who was she?'

'Does it make any difference? OK, OK. She did know me. I was there when she got involved in the first place. She knew she could trust me.'

'What happened to her? Where is she? If she's alive somewhere, couldn't you have put our minds at rest when we were scouring the mortuaries and hospitals?'

'She *is* alive. She wanted a fresh start, a new life and, to be honest, didn't feel safe here in London.'

Lewin stared at her. He felt old and tired. 'We were supposed to be caring for these youngsters, looking after them... her parents... do they know she's alive?'

Emmeline leaned over and squeezed his hand. 'Her mother knows, as much as she knows anything. Her father, well, he's no loss and probably hasn't missed her yet. A couple of ageing hippies by all accounts and none too responsible. Her grandma, who largely brought her up, died before Emmy Lou could contact her.'

There was a bitterness in her tone that made him lift his eyes to her face.

'Emmeline, I may be way out of line here but... something occurs to me. Humour me, please. You. This girl, Emmy Lou. She isn't by any chance a relative of yours, is she? Not your *daughter*?'

Emmeline laughed. 'No, no. She's not my daughter. Rest assured. I do have a daughter, mind. I kept quiet about her because I wanted this job and she, well, she was born out of wedlock as they say. Maggie's her name. She's an adventurous wee thing. Not much older than Emmy Lou was when we sent her off. She'd have jumped at the chance, too!'

'Yes, silly of me, really. It was just a thought that flashed through my mind. I think I'd better put the kettle on, make a sandwich or something. Or do you fancy that wine now?'

'A sandwich would be great – don't worry about the kettle. I'll come and help. You know, I think you should meet Maggie. You'd get on and I think she might be able to help us.'

It was half an hour later when, ensconced by the gas fire again, Lewin remembered his second question.

'The tape, did Emmy Lou tell you why she took a tape recorder into her de-briefing? She must have kept it hidden; she must have been suspicious.'

'Yes, I think she was. Something odd was going on in the Mojave that she hadn't been warned about, something fishy. She says she was expected at the desert camp – who could have told them? Could only have been someone this end. I think she probably suspected you, as it happened, which was why she was so open when just Anstruther turned up, but she left the recorder on anyway. Fortunately. She hadn't ever been properly introduced to him, you know. Maybe if she had, things might have gone differently. They'd made a mistake, though, a stupid, schoolboy mistake that led her to hide the tape here at the hospital until she could retrieve it or tell someone else to.'

'Who made a mistake? You've lost me, I'm afraid. What mistake?'

96

'They shouldna' ha' picked a Scottish lass, Roland.'

Emmeline dug an old road atlas out from her capacious bag. 'Look here,' she said, placing it in front of him. 'This is a map of Fife – here, on the east coast, just above Edinburgh. Look at it.'

Lewin studied the map while she watched and waited. Eventually he looked up and met her amused gaze. 'Who the hell are these people, Emmeline? Elie, Andrews, Anstruther? I'm surprised there wasn't a Pittenweem!'

She laughed. 'Well, *that* might have given the game away a bit sooner! It was enough for Emmy Lou, though. Every summer when I was a wee one my granny used to take me to St Andrews to freeze on the beach and then we'd have a fish supper. The best fish and chips were always in Anstruther. Emmy Lou would have done the same at some point, I expect.'

'Jesus wept!' said Lewin, feeling weak.

They talked long into the night, coming eventually to the conclusion that another meeting was called for and that they should perhaps put out some feelers to Weatherspoon as the least likely to be in cahoots with Anstruther, Emmeline having finally convinced Lewin that Anstruther was in it, whatever it was, up to his neck. They would also extend an invitation to Maggie.

Emmeline spent that night in the musty little bedroom that had once been Lewin's. They had struggled to make up the bed between them because Emmeline kept collapsing on it in fits of giggles and Lewin managed to trip over a sheet and fall flat on his face at one point. For breakfast they had eggs on toast and Alkaseltzer. It was a companionable, if silent, meal and then they both set off by train together for St Jude's and Waterloo. It was tacitly assumed that Lewin's old bedroom was now Emmeline's – Beano Annuals, Wisden Almanacks and all.

12

An Inner Circle

It was six o'clock on a Thursday, ten days before the planned general meeting was due, when Julian pre-empted Lewis and Emmeline's plans by turning up unannounced in Lewin's office. He sat back in the chair facing the desk. He nodded his greeting and drummed his hands on his thighs for a moment or two. Finally he spoke.

'Professor Lewin, I've come here after some hard thinking because I feel I need to talk to you before the next meeting, to put my case. I just hope I am not making a mistake.'

'I'm glad you came. Carry on. Actually, there was something I wanted to say to you privately, too.'

'I know. But please hear me out. You were at that last meeting and you know that after my last trip into the future I feel it's crucial that someone goes forward again – to a different location, of course, but either the same time or a few years later – just to find out what was going on. I'm still not sure what the connection was between what I saw in Manchester and what I saw in the Gobi. I've been assuming till now that I only moved laterally and stayed in the same time but I couldn't see or feel what I was doing with the chip face and can't really be sure. Something had gone seriously wrong, though, and I can't see that we should just walk into it without even trying to avoid it – just because of some odd idea that leaving footprints

98

might make it worse!'

'Well, I tend to agree,' said Lewin. 'It's hard to see how things could be a lot worse than what you found: part of England devastated and Central Asia returned to the dark ages. The Mongolians seem to have coped amazingly but I doubt a more urban society would have fared as well.' He paused and looked at Julian thoughtfully before continuing. 'My one reservation is that, so far, we've not seen any of the footprints we know about, the ones left in the past, actually making much difference – we can't be really sure that we *can* make a difference, can we?'

'We only have what we have and don't know what might have been without them, though, do we?' Julian leant forward and slapped his hands on the table. 'We just know we've been given a chance to try and change things and, as you say, it doesn't look as if the future could get much worse if we did leave footprints we didn't intend. So, if you agree with that, why did you veto it? Why can't I go?'

'Who said I vetoed it? I thought we were all going to go off and think about it.'

'I know, Lewin! But Anstruther *told* me.' Julian was almost shouting now. 'He said he was breaking ranks and you would be upset with him if I told you he had let on – but this is too important for silly bureaucratic games. He told me that if it had been up to him he could have fixed ID for me, everything. He even said he might be able to wangle an unofficial trip for me without you knowing. But that's not good enough. Is someone leaning on you? Is that it?'

'Slow down, slow down. He told you what? That I vetoed it, personally?'

Julian nodded slowly. 'He told me you were thinking of sacking me from the group as you were unhappy with the campaigning I've been doing and there was no way I was going anywhere again–'

'–that's untrue, Julian. I'm afraid Anstruther hasn't been telling you the truth. If anyone is leaning on anyone it is him, I think you'll find. To be honest, from what I have been learning recently about Anstruther, all this is par for the course. As for what his agenda is, we don't really know as yet.'

'We?'

'Yes. Dr Harrison came to me earlier this week with some very alarming information. We've not been sure who to trust with it or what to do about it. We are meeting again at my house on Saturday. Come along and I'll tell you more then. I'm beginning to think this place may have eyes. I trust you didn't tell Anstruther you were coming?' Julian shook his head. 'If you are still not sure of my reliability,' added Lewin, 'give Emmeline a ring and check it with her, by all means.' So saying, he rapidly scribbled his own address on a scrap of paper and pushed it across the desk. 'Please come.'

Julian took the paper and stared at it and back at Lewin for a moment as if unsure. Then he shrugged and smiled. 'Very mysterious! I'll give it some thought.'

Saturday dawned crisp and dewy and Lewin got up early to go for a walk; the morning mist lent a fairytale quality to the river and as the tarmac path gave way to a cinder track he felt he could be anywhere at any time in the river's history. He loved London, he acknowledged, somewhat surprised. He hadn't thought himself such a sentimental fool. He walked on longer than he had intended and returned to find Emmeline sitting on the doorstep reading a book.

'Good book?' he asked, letting her in. 'Julian should be along soon. What about Maggie?'

'In about an hour. Thanks for letting me include her in the meeting. She knows something of what's been going on and I'm sure she can help us. If you think otherwise after meeting her, she'll just leave. She'll understand. When do we expect Julian?'

'Now! He should be here.' Lewin paced up and down looking at his watch until Emmeline, exasperated, told him to sit down.

'He'll come, Roland. I'm sure he will.'

'But what if he doesn't? What if he goes to Anstruther instead?'

Emmeline was saved from having to answer by the ring of the doorbell.

'Julian! At last!' she said as she opened the door. 'We were getting worried!'

Getting Julian up to speed with events once they had brushed away his apologies and settled him down with a cup of coffee was easier than they had thought. Emmeline played the tape, telling Julian that she had been told where to find it by Emmy Lou some time after her disappearance. Julian stretched out his long legs and looked thoughtful. The minutes ticked by and Emmeline had just shot Lewin a worried look when Julian finally spoke.

'It's a pattern, isn't it? Playing one off against another – running the show from behind the scenes... how did you let that happen, Lewin? Couldn't you see?'

'No. That is, I knew he was at least a full partner rather than an assistant – but he said he liked to take a back seat and just watch what was going on. Said he was not a political type – more for the technical side. I did sometimes find myself wondering. I can see now he has been playing me–'

'–for a sucker?' suggested Emmeline helpfully.

'I was thinking more of *like a fish*. Playing me like a fish. Where on earth do you get these expressions from, Emmeline?'

'The telly. I watch it a lot. Anyway, there's no point

beating ourselves up about it. What we do next is what matters.'

'I still want to go to Australia or New Zealand – ten years or so after my last trip,' said Julian. 'How do we handle that? Do we just dig our heels in?'

'And alert Anstruther to the fact that he has a problem?' Emmeline was frowning.

'I'm not sure we have to involve Anstruther,' said Lewin. 'My research programme was subverted and, well, guided by the man. I can see that now, humbling thought though it is – but I did put it all into effect and am perfectly capable of running the machine on my own. Once we have agreed coordinates, I usually do that anyway. It may have been just a way of giving me the illusion of being in control but the fact remains–'

'–we can do it without him!' Weatherspoon interjected, sitting forward on his chair. 'I'll get thinking about the best time and location – when can we do it?'

Emmeline was looking at Lewin curiously. 'As soon as we have the coordinates and the coast is clear, I imagine. You didn't tell me you could do this, Roland. It opens up a load of possibilities for us in the other matter, too, don't you think?'

'I'm not a complete idiot, Emmeline! I wouldn't have laboured under the illusion that I was in charge of this project if I didn't understand the technology! I built the thing!'

'Sorry, of course. But you have to admit that you weren't the only person building it.'

'Children, children!' interjected Julian, an amused expression in his eyes. 'Enough of this bickering. And, ah, I think I hear someone coming up the path. We are to be saved by the bell... your daughter, I assume, Emmeline?'

Emmeline leapt to her feet and a moment later was

ushering in a tall young woman in a dark green, figure hugging T-shirt and blue denim jeans. She had a mane of auburn hair piled up in a profusion of curls and green, green eyes. She put her canvas satchel on the floor and shook hands with Lewin and Julian, the latter looking from her to her mother, a trifle bemused.

'I have heard so much about you,' Maggie said smiling at the two men and proffering her hand.

'Whereas we,' responded Julian with his most charming smile, 'knew nothing of your existence. Emmeline, you have deprived us.'

'Yes, well, I may as well warn you, she is not quite as impressionable as she may look, Julian. And she is only twenty-three.'

Julian sighed. 'Why don't I go and make some coffee while you explain to Maggie what this is all about and then perhaps you can explain to me what *possibilities* you were referring to earlier.'

Half an hour later, Maggie's addition to the inner circle had been approved and Emmeline was telling them about the anomaly of the Romans in Reculver and her theories about the explosive-making Nubian.

'You see, we do, it seems, have a way of checking once and for all whether I'm right or not. Of finding out more. If this man was a time traveller, was he a private project of Anstruther's? If so, why private? And why was he there so long? Did he go AWOL, like Mark? Assuming he'll talk to us, we can get answers to all these questions. If he isn't or doesn't want to know – we beat a retreat and leave him there. It will have been interesting to see something of what was going on then anyway. It was a unique community however you look at it.'

'How's your Latin, Emmeline?' asked Julian. 'Mine's somewhat rusty these days.'

'Mine isn't.' Julian and Lewin turned to look at

Maggie who had been sitting in silence on a cushion on the floor, leaning against her mother's chair. 'And classical Latin wouldn't be much use in 5th century Britain anyway. What they spoke was more like Spanish or Italian. Even the written language was different.'

'Classics. Cambridge,' explained Emmeline. 'I thought that could be useful. She did Duke of Edinburgh, too, when she was at school. Resourceful.'

'Thanks, Mum. I *am*, though. And I need an adventure! I would really, really like to go. I can suss out this settlement and make contact with Antonius. I don't have to stay long or get too involved. In fact you'll want me back quickly to report. I realise that.'

'Maggie, a trip like this is potentially full of dangers – of all kinds.' Lewin looked worried.

'I know, Professor. Of course I do. And I have been through all that with Mum. But I really want to go and I know I could do it. Please.'

It was nine o'clock before Maggie sighed and announced that it was time for her to get back to her flat in Camden and Julian offered her a lift to the station. They left a sitting room littered with fish and chip wrappers and wine bottles, the last of which Emmeline and Lewin finished off between them.

'This feels a lot better doesn't it, Roland? A problem shared...'

'Yes, you're right, of course. Although we're no nearer knowing what we do about it when we find whatever we do find. If we are not the only programme running, or if Anstruther is running his own game – what then? On the other hand, it was always a matter of time, so to speak, before the technology became known more widely. I stuck my head in the sand over that, too, because it didn't really bear thinking about but now...' He shrugged.

'It's a start, though. We might find out what

Anstruther, at least, is up to – what this place in the desert was, perhaps. It's got to be better than *not* knowing anything, hasn't it? And if this man got himself stranded in the 5th century accidentally, we could help him get back home.'

'If he got himself stranded, he probably wanted to. No-one would abandon such a valuable investment or just forget about him! He seems to have got himself a nice billet there with this Flavia woman. Mark made the same decision, after all.'

Emmeline stared at him for a moment and looked as if she was about to argue the point. Then throwing her hands up in surrender she set about clearing away the greasy newspaper wrappings and bottles.

13
Purple Ring Virus

2090
Queensland

Julian stretched out on the recliner on the shaded veranda and reached for his beer. He closed his eyes and let his body adjust to the intense heat. It was mind over matter he told himself – and the beer helped. This was so much hotter than he remembered from his last trip to Australia. This time there was no air-conditioning, either, and no pool. That signature of Aussie life appeared to have had its day. He reflected on the events of the last couple of weeks. Things had gone surprisingly well in the circumstances.

He had won the right to be here now mainly because Emmeline had insisted that Maggie got a grounding in the Celtic languages and a bit of Anglo-Saxon before she went on her own trip: she didn't look very Mediterranean, after all and it might help her chances of going unnoticed. He smiled at the thought of the poor girl trying to learn Welsh, let alone Cornish! She was a looker that was for sure. He hoped she could look after herself. A looker was a looker in any world.

He had chosen to arrive in Hervey Bay – a town he knew of old from a 70s book tour – as he was wary of heading straight into a big city again. His instincts had told him to avoid Sydney and Melbourne in particular. He had soon discovered that his choice had been wise.

Here, at least, life had a semblance of normality. The architecture was eclectic, to put it mildly: old veranda'd wooden buildings rubbed shoulders with the kind of glass skyscrapers he would have associated more readily with New York and streets of whitewashed houses were reminiscent of Mexico. The most striking thing was the air of peacefulness; electric cars and vans and people on push bikes coasted up and down streets that previously had resonated to the noise of nose to tail traffic stopping and starting, braking and accelerating. Last time he had been here, too, the front had been pulsating with music from stores and bars and the thrum of motor boats in the bay. Now there was no music blaring and just a handful of sailing boats and canoes drifted across the calm blue bay. Out to sea, was an army of enormous white windmills, rank upon rank of them. He noticed panels similar to the ones he had seen in the desert on the roofs of every building.

He had been ashamed of what he had had to do next. The people of Hervey Bay were a trusting bunch and it had not been too difficult to pick purses out of bags and steal clothes off racks. He had gleaned the address of the head office of *New Australia* from an edition he had lifted from a small store in Hervey Bay. After that first busy morning he had decided not to push his luck and had headed for the bus station. If he had expected the ride to Brisbane on the electric bus to be like the ride he had once hitched on a milk float after a heavy night, he was to be pleasantly surprised. The coach travelled at normal speeds along well-maintained roads and did the whole four hours in one hop.

He had turned up at the head office of the paper and tried to bluster his way past the receptionist. The editor, one Bill Edison, hearing the racket, had come out of his office and been persuaded to give him a

107

hearing. He seemed to have been impressed by Julian's well-rehearsed story and here they were – at the man's house with Julian lying back listening to the cicadas while his host prepared a barbecue. The swing door clicked behind him and Bill appeared with another jug of beer in one hand and a glass for himself in the other.

'Time for a top up before stage two. Now, where did we get up to? West Papua. I'm amazed you got permission to go there. The Heritage People were pretty hot on keeping foreigners out of there even in '78. I remember I tried to get a reporter in around then, myself. Who did you work for?'

'I got my NUJ card through the *New Manchester Evening News*, as you saw, but this was a freelance job. I write books. I did a book on the herders of the Gobi way back in '69, I think it was, and built up a bit of a reputation from there. I had taken the trouble to learn the local lingo a bit for this job, which helped.'

'Tok Pisin?' asked Bill.

Julian realised he was being tested. 'A bit. Ternate is the best bet in that area, though. And I had picked up some Indonesian in Borneo, too.' That much was true, at least!

'So you missed the whole thing! It's unbelievable.'

'Yeah, I need to do some reading up. I was there from '68 and due to come home in '70 but oh, I got ill and had to be hospitalised, and then went back because I hadn't finished. Time passed and then when I did try to leave I couldn't get anywhere – no buses or taxis from where I was. I had to travel by canoe and on foot. That was no joke. Got ill again. By the time I got to the old Sorong airport, or whatever it's called now, there was nothing. I nearly got locked up when I asked when the next flight was!'

'You must have felt like Rip Van Winkle.'

'More like Odysseus. I can't wait to get home!'

'Yuh, well...' Bill looked as if he was about to say more but thought better of it. 'Hey, steak o'clock, you reckon? We got a lot to talk about but we can't do it on an empty stomach.'

That evening Julian faced his first major challenge. When they had eaten Bill showed him through to his office and went over to a blank screen on the wall. He typed rapidly on a keyboard on the table below it and on the screen appeared a banner for Time magazine, 2080 Special Edition. He stroked a pad on the table and the page turned.

'I got all these on file,' he said to the dumb-struck Julian without looking round. 'You're welcome to browse but I think I'll get out of your hair while you do. You are going to find this a bit of a shock, I'm afraid. I've got mail to catch up on, anyway. I'll be in the other room.' With that, he left.

Julian walked gingerly over to the office chair and stroked the pad this way and that. The screen went mad as pages flipped across it and grew bigger and smaller for no obvious reason. At one point he found himself with eight miniature pages up simultaneously. He peered closely at them placing his finger on one of them as he did so. The page immediately filled the screen. By the time Bill came in to say goodnight he was up and running and engrossed in a review of the events of 2080 in Great Britain. It made grim reading.

Even in his own day, people had been aware that coal and oil were finite resources and the implications of that had been brought home to the British to some extent by the coalminers' strikes and the three-day week. The United States had had its own wakeup call with the OPEC boycott. There were some expensive wind and solar energy projects in various parts of the world that he had read about at the time but the great hope was nuclear power. This much he knew already.

What came as news to him was the rate at which the fuel reserves had declined and the reckless speed at which the (inevitable) changeover had had to be made in the end. It appeared that people had continued to stick their heads in the sand about fuel consumption and had refused to invest in research into alternative solutions until right at the last minute, when it was too late. At that point the only option up and ready to go was nuclear. Reactors had mushroomed up all over the globe in the 2030s and 40s, providing unlimited energy and making a few people extremely rich. It was strange to see China described as being a major player in this industry – but why not? Great Britain had been too busy debating the future of the mining industry and drilling for oil in the North Sea to have made any serious investment in the 1970s and 1980s when, arguably, the writing should have been visible on the wall. The hunt for fossil fuels had just gone on, it seemed, devoting more and more time and money for less and less reward. The Chinese had merely found their own niche.

The limited capacity of human beings to worry about anything other than their own personal problems had been completely taken up with the effects of wars and extreme weather on the migrations of millions of people. The reactors had worked away, requiring minimal maintenance and providing enough electricity for domestic transport, heating, lights and manufacturing. The last reserves of oil were used for long-haul flights (which were becoming increasingly expensive) and, of course, the military had their own back up reserves. Most of this Julian, in his new 21st century role, would have already known about and he now paid particular attention to it in order not to get caught out. He skimmed through the rest as dawn lightened the skies and he realised how tired he was. He had no idea how to turn off the machine, of course. He tried various buttons and ways of stroking the screen and the pad: all sorts of things happened but it stayed on. It was only when he finally got up, saying out loud, in exasperation: 'Turn off, damn you!' that the screen went blank.

The next morning he got up late and found Bill sitting over a pot of coffee on the veranda.

'Late one?' asked Bill offering him a coffee. 'Did you get up to speed on the years you missed?'

'Kind of. I think I need to hear it from someone who was there at the time, though. I've missed ten years of my life – even the technology seems weird to me now.'

'That hasn't changed so much. People have had more urgent things to occupy them. I guess you tried the internet. That's not what it once was, obviously. So many major players out of action.'

'Mmm,' said Julian. Christ, this was a minefield!

'Well, what do you want to know?' asked Bill. 'We'll never know how many failures there were in Central Asia and China, but we could see general radiation levels going up. The scientists couldn't work out why, that's all. Hard as that is to believe, now. But then, I guess, no-one really wanted to believe it. That all must have started before you went away, though. We tried to run a story on it and we were told to drop it. The word came down that there was no point creating public panic. There was no proof and, anyway, there was nothing that could be done about it if it *was* true. Then there was Bugey and Gravelines (he pronounced them Boogie and Grave Lines) and, finally, that one near Manchester. That was sure the biggy! Why on earth they built a power plant so close to a major city I will never understand. But that was the biggest of all – and the one they didn't catch. By the time the blast had finished setting off fires a great hunk of the city suburbs had gone and thousands were dead. People couldn't wait to come forward then, of course, self-righteous bastards, saying that all the plants had been showing signs of cracks and wear for years. It turned out everyone knew but Joe Public and the Australian press. They shut down the reactors in highly populated areas within a couple of months and then started sending inspectors out to the others and it was true – they were all showing cracks. Every one of that generation of plants. There were demos – the lot. Governments fell or were pushed. News blackouts. You can have no idea what it was like. We still don't really know what is going on over there in Europe or America.'

'But you, you're up and running here in Oz. How come?'

'Well, obviously, our Pacific Rim countries hadn't gone quite so flat out for nuclear. Not after the quakes and tsunamis.'

Bill looked curiously at Julian. 'Even Japan had given up on it after Kashiwazaki. We had more fossil fuels left than some to tide us over and we just got going with our wind and solar programmes. They were pretty far advanced anyway, as you probably know. We're still struggling with long distance flights but it's amazing what the brains can come up with if the money's there. We can get to Perth, at least, now.'

'You've not been over there, to England, then?'

'No. No-one has from here. The yanks may have, of course. They were pretty badly damaged themselves, though. I doubt the lights have come back on up the eastern seaboard and LA is a write off, I know. No-one really knows the full extent because we can't get there either. England will have been hit harder than most, I'm pretty sure. Too many people – nowhere for them to go. No point going to France – they were hit bad, too. I don't know what they will have done for food but I wouldn't fancy eating anything grown within a thousand miles of Manchester!'

He looked at Julian. 'I haven't pulled my punches, I know, mate. But that's how it is. You must have loads of family and friends over there. For what it's worth, you know you are welcome here for as long as you like.' With that, Bill got up and went indoors, leaving Julian to absorb what he had heard.

'No. No friends, no family, mate,' murmured Julian into his glass, 'and, thank God, no descendants – nor will there be if I can help it.'

Over the next couple of days, with a sense of rising panic, Julian gradually became aware of a change in Bill. The Aussie journalist was frequently silent and thoughtful and had acquired an almost permanent crease on his brow, as if perplexed. Julian wondered if he was outstaying his welcome and tentatively suggested he might move on.

'No, mate,' Bill reassured him. 'You stay here – make yourself at home. You still need time to adjust and, remember, I'm still counting on getting the scoop of the year when you get round to writing up your Papua experiences. I don't know what we'll do for pictures, though. What did you say happened to your camera?'

Julian cast his mind back over every conversation he had had with Bill. Keeping his story consistent was yet another strain in what was proving a challenging couple of weeks. In fact, he was fast coming round to the conclusion that he was going to have to cut and run before long. It was all so much more difficult than he had anticipated.

'Didn't I tell you? I had it stolen in Daru when I was waiting for a boat?'

'You lost all the pictures, too? That was tough!'

'Yeah, well. I'd obviously run out of film years before and God knows if what I had got would have been any good after all that time. Perhaps we could use some pictures from the archives. I want to earn my keep, Bill!'

'You can use the computer in the office any time, of course, or I can find you an old tablet – that might be better. You can sit out here, then.'

'Yeah, right. Thanks!' Julian tried to hide his puzzlement at the offer.

'First things first, though,' said Bill. 'I've managed to swing an appointment with the medical centre. Pulled a few strings to get round your lack of paperwork. Shall we run into town this afternoon or do you feel up to driving yourself?'

'It's so long since I've driven, Bill, I don't know... I probably should get a bit of practice in before I tackle the city.'

'It's this side of the city – an easy drive really. But I'll run you along.'

'That'd be great. Probably a good idea to have a check up. I haven't felt quite right since my return to civilisation. I've been putting it down to the shock of everything! But I might have picked something up on my travels. Or do you think I'm losing my marbles? I wouldn't blame you!'

Bill laughed. 'I haven't heard that expression for a while! But it's not really that kind of check up – neither of those kinds of check up. We all have to go for REM checks these days. When I say us Pacific Rim countries had been phasing out the nuclear plants, obviously that didn't include China! And you were that much nearer them in Papua. For what it's worth, I think you being a bit spaced out is probably just psychological and very understandable in the circumstances, but lack of focus and all that shit is part of the symptom picture for radiation poisoning,

114

isn't it? And you say you were ill a couple of times when you were over there. We should go to the general clinic and get you checked out for the bugs and cooties another time.'

'Yeah, you're right!' Julian didn't have to try to look concerned. Medical tests could make a liar of him in so many ways.

In the end he decided to brazen it out at the clinic; if he wanted to stay he had no choice. And if the worst came to the worst he would just have to activate his chip and go.

The following day they got up early; Bill drove him to a bright, modern building in a leafy suburb of Brisbane. Bill had pulled strings to wangle an out of hours appointment and Julian didn't have to wait to be seen. As the nurse, an attractive blonde girl who looked like she would be more at home on the beach and was helpfully labelled 'Delilah Taylor' ushered him into the scan room he gave her his most engaging smile. 'I appreciate you doing this, love,' he said. 'I expect Bill told you I've been out of the loop for a while.'

She smiled back somewhat icily. 'He did and I understand you are a Brit, too. Which is why I'll ignore the *love*, just this once. I don't suggest you try it again, here or anywhere else, though. Let's get on with the paperwork, shall we?'

It was a bad start and he cursed himself as he struggled with the eight-page questionnaire. When was he born? What jabs had he had? Where had he been on his travels and when? So many dates to get wrong; so many details that might give him away. Fortunately, Delilah did little more than glance at it before putting it in a file and standing up with an impatient glance at her watch and ushering him through to the adjacent room.

The scanner was a hand held instrument and the process seemed to take for ever. Delilah finally stood back and returned it to its stand and Julian moved to stand up and gather his possessions but she put her hand on his shoulder. 'I'm sorry. But if you wouldn't mind waiting – I need to check something with my boss.'

When Dr Feldman, a bespectacled and balding young man, came in he referred to the form and looked at Delilah's readings for some moments. And then went through the whole process again. It was obvious that there was something wrong. Julian's heart sank.

'Mr Weatherspoon,' said Dr Feldman eventually, 'I understand that you are British and have not been on our system before but that you have been in PNG for the last few years, from before the Crisis. Is that correct?'

Julian nodded.

'Well, I would have expected from that to find readings broadly similar to what we get here on this coast of Australia – but yours are sky high. At some point you have been exposed to massive doses of radiation. I see no mention of that in the form you have just filled in. You must have some idea of where and when this happened?'

Julian thought quickly. 'I suppose I did travel through Russia around fifteen years ago, for a book. I wasn't aware of any exposure at the time or I would have mentioned it. Could it date back that long? Should I be worried?'

'If it dates back that long, Mr Weatherspoon, I wouldn't worry about anything at all. You are a walking miracle! It wouldn't be a bad idea to put you through the decontamination procedures, anyway, though, just to be on the safe side.' He frowned, evidently   not   totally   convinced   by   Julian's

116

explanation.

It was several uncomfortable hours later that Bill came back to pick him up and it was obvious that the doctor had shared his concerns. 'Walking miracle, eh?' he chuckled ushering Julian to the car.

Julian's sense of impending doom was not lessened.

Sure enough, that evening after he had cleared the plates, Bill invited him to come and sit with him on the veranda to try some wine he had just been sent from a local vineyard.

'Doing the occasional wine review is one of my perks,' he explained. 'I'd appreciate your opinion.'

They talked wine for a while in a desultory way. Then Bill sat back and said with a shrug, 'Of course, the purple ring virus that did for the Californian vines in 2050 really got our industry on the map.' Julian nodded sagely in agreement. 'Which was odd,' Bill continued, 'as there has never been such thing as purple ring virus in California or anywhere else. But you don't know that, do you?'

The silence drowned out the cicadas for a few moments. Where do I go from here? thought Julian. His mind was blank.

'Julian, strange as it may seem, I think you're a good guy,' Bill went on eventually. 'I like you. But I also think it is past time you told me what's going on here. I can't make it out. And no bullshit about some trip to West Papua, which you would never have got out of alive, I might add.'

'I – I'm not sure...I mean, what exactly–'

'–am I suggesting? Well, I don't know myself *exactly* what I'm suggesting. All I know is, you come here as a bloke who grew up in Europe in the 21st century and you're like a baby, like an Elizabethan. You know nothing. You can't work a computer that is

117

getting on for fifteen years old; you had *film* in your camera? I'm a newsman, myself, foreign correspondent in England and Europe for a couple of years before the Crisis. I have no recollection of the *New Manchester Evening News,* or of a writer called Weatherspoon. I don't know who you are or what the hell is going on – I have racked my brains and I can't begin to fathom it out. Today I hear that your REMs are atypical to say the least. And don't tell me you were in China! I just wouldn't believe it. Apart from anything else, they had computers and tablets and cameras in China just like here – they made most of them for Christ's sake!'

Julian sat with his head in his hands, his fingers buried in his hair. After some moments he sat back and stretched out his legs, eyes closed. The time had come – he had either to trust Bill or use his chip to make a break for it.

'Like an Elizabethan, you say?' he started. 'Well, Bill. I've never thought of myself that way but – I suppose I am just that. I don't suppose you believe in time travel, do you?'

'You don't suppose correctly.' Bill's face was inscrutable in the darkening shadows.

'OK, then, let me tell you a story. About the real Julian Weatherspoon. Born in 1931 in Manchester. His father was killed in Africa but young Julian couldn't wait to do his bit and just hoped and prayed the war would last long enough. The old story. He was to be disappointed, though, and had to make do with National Service. That took him to Palestine and was, as it happened, the making of him. He discovered a passion for travel and an ability to write. He also developed a lasting interest in what makes people and countries tick. Politics, really, you could say. When he came back, he joined the Manchester Evening News as a tea boy and, to cut a long story short, worked his way up. It was tough and what he was after, of course, was a War Correspondent's job. Eventually he got one with the Express in London and stayed with them until he got shot in the leg in Biafra and was sent home early. After that he began a series of travel books which took him to remote parts of South East Asia and the Middle East. And, significantly, some sci-fi novels that made it to the awards lists. In the course of all these activities he also made some contacts, I suppose, and one day he was phoned out of the blue by a guy he'd met in Lagos who had a proposition for him.

'This guy put him in touch with a charitable foundation that was funding a group of academics to set up a ground-breaking research programme. It was kind of hush hush; he *might* have to travel; he would be a consultant; he'd be doing a useful job in the national interest... that kind of stuff. It seemed a bit tame, really, but his curiosity was piqued and he signed up. It was far from tame, Bill.'

Julian leaned forward, peering into the gloom at his companion who was sitting silent and immobile. 'It took a couple of meetings to get round to what exactly was going on – but these people had developed a machine, or a couple of them had. The others were academics called in to decide how it could best be used. The machine could send people backwards and forwards in time. It sounded like science fantasy, but seeing was believing, Bill, and Julian, sat through enough demonstrations.

'Anyway, feelers went out for youngsters, students or recent graduates, with the right skills and background to be the first travellers. They went through a selection process of sorts and then back to various points in the past. Crazy idea to choose students, I thought – until I remembered that at that age I was in Palestine. The youngsters just seem so much younger now, somehow.'

'That much is true,' agreed Bill with a sigh, 'but do carry on. The first person format is fine with me, by the way, if easier for you.'

'If you say so,' said Julian, wrong-footed for a moment. 'We did three of those, with mixed success. Then I started pushing to get the chance to go forward in time myself, believing that was probably what I was there for, apart from anything else. It was the first time we'd gone into the future and there was some resistance but in the end they agreed. I picked a date more or less at random – a hundred years ahead – and I picked a place I knew, Manchester. My timing was perfect–'

'God, no!' Bill leant forward into the pool of light that was spilling out from the window.

'I arrived into this choking smog. Flipped a switch as quick as I could and ended up in the Gobi desert, of all places. At least the air was breathable there. In fact it was great. I picked up some idea of what had happened but – it was difficult. I worked out that the nuclear power plants were somehow to blame and it looked as if the whole world might have been thrown back into the dark ages.'

'I think much of it has been.'

'Well, when I got back I told the team about it. It was strange – one or two didn't seem to think I should be speaking out about fuel shortages and the dangers of nuclear power. There was this weird idea about not being allowed to try to change things. I decided I needed to go back to a later time to find out exactly what had happened. At first they agreed and then I heard that Lewin, the man in charge, was blocking me. I went to see him and it turned out that he wasn't but he and another team member had already decided that this other guy on our committee, the one I'd been talking to, wasn't being quite straight with us – had his own agenda. Lewin not only supported my proposal but he invited me to join their little cabal. They had some pretty convincing evidence that this guy, Anstruther, was playing a deep game and that there might even be other time projects around that we knew nothing about. Anyway, to cut a long story short, we decided I should come here unofficially, without Anstruther or the others knowing about the trip. I was supposed to find out what was going on, what had happened, and what, if anything, we could do about it.'

'And have you found out enough – do you know what you are going to do?' asked Bill.

'I'd already started funding research into non-nuclear energy sources and anti-nuclear campaigns before I left and it's been helpful just knowing you lot are still here and seeing how you're adapting. My secondary aim, I have to say – apart from getting more information generally – was to get back to England and see how bad it was, although I can see that's not going to happen now. I also wanted to find out if time travel technology is common knowledge now, what other programmes there may have been, and what they were up to.'

'I can't help you very much, I'm afraid, except to say that that knowledge hasn't existed in my life time, or at least not that I am aware of. As far as getting over to the UK goes, there is a chance. The solar-powered aeroplanes that we use here in Australia and around the Pacific – they might be able to do it in a couple of years.'

'By then we may have made contact with one of these other travellers, too,' mused Julian. It was good to think he had an ally. 'I'll have to go back soon to tell them what I've discovered. I've got to try and change things, Bill! That has to be my priority. We don't even know if it's possible – but that was my country. That *is* my country. I'll think about coming back in a couple of years, though.'

'I must admit, I can't begin to get my head round what might happen if you do manage to change things. Desirable though it obviously would be. Do I vanish in a puff of smoke. I'm still not sure I can believe any of this.'

It was late that night when Julian finally said goodnight to Bill and went to bed. The heat was stifling as he lay awake under his mosquito net. He had found out enough to clarify what he must do next. He, or someone else, would have to come back here – if only to find out what the outcome of any attempts to change things might be. What he couldn't understand was how anyone would *not* want to know. Why would Anstruther block him? What was Carew's problem? And if Anstruther did have access to another project – had no-one in that project ever thought to travel into the future before? His head was spinning but eventually he fell into an uneasy sleep.

He was in a balloon drifting in a cloudless sky over a blue sea, speckled with white horses. There was land ahead, with green fields coming down to stony beaches. He turned to the man next to him and said, 'That looks like Essex.' The man, dressed top to toe in protective clothing including a full visor, nodded. Carew was there, too, incongruous in a leather helmet and goggles like a wartime pilot. Julian turned back to watch the land approach. They were gliding up a broad estuary now. A solitary seagull approached and squawked in his face before flying off. He was surprised at how big it was, what a broad wing span it had.

After a while, below him, he saw a sandy beach and then what looked like a church, two towers rising up on a small headland. He knew it was Reculver. There were the remains of a walled village around it to the land side but as he watched, the cliff fell away and the church and village started sliding into the sea. The sea was slate black now, and the breakers were cruel and menacing as they rose up towards the balloon and its passengers. The sky was pearlescent grey. The balloon floated higher. Ahead they could see the remains of a pier, a wooden structure abandoned in the middle of the estuary. Along the edge of a pebble beach with its wooden groins stretching forwards like fingers, were houses; their windows were empty eye sockets, the streets deserted. Near one of the groins there was a solitary figure, a boy. He looked up and waved. Then he returned to poking at a dark pile of rags on the edge of the water. Julian knew what it was. As he watched the boy managed to turn the body over, revealing a pale face trailing seaweed; a white hand appeared, claw like, grasping at the air and then fell back into the water. The balloon drifted on. The cold wind rushed past them snatching at Julian's clothes and making the balloon tip from side to side. He was indifferent to fear and danger. Maggie was beside him, her bright hair flying back, a pre-Raphaelite figurehead.

They arrived in London and landed in a park. Julian recognised it from the proximity of the river and the domed structure that he knew led into a tunnel under the dark Thames – one hundred steps or go by lift. They climbed out of the balloon basket and looked around. Carew produced a heavy wooden box, bound with iron bands, and opened it. He took out of it a packet of custard creams and an A-Z of London. He gave Julian the A-Z and began to eat the biscuits. Julian opened the book and started turning the pages. As he did so, the print shifted and broke

up. The pages were turning more and more rapidly.
He felt a sense of rising panic. He couldn't stop the
pages. He couldn't stop the pages. But he had to have
a map. How could he know what to do without a
map? He saw Maggie walking away. 'Maggie!' he
shouted. She turned to him and smiled. She had
flowers in her hair. 'I must go back to my garden,'
she said. And, with a shimmer of light, she was gone.

In the end Julian was persuaded into staying a few
more weeks in Queensland. Bill threw himself into
educating the traveller in time. He took him round the
factories that made the windmills and those that made
the solar panels ('Will they be any use in Britain, do
you think?') They took a trip to Broad Sound where
they visited the Museum of Ocean Energy and the
curator was lured into a discussion of how that could
have been used around the British Isles – if only they
had bothered. 'The Brits had all the technology, you
know, in the early days. World leaders at one point –
but they didn't do anything with it.'

They travelled in silent cars and flew in silent
aeroplanes. The weather grew hotter and hotter as the
Australian summer approached. This, too, Bill told
him was in some way connected with the energy
choices and excesses of the previous century.

Eventually he decided it was time to go home. His
game plan was clear and he was beginning to feel
guilty about Maggie who was, no doubt, champing at
the bit to do her own bit of travelling. Anstruther, the
existence of other travellers, the truth about Area 51, if
that was what Emmy Lou had seen, seemed quite
trivial in the light of what he now knew was awaiting
around the corner for the whole world – but it was
still important and he had had his turn.

14
Saturnalia

London
1980

Back in London, Maggie's patience had been further stretched by a seemingly interminable wait for Lewin to be sure Anstruther would not be around. Then, one day just before Christmas, when the trees were bare and the Yorkshire Ripper was keeping God-fearing Yorkshire women indoors after dark, Maggie set off for St Jude's with her mother. They made their way through institutionally be-tinselled corridors and down into the basement where the machine was stored in a room full of various types of scanning equipment and orthopaedic beds. They found Lewin waiting for them.

'He's gone to family for Christmas,' he said. 'Can't imagine Anstruther having family.'

'Do you think he just arrived, like Damien?' asked Maggie glancing sideways out of the corner of her eye in mock-horror. 'Do you think there's a host family out there *and they don't know?*'

She settled herself into the chair and adjusted the straps.

Lewin looked puzzled. 'Damien who?'

'Never mind,' sighed Emmeline. 'I'll explain later. Remember, Maggie darling, you are quite likely to be arriving bang in the middle of the midwinter festival. That might make it easier not to be noticed, of course, as everyone will be drunk and in costume. What you are wearing now should be OK... there's so much to think of–'

'–and I will be careful! Don't worry, Mum. I'll be fine. Ready, Professor? Here goes. Lo Saturnalia – that's what they say!'

Maggie landed with a bump, half in a hedge. She sat up, looked about her and listened for a moment or two. She could hear voices approaching and realised there must be a path on the other side of the hedge so she lay still, trying not to breathe, until the chatter passed and receded in the distance. She sat there for an hour or more huddled in her cloak, checking the trajectory of the sun until she was sure which way she needed to go to get to the coast. She had arrived, by design, to the north of the settlement of Canterbury, still tucked behind its walls as it was to be for centuries. Her path, the one the other side of the hedge, lay through the woods and her plan was to get within sight of the sea before dark.

Although still daytime in the outside world, the oak woods were already gloomy and a thick bed of leaves scrunched under foot as she walked. She had the illusion that the sound must be reverberating for miles. From time to time she stopped and listened but could only hear the scuttling of small creatures and the protest of pigeons as her approach disturbed them. After a while she thought she heard voices and laughter ahead. She must be catching up with the group she had heard earlier. She slowed right down and wondered what to do. They had sounded a cheerful and friendly crowd and the thought of wolves had been preying increasingly on her mind – but would it be safe? Would she be able to make herself understood? Wouldn't it be better to lie low, concentrate on finding Antonius and make as little contact with others as possible? The decision had been taken out of her hands, she realised, when she

126

suddenly became aware of two large brown eyes peering at her from under a thatch of hair. Maggie smiled and waved, 'Lo Saturnalia!' There was a quick grin and a 'Lo Saturnalia' from the retreating back as the small spy disappeared in the direction of his family.

When the child returned, he (or she) had a man in tow. When he saw her, the man's hand went instinctively to the knife at his belt but, to Maggie's relief, he was brought up short by a female voice calling out to him. A slight woman in a long red cloak appeared and stared at Maggie.

'Good afternoon,' said Maggie in halting Latin and then repeated it in the Old English her mother had thought might serve her best in the countryside. 'I am going to Reculver.'

After a brief, rapid discussion the woman gestured for her to come along with them, smiling and laughing as she did so. The child pranced along beside them talking nineteen to the dozen.

Waiting for them a couple of hundred yards further along were another five people including an older woman carrying a small baby and her husband, who was resting by the path. As he rose to greet them, Maggie could see how she had managed to catch up with them. He was obviously in some pain and supported his weight on a stick.

'Lo Saturnalia!' he said.

The rest of the journey went quickly. The family laughed and sang and joked with each other, and made attempts to communicate with Maggie which regularly brought the whole troupe to a halt as they laughed so much they couldn't put one foot in front of the other. It would be a brave wolf that tackled this family, Maggie thought.

Eventually, they reached a small settlement of thatched huts on a rise overlooking the sea. Maggie could see the stony bay ahead of her and a headland to the right that must be Reculver, but Reculver with a difference. Instead of the ruined church on a promontory there was a stone fortress, guarding the northern side of a wide river, a river with large wooden boats moored along it. The family stopped at one of the houses and signed that she should come in with them. She was tempted but already others were coming out of the house to greet them. She sighed regretfully (resisting the temptation to look meaningfully at a non-existent watch on her wrist) and pointed over towards the camp with a shrug. With a final 'Vale', she set off purposefully towards the bay, hoping she looked more confident than she felt.

As darkness fell she looked for somewhere to shelter. The temperature dropped to close on freezing as the stars came out and Maggie dozed fitfully through the night, curled up in her cloak in a hollow hidden from the path. Her new friends had pressed some bread and cheese on her before she left them but her stomach still ached with hunger. She knew this place; she had come here many a time with her mother to pick blackberries; she wished there were some left now. She set off towards the camp just as the rising sun was tingeing the sky behind it with pink and gold.

As she crested the hill she saw the stone walls ahead of her; they must have been fifteen foot high. Off to the right was a heavy gate, closed, and directly ahead of her a small group of thatched buildings. There was a dog tied up outside one of them – she realised with a sinking heart that she hadn't considered the possibility of dogs. She decided to wait until the camp awoke and there were more people around before approaching nearer to the walls – and the dogs.

She didn't have long to wait. Before long she saw

the gate open slowly. First a bleary-eyed soldier emerged. He wore a cloak open over his tunic and his legs were wrapped in bindings against the cold; he was carrying the short sword familiar to her from countless pictures.

'Oh Mummy, Mummy,' breathed Maggie. 'A real Roman soldier! If you could see me now, Mum.'

The soldier called across to the little house nearest to him and a slatternly woman emerged and shouted something back at him as she went to let ducks and geese out of a pen round the back. They both looked and sounded hung over. The woman presented the soldier with a couple of ducks' eggs looking at them distastefully as she did so. Maggie was enthralled.

It was as if this exchange was the signal awakening the whole village from its drunken slumbers. Just in time, Maggie heard people approaching down the path behind her. She retreated into the bushes and watched as a procession of women carrying baskets of cabbages, onions and withered looking apples chattered down the hill towards the camp, where they were waved on, it appeared, with no more than an exchange of cheery insults.

Next to come down the track were the fisherman with baskets of oysters and live squirming eels. Maggie took out the little case containing the two medallions for the return journey and found one of the tiny silver coins that her mother had bought from a shop in Canterbury for her journey. She waited until most of the traders had passed and a solitary man she had spotted bringing up the rear approached; she stepped out to greet him. He grinned up at her toothlessly and returned her greeting. He looked a bit simple – that was good. Maggie held out the coin and pointed from it to his overflowing basket of oysters and mussels. At first he looked puzzled, then he put the basket down and took the coin from her gingerly.

He turned it this way and that and put it in his mouth as if to test it for quality. He then remembered he had no teeth and frowned at the coin as he passed it back and forth from one gnarled hand to the other. A crafty gleam came into his eye and he peered more closely at Maggie. With the dirtiest chuckle she had ever heard he pointed down at the camp, mimed a helmet and a sword and made a crude but age-old gesture with his fingers that Maggie had no trouble understanding. She felt herself blushing. The man buried the coin deep in the folds of his grubby smock and turned to make as much haste as he could back the way he had come, leaving his basket for Maggie to pick up.

When she reached the gate, she braved the lecherous leers of the two soldiers who were now positioned there and walked past as quickly and confidently as she could, ignoring the comments that followed her through into the central square as she stepped carefully to avoid puddles of vomit. It must have been a good party.

The first arrivals had already set up and she looked around in vain for a space for herself. Several of the traders waved her away brusquely as she approached them but eventually one of soldiers came over and swore roundly at them forcing them to make space. Gradually, the market filled with men and women moving from stall to stall haggling and bargaining. Maggie shrugged and pointed at her mouth as if dumb when they approached her and must, she reckoned, have been the cheapest stall in the market judging by the rate at which her stock diminished and the dirty looks from the other traders; she began to wonder if she had made a mistake in choosing this method of gaining entry.

Then, at last, she saw a group of men walking across the square talking earnestly amongst themselves. One stood head and shoulders above the others – and he was black.

'Ostreae, ostreae, ostreae vivae!' She called out as loud as she could. 'Come and buy your oysters here!'

She saw the man hesitate and then carry on walking. She called out again, in English, 'Fresh oysters for sale!'

This time he stopped and turned to look at her. She raised her head and met his gaze squarely, challenging him with her eyes. He turned back to his friends and moved on. She felt tears of disappointment well up. Then she realised the man next to her was watching her, a smirk on his face; she couldn't understand what he said next but could guess. She blinked her tears away and turned her back on him pointedly.

When her basket was finally empty and she had no excuse to remain, Maggie stood up and, with a small wave and a murmured 'Vale', headed for the gate. She trudged up the hill lost in thought, unsure of what to do next. As she descended again through woods towards the bay on the other side she heard a rustle in the bushes beside the path and a young boy, about fourteen or fifteen years old, stepped forward.

'Lo Saturnalia,' he greeted her and held out a small clay tablet. The inscription read, in stiff angular capital letters, *FOLLOW THIS BOY*. She nodded.

They carried on down the hill as far as a small track off to the left. It led into a sheltered clearing that smelt of fish and smoke. Around the outside of the hut Maggie could see strings of dried fish. The boy disappeared into the hut and moments later a wrinkled woman of indeterminate age came out to greet her and showed her to a bench to the side of the hut, upwind of the smoke. The woman gave her a small smoked fish, a piece of hard bread and a clay cup of vinegary water. Maggie wolfed it down much to her host's amusement. The boy ran off with a wave and then there followed a long wait as the sun rose in the sky and continued its arc to the west. It was beginning to get chilly and gloomy when the tall, black man appeared in the little clearing.

Maggie and the newcomer stared at each other for what seemed like an age. A puzzled frown creased his brow but he didn't speak. It was up to her, then. She smiled tentatively.

'Happy Christmas?' she tried.

The frown disappeared and Antonius' face split into an incredulous grin. He approached her, laughing, and wrapped her in a bear hug that left her breathless. The lady of the house had vanished discreetly indoors and the two travellers sat on the bench and talked until night had fallen and the first stars had begun to appear. At first Antonius stumbled from time to time, unable to find the right word in English. He came from Virginia, it seemed, and his southern accent sounded incongruous and funny to Maggie – as did hers to him.

'It's like you strayed into Spartacus from the Gone With The Wind set,' she commented.

'Well, I never thought Romans spoke with Scottish accents either, you know,' he protested. 'They spoke English English in Spartacus!'

'Apart from Kirk Douglas! You know, that really offended our sense of what was proper at the time.'

Later, Maggie explained about the project in London and how she had got involved. She told him briefly about how Emmeline had tracked him down, and about her own journey to Reculver. In response, Antonius, at first, merely said that he had been involved in 'something similar in the sixties,' and went on to ask her more about the Janus Foundation and the specific destinations that had been chosen to date. He seemed particularly interested in how decisions were made within the group. Eventually, he told her about how he himself had got where he was. Maggie was shocked into silence.

Antonius gave her a squeeze. 'I'm sorry. No need to get all upset. I'm here now. And, hey, let me tell you, there's an oyster fisherman who'll be celebrating well this Christmas, Maggie. They'll be talking about you for years to come.'

Maggie gave a little laugh. 'It was that much, was it? Oh dear. But there'll be a traveller celebrating, too, I hope?'

'Yes, of course. But I *am* wondering what's gonna happen now, Maggie. To me. To you.'

'You come home with me, of course. I brought a second medallion for you. It won't get you home to 1965 but 1981 isn't bad – and who knows? I'm sure the Prof can get you where you want to go from there.'

'I sure as hell don't want to be landing back at the Base, anyway. But I need to think, Maggie.'

'What's there to think about?'

'I've been here a long time – fifteen years. I have children, obligations. I have Flavia. I owe her everything. I need to think – that's all. I need some space to get my head round all this. I'm going home now but I'll be back tomorrow. Fritha will look after you. Just keep your head down.'

The next day dragged. Fritha rose early and worked non-stop, pulling Maggie into the dark, low hut when the fisherman arrived with their catches and again when the traders came to collect the smoked fish. Every now and then she would thrust a small fish and a lump of the dry hard-tack into Maggie's hands. Maggie tried to smile gratefully.

Finally, as the sun sank towards the horizon, Antonius appeared as he had said he would.

'Listen, Maggie. I don't know how this fits in with you and your plans but this is what I'm thinking. I can't just walk out on Flavia. I've kept this place safe and she's stayed on here because I could do that. I do

133

want to leave – of course I do – but I have to make some preparations? Do you understand?' Maggie nodded.

'I need to make sure my side-kick, the boy who brought you here, knows how to make the explosives,' Antonius continued. 'I've kept that close to my chest up till now as an insurance. I also need to make sure someone knows how to set about building the new fort that I've designed. It's going to take a little time. And then I'll have to say goodbye to my boys, somehow, and prepare Flavia for my going. I won't go into details, of course, but she deserves that at least. She deserves much more.'

Maggie sighed. 'I suppose I understand. I can't deny that I'm sick to death of dried fish and vinegar – but I can give you a few days. How long do you need?'

'A few days. I'll send Felix over with some supplies and to keep an eye on things. He'll tell you when I'm coming.'

He was true to his word and the young lad who had brought her to the fish wife's hut appeared the next day bearing goats' cheese and a clay jug of almost drinkable wine. The next day he brought stewed meat and some dried fruit. Maggie noticed he had small burn marks on his hands and face and guessed that his gunpowder lessons were underway.

In the end, though, just when Maggie was beginning to think she'd have to send him an ultimatum, it was Antonius himself who arrived, breathless, to tell her it was time to leave.

'Honey, I hope these medallions work quick! I gotta load of soldiers comin' on my heels and they got orders to drag me back by my ears!'

Maggie pulled out the little leaden case. 'How come? What's happened?'

'I guess Flavia took it harder than I thought. Someone told her about a red-haired girl in the market – she put two and two together. Here, give me that and show me what to do!'

'*Red?*' Maggie was exclaiming indignantly as she, too, disappeared in shimmer of air.

Ten minutes later, they emerged laughing from the door at the top of the stairs that led into the hospital basement. They had got themselves changed and Antonius was looking comical in too-short jeans and a t-shirt that barely reached his belt. As they rounded the corner of the corridor they came face to face with a slight, dapper man who pulled up short and stared at them, shocked.

'What the... what are you doing here? This is not a public area.'

Maggie flung her arm around Antonius and laughed. 'Oh, I know it isn't, but I'm a trainee here and I wanted to wish my boyfriend Happy New Year in private, if you know what I mean!' She doubled over laughing and Antonius pulled her round to face him and started kissing her.

With a snort of disgust, the man walked past them in the direction they had come.

15
Coming Home

London
1981

Emmeline did a circuit of the sitting room, plumping up cushions and aligning newspapers and journals neatly in their piles. Then she went into the kitchen and cast a critical eye over the bowl of peanuts, the plates of sandwiches and biscuits, the five matching tumblers and the five assorted mugs. She counted the sandwiches again. Would there be enough? She wasn't sure there was any more bread anyway. She should have asked Lewin to get some at the off-licence. They probably sold it. She sighed. Too late now. He had stomped off ten minutes ago muttering something about not being able to sit down anywhere in his own house and needing more beer. It'd have to do.

The off-key chime of the doorbell stopped her in her tracks. She wiped her hands on her skirt and went to the door. 'Oh, Maggie! Oh, Maggie, come in, come in!' She held her daughter away from her for a moment and drank in her laughing face and her beauty before enveloping her in a smothering embrace 'Oh, my darling Maggie!'

Maggie extracted herself smiling affectionately down at her mother. 'Mum, we will come in if you let us past! And you may have noticed that I'm not alone.'

Emmeline had been vaguely aware of the tall figure standing back from the reunion and now turned to face him – her hand outstretched.

'Of course, I noticed! I must apologise for being so

rude... you have no idea how I much I've been looking forward to meeting you, Antonius, ever since I found you in those scrolls.'

Antonius stepped forward and took her hand. His voice when he spoke was deep and melodic and his accent took her aback, as it had Maggie. 'Why, ma'am, I do understand. And I am so appreciative that you did find me.'

He was a good-looking man, late thirties she guessed, but it was hard to tell. His smooth, black face was barely lined but his hair was grizzled at the temples.

'He's not Antonius any more, Mum, either. Meet Tony, Tony Bennett.'

'Tony Bennett?'

'Yes,' he said. 'Tony Bennett.'

They went in. Emmeline had barely got them settled when they heard the key turn in the lock and Lewin appeared bearing a plastic bag, bottles chinking. Tony unpeeled himself from the armchair and rose to his feet.

'Professor Lewin. It's a real pleasure to meet you, sir. I'm Tony – Tony Bennett.'

'Tony Bennett?'

'Yes, Tony Bennett.'

'I am so glad we've got that sorted out,' said Maggie settling herself on the footstool near Tony's chair.

'Would you like coffee or tea, Tony?' asked Emmeline. 'Or would you prefer a beer?'

'Beer would be great, ma'am, thank you.'

'I don't expect you've had a beer for what, fifteen years or fifteen hundred?' Lewin laughed at his own joke.

'Well not for a couple of hours, anyway,' replied Tony. 'Maggie has looked after me well. Eggs with bacon, chips, pickled onions and what were they? Itchies – no – scratchings! And warm beer.'

'Not all at once, I trust!' said Emmeline, feigning horror. 'We're waiting for the last member of our inner circle to arrive before we get to the serious stuff – but first you can tell us about how Maggie found you. Oh, I'm so looking forward to hearing about your life in Kent. You know it isn't far from where I live. I know that bit of coast well.'

'And I want to find out what happened after I left,' said Tony. 'They were good to me, you know. I felt bad leaving like I did. And what seemed like good ideas at the time... well, I'm less sure than I was. I maybe wasn't helping as much as I had thought I was.'

'I can tell you what I know, certainly,' said Emmeline. 'The records we found do get sketchier after you left. Aquilia Severa wrote of your departure but her journal stopped altogether within a few months – maybe she died.'

'Aquilia was writing a journal? Wow! Who'd a thought it? That I must read! Full of all the gossip, I'd guess.'

'You'd be right,' Emmeline laughed. 'She wrote about you and your little hobbies – they're what first rang the alarm bells for me. You should be glad she did. She did also speculate, I must admit, about the parentage of Flavia's boys.'

Emmeline didn't miss the quick sideways glance in Maggie's direction.

'They were mine, of course. Not much need for speculation, I'm afraid. You know, there are parts of the States where I'd have been lynched but – not there. They had coloured emperors in Rome, did you know that? But, please, do you know what happened to the boys? It's a strange feeling. Last week I had sons. Now I'm here and they're dust. Not a right good feeling.'

'Hmm... the community outlasted them by a couple of hundred years,' Emmeline continued. 'They each

138

took their turn as Proconsul, it seems, and the family monopoly of power continued. The Rule of Three kept them and their respective families on reasonably amicable terms, which, as you may know, makes it a pretty unique dynasty for Romans. For anywhere. It did lose its matriarchal tradition, of course, which some of us might see as a shame. That was a bold, imaginative move, Tony.'

'That was Flavia. She was the only one who could have held them together at the beginning. An amazing woman, you know. Educated, well-read, charming – and a real politician. But I had no problem with it. Negro families in the South were always ruled by strong women – like my grandma, Elsie Bouvier. I don't even know if she's still alive but if she ain't I guess my Mom will have taken over the role. Do I get to find out? I guess I do.'

'Yes, of course. You'd have to go back nearer to 1981, you know, or you'd look too old – and we can't do anything about those lost years. Don't rush, though.' Emmeline reached over and took his hand. 'Learn from Julian's experience – did Maggie tell you about him?'

'Yeah, the guy who didn't know the history and couldn't work the gizmos to find out? I'll have to do a bit of research here before I go, I guess. You still have books, I hope?'

'We do.' Lewin gestured in the direction of the piles of papers 'And newspapers and periodicals, British and American. You'll be fine. Julian will be along any minute. He had to put in an appearance at a birthday party or something. You can pick his brains, too.'

Tony turned back to Emmeline. 'Right, so what else happened after I left, ma'am?'

'Emmeline, please. I'm not the Queen! Well, your tall fortress was built as you designed it. Your grandson, Marcus Antonius did that using stone from

139

the old Roman camp. Oh, and they still had stocks of gunpowder, it seems, enough to put off the raiders for many years. It looks from the receipts as if trade with the local fisherman got more formalised over the years. Pots for fish, mainly. Those scrolls and tablets really have provided a unique source of information for us – when I can find a way of presenting it. I only wish we had the box – I can't imagine what it was made of to preserve vellum like that.'

'Marble, lined with tin. It was an urn for ashes originally – it was old before I ever saw it. Family heirloom. Flavia said it would be good to store the codex in and all the letters they had written that never got sent. We kept it in the tunnels.'

'A cinerary urn! We can look out for that now in the auction houses. You know it came down in a cliff fall and killed someone?'

'Right. Maggie told me. Poor guy. Wrong place at the wrong time. So they built the fort! I modelled it on a church – with two towers – so later on it wouldn't look out of place. How long did that last for?'

'Right through to the Norman invasion. It was described as a monastery in the normal history books. But then someone made the mistake of firing on a Norman platoon from the arrow holes and that was that. It was pulled down. Rebuilt later as a proper church but always called the Roman fort – right up to the present day by some people. I am not sure how many of your people were left, by the time of the rebuild, though. The community had declined in numbers and it looks as if they had been mixing in more and more with the locals. Got on better with the Saxons than the Celts – or maybe they had to. There was an Anglo-Saxon King of Kent, Ethelbert, in the 6th century. He had a lot of local connections and was the first English king to convert to Christianity. An educated man himself by all accounts. Maybe that was when the integration started. The community did seem able to maintain a wall of silence around its doings, though. It is quite amazing that there are just no records apart from the ones we found from the urn, not accurate ones, at least. It is like your community never happened as far as anyone else was concerned.'

'This is a phenomenon we've noticed before, isn't it, though, Emmeline?' Lewin put down his glass. 'I once thought it reassuring that what should, by rights, be the most enormous of footprints just seem to fade away. Now, I'm not so sure. After what Weatherspoon has reported, not being able to make any impact doesn't sound quite so good, does it?'

Weatherspoon, when he arrived an hour or so later, had no such reservations. Or, if he did, he was ignoring them and prepared to carry on regardless. He launched into an account of his latest activities before he had even sat down, so wrapped up in his own preoccupations that he barely acknowledged Tony.

'Julian! Please!' interrupted Lewin. 'This meeting was arranged, primarily, to welcome a new member to our group. I'm sure he's going to add hugely to our understanding of what has been going on at St Jude's and elsewhere if you just give him a chance. Tony, this is Julian Weatherspoon, a writer and traveller himself – but into the future. Julian meet Antonius, born Tony Bennett.'

'Tony Bennett?' Julian looked startled.

'Yes. Tony Bennett,' sighed Tony. He leant back and pushed his fingers through his hair. 'Maybe I should stick to Antonius.'

Lewin seemed somewhat confused by this exchange but as no-one seemed to want to enlighten him he turned to Julian 'Just grab a beer, Julian, the bottle opener is over there and I'll get you a glass. Maggie has told Tony something about what you found out. Perhaps you should get him up to speed, as

141

they say, with what you are trying to do about it. We've been talking about the long term impact of his activities in Roman Kent and – I don't know. Just tell him.'

'You'll have gathered, Tony, that the Professor thinks I'm whistling in the wind trying to change the future. Personally, I don't think we can afford to think like that. We have to try. That's why all my money is going into campaigning against nuclear energy, funding research into windmills – and sun panels like they had in Australia and Mongolia. Much to the disgust of my loving sister, I might add!'

'Oh dear,' said Emmeline. 'Is that where you have just come from?'

'Yes. It is. I have to say my nephew got more fun out of his box of ball bearings than from his Cosmic Convoy game machine and his sister couldn't be parted from her little mirror. My own sister was less impressed, needless to say. She made a remark about me being a true Midas, disgustingly rich but mean to the core, just within my hearing. I asked her if she really wanted her children turned into gold figurines. The allusion was lost on her, sadly. I might offer to pay for them to go to boarding school, though,' he added thoughtfully. 'Where was that place Prince Charles went to in Australia? Geelong or something. Could be doing the kids the biggest favour ever.'

'That would be a footprint in the future, wouldn't it?' suggested Maggie.

'I'd be giving them the chance but whether they took it – I'd never know. This is all an act of faith, what I am doing. I know that.'

'You could find out,' Tony intervened. 'Haven't you thought of going back to check how things turn out?'

'Of course I have but – just keeping going backwards and forwards to see what works? I don't know. I suppose I could. I'm not even sure I want to know. Perhaps part of me is in agreement with the Prof, after all. Your little Roman settlement didn't even make it into the history books did it? We certainly aren't speaking Latin! Or am I being a bit hard, do you think?'

'No, of course not,' said Tony. 'You're right. But Emmeline was talking about this local king – Ethel something – who had dealings with the community. Maybe those dealings led to more integration – well, we don't know what effect the Romans had in that relationship, do we? I am sure the people at the camp were still educated and I bet the women were still learning to read and write. If this Ethel feller was such an educated man, it may be my great, great, great granddaughter who educated him. Why not? And as for what I set up – you could say it was bucking the trend of the disintegration of an empire and the rise of a new nation. How could Reculver ever have made a real difference to something as big as that? It's the way of the world. And think about why was there nothing about it in contemporary records? It's like Da Vinci's stuff. Maggie told me about that. There were far more people writing things down by then and no-one says "Hey, isn't it amazing that this guy in Italy is drawing bicycles and aeroplanes?" Why would they? You need to be alive now to see the significance of what he was doing and even then – well, it took long enough before someone worked it out. They would have needed some advanced technical skills to do anything with those designs at the time, anyway. There just wasn't the backup knowledge around – or the right materials. My gunpowder was the same – so far out of time that no-one could ever have picked up the idea and run with it.'

'So what are you saying? That it *is* worthwhile trying to change things or that ideas out of time are lost causes from the word go?'

'No, I am not saying that you can't change things. I am pretty sure you can. It wasn't my first trip and – believe me – not everyone has this hang-up about footprints that you have here in England!'

'This is it, Mum!' interrupted Maggie, excited. 'Listen to this! Tony was at Area 51 – the place in the Mojave. He knows all about Andrews and Ely! He knows what it was all about!'

16
Tony

'OK, guys. I don't really know where to begin – but I'll start with how I got involved in the first place. If you have any questions, that's fine but it may be worth waiting till I'm through – it's complicated.'

'Fire away, Tony. We're all ears,' said Julian passing round the remaining beers. Emmeline handed round the sandwiches and they all sat back to listen.

Tony Bennett had been born in Virginia in 1942. His parents were teachers. He had been twelve in the year that the Supreme Court ruled against segregation in schools but the ruling, he said, hadn't made a whole lot of difference in Virginia. He'd done well at school and gone on to Junior College and teacher training at Hampton. His parents had been among those opposed to desegregation in education, believing that blacks would do better in black colleges and black teachers would never be accepted in mixed race institutions. The young Tony, in turn, had not got involved in the radical movements of the early sixties – but neither had he wanted to be a teacher. It was in his final year at college that he was approached by an older black man who said that he was looking for potential candidates for a post-graduate, federal, programme. The government department in question was offering to pay the last year's tuition fees plus a small salary to successful candidates. Tony did not ask questions – he applied. Things had been tight for his parents paying his fees through college and this looked like it could be his passport out of teaching.

Over the course of that year he had attended several 'induction' weekends in Richmond and it had been explained to him that the government department in question (as yet un-named to candidates) was building a crack team of investigators to tackle organised crime. There would be analysts and specialists in various fields working at the head office in Nevada and field operatives training alongside them so that everyone would have some understanding of the role of others. There would be men and women, white and black, all working together. This is in itself was an exciting prospect for Tony. Here he was being offered freely what others, in the Civil Rights movement, felt they had to take by force and vociferous protest. His father was saddened by his decision to abandon teaching and a career of helping his people and also by the thought that his only son was going to be making his life thousands of miles away – but he could see that it what was what Tony wanted and he would obviously have many more opportunities away from the racial divide of the South. How could he refuse to let him go?

Tony graduated top of his class, as expected, and set off across America by bus. His first few months in Nevada involved a rigorous physical fitness regime, endurance runs and training in use of weapons. He trained in the martial arts and learned how to defend himself from knife wielding opponents, giving as good as he got, if necessary. He and his classmates spent two months in the Canadian wilds learning to hunt and trap, and basically just survive. It was every schoolboy's dream come true. There was time in the classroom, too. They all learned Spanish and Portuguese, basic sciences, history and geography, particularly of their own continent. They did a course entitled *Political Realities* which gave them some background to understanding what was going on in

South America and the Far East – namely the battle against communism. The lecturers painted a grim picture of life in communist countries and explained how perilously close America itself had come at times to being undermined and subverted by the cells that had infiltrated everywhere.

Sometimes he thought this might be over the top but, all in all, he was having a ball. Every month the pay check came in and, unable to spend it all, he was able to send money home. He discovered sex. He discovered alcohol. He put any reservations aside and threw himself into his training. When the other guys questioned what they were doing, as they did sometimes over a beer at the bar in the camp, he was the one who told them to just get on with it and enjoy. Life was good. Go with it!

At the end of the year he and four of the others, three guys and a girl, had been separated off from the rest and the five of them had gone out to the isolated desert base for special training. First they had been shown the machines and made to watch party tricks where objects were displaced backwards and forwards in time. Then it was small creatures and then, finally, they had been invited to participate themselves. It was only at that point that they were totally convinced. Then, one by one they were taken aside and prepared for their 'missions'. Tony had never seen any of the others again. The only people he saw at the base were the people who worked there permanently: the guards, the fitness guy, known as Sergeant Joe, Dr Ely, his wife, known by her maiden name of Andrews, and the young guy who had taken on the role of personal supervisor or tutor. His name was Frank Lundin. ('What a surprise!' interjected Emmeline. 'Lundin Links, half an hour up the road from Anstruther!') The handful of lecturers who were flown in and out to give him one to one teaching in specific

147

subjects seemed to each know part of the project but not all and he had been warned to be circumspect around them.

For his first mission, he had been transported back to Alabama in 1958. He had grown up with segregation but it was still a shock. Virginia seemed relatively emancipated compared to what he now experienced but the time in Nevada had given him a new perspective on life; he had learned to hold his head high and look about him even if here in Alabama, catching the wrong eye, at the wrong moment, could earn him a kicking. Going so far as to fight back would get him killed. He could have given them a good run for their money now but he knew that that was not what he was there for. His mission was to find the Reverend King and sign up to be part of his support network of volunteers.

'He's such a great guy,' said Lundin. 'History will want to know about his early years and you get the bonus of being able to help. You might never be able to tell your grandkids but you will always have that, that you were part of it. Consider it a reward for being top of the class in training!'

A six month whirlwind of activity had followed. The Reverend King had just published his first book *Stride Toward Freedom* and had a book tour planned. He'd been pleased to welcome the bright newcomer from Virginia – and the fact that he had experience of life beyond Montgomery got him on the tour. He found himself frequently in tense situations as the crowds that followed King everywhere were targeted by police and redneck demonstrators alike. Several times he waded in to clear a space round Dr King's immediate group. He knew better than to come up with the flash tactics he had learned at the base but there was much he could do more subtly. Non-violence was the message, after all.

He felt sure, at that time, that this was the role that had been planned for him by Lundin back in Nevada in '64. By then, Dr King was already listed for a Nobel Prize and they maybe felt he needed help getting there in one piece.

Keeping in touch with the Base was easy; Tony had a list of safe boxes where he left his reports, who they had met and what everyone had got up to and he would also send more precise details of where they would be at any given time so that Base could contact him in an emergency. On the rare occasions he needed to use the same box twice he would return to it and find it empty – or with a brief message from the future in it. He knew that his return instructions would be fed to him via the drop-boxes by 'ghosts' whose sole function this was.

'Frank used to send me personal stuff, letters from home and so on and I used to give him the low down on some of the gossip. Dr King wasn't quite the saint he should have been and I was having a ball if you know what I mean!' Tony paused for a few moments in reflection and then continued.

'It all came to a head in a department store in Harlem. Dr King was doing a book signing and there were the usual queues and crowds. I was watching from my place behind him, keeping an eye on the white folk heckling from the back of the room and on the crowds pressing in. What drew my attention to that middle-aged black woman, I can't tell you. Just practice and experience, I guess. She had pushed her way to the front of the line and, as I watched, she put her right hand into her purse and reached forward with her left. Everything seemed to go real slow at that point. I saw a flicker of something shiny and threw myself at her but it was too late, almost. She moved like lightning and got the knife into Dr King's chest. I pushed her to the floor and yelled for the police and

149

an ambulance.'

Tony went on to describe how King was eventually carried away with the knife handle still sticking out of his chest and how the police had dispersed the crowd and arrested the woman. As he had knocked her aside, Tony had felt a gun in the folds of her dress; it was a smart little gun, he noted with some surprise as he now handed it over to the police.

The next few hours were spent in the waiting room of the hospital as one delay after another kept King from the operation that would save his life. Finally, it was all over. The message came through that the knife had come out and the operation had been successful. Tony stayed for a further day, watching everyone who came and went. There had been something odd about the whole affair.

Whilst waiting, he passed his time writing up his report. He felt that his last minute intervention had possibly made all the difference in deflecting the knife and he saw no point in not mentioning that, even if he had to apologise for not spotting the danger sooner. He mentioned his concerns about the gun and the delays in King's treatment, as well. When he went back to his room after a further couple of days on duty at the hospital, he found his recall notice awaiting him.

There was silence in Lewin's living room as everyone struggled to digest what they'd just heard.

'What happened to the woman?' asked Maggie eventually.

'She was certified insane, paranoid schizophrenic, and locked away. Still is, I think. Apparently she was shooting off her mouth about looking for King for years, "having instructions to kill him" and "being betrayed". She accused him of being a communist stooge, even.'

150

'Well, she wasn't the only one to do that, I'm afraid. It was an accusation that haunted him until he died,' sighed Weatherspoon.

'He died?' Tony sat up sharply. 'When? How? We're in 1981, right? He can't be that old!'

'He was shot in '68 by a chap called James Earl Ray, a racist nobody from the sticks somewhere. The chap got away, amazingly. Travelled all over the place and ended up being arrested here, in London, a few months later. *He* always said he was set up by someone else, too – even that this other guy fired the shot. Some Canadian sharp shooter, I think he said.' Weatherspoon was looking thoughtful.

'Jeez! You know, apart from anything else, it's hard to see how a small town loser would get to London in the first place without help. Most of us don't even have passports. Anyway, to get back to my story, my reception when I got back was a bit like a Canadian winter itself. They said I'd done well and King was there to prove it, which I knew, but that maybe I had been there as a researcher and hadn't been meant to interfere with history. Just a thought, they said. I told them I wished I'd made sure Dr King never went anywhere near Harlem! *History happens,* Frank said. Some other nutter would have tracked him down somewhere else when I wasn't around. And now you are telling me they did. That's shit, man. My apologies, ma'am, Maggie!'

'Listening to what you have just told us, Tony, I think, well, from here – at a later point in time – we've maybe got a slightly different perspective on the story.' Weatherspoon hesitated, unsure of where to go next. 'We can come back to that, though. Did they use you again? Or was that it until you came to Kent?'

'Believe me, I have a much different perspective on it now than I did then, too! But at the time... it's hard to explain to you here in England – but you have to remember this. My parents were good to me, gave me an education and so on, but we were still poor folk by white folks' standards. Some restaurants would serve me, some not. I could sit on a white bus by then, sure – but I had to be careful how I spoke to people, you know what I mean? If I had stayed home in Virginia I would have been living a few streets away from my parents. No question of buying a nice house in a good neighbourhood and sending my kids to a good white school. The Project had been my pass to get out of there. I had been treated like someone of value by white people for the first time in my life. I didn't *want* to believe bad of it, of them. I didn't want to think too hard at all. Can you understand?'

'Yes, Tony. I think so.' Emmeline stood up and rested her hand on his shoulder briefly. She sighed. 'I also think we all need a break now, though. How about I go out and bring back some food for us and then we can hear what happened after that – how you got to Reculver at least. Can everyone stay? Will Indian do?'

It was early evening by the time the last dishes were cleared away and Tony picked up his story.

'They evidently gave up on sending me back into the fifties, Civil Rights and all. Reckoned I couldn't be neutral enough, I guess, but my Spanish and Portuguese were fluent and being black was still a pretty good disguise if you worked for the government and didn't want people to know. How much of this was official CIA, I never really knew. Never had an ID card or anything.'

'South America! Where did you start?' Weatherspoon had his head in his hands. 'And you are saying you never really knew who you were working for? Who was pulling the strings?'

'Well, no. I guess there was never anything signed

152

– just implied and assumed. First stop was Brazil, anyways. Early fifties. I was to get to know the local commies – find out what they were up to and whether we should be worried. Vargas was the feller in charge at the time and he wasn't much better than the commies, as it happens. I found out that they were all drinking buddies. Reported that back. And then they said was there anything else about Vargas we should know about. Well, he had his skeletons you can imagine... not all political, either. He had managed to get himself elected by suppressing a lot of stuff he wouldn't have wanted people to know about. But people did find out. I warned him to be careful, told him that kind of thing could get him into trouble – and I was right. Someone leant on him and he shot himself.'

'You don't think that could have been due to information supplied by you?' asked Julian.

'I guess it might have been. I didn't think of that at the time. The letter he left sure blamed us – the CIA, that is. I felt bad but I had tried to warn him. If it *was* us, it backfired anyway, because the people who Base thought were commies took over. The letter only helped them do it. They weren't really commies, you know. They just didn't have their fingers in the till as much as some others and didn't want to know about American investment. I reported that as my opinion but I was called back soon after because something was going off in Africa and they needed my skin. I did hear the guys we'd wanted to get in did get in, in the end.'

'And Africa? What was going on there?' Julian was making notes of dates and names as Tony spoke, frowning.

'That was the Congo. My French was just basic but I passed for Angolan on account of speaking Portuguese. It's safer travelling like that, having an excuse for being a bit different. People are much less suspicious of you. I was to get in with Patrice Lamumba. He had been chucked out for being in cahoots with the Russians – I think we may have had something to do with that – but he was still around causing trouble. More straightforward than the South American stuff, I thought.

'We were definitely on the side of the good guys here. It was past time the white people left Africa alone – but it was important that what came next was going to be stable and, above all, not communist. That was all the people at Base were worried about, that and whether whoever it was would continue to let our businesses operate. Our companies built roads and railways and needed to know it wasn't going to be money wasted.'

'That's one way of looking at it,' said Julian.

'I can see you think I was naïve, Mr Weatherspoon – and I was. But I had only learned what I had heard in school and training. I believed, I believe, the United States has a role and a duty in helping other countries get the kind of freedom and democracy we have. We have fought in two world wars for that!'

'Fair enough. I shouldn't interrupt. Carry on.'

'It wasn't that easy getting in with Lamumba's lot. They all knew the government was after him and they didn't trust anyone. One day, when I was in Leopoldville, I met a guy, Antoine; he and his wife were both teachers and they reminded me of my mom and pa. Kind folk, books everywhere, kids knocking on the doors at all hours for help and advice. More political, though. Friends came round and we talked late into the night. I ended up staying with them. I had been left a cache of money by the guys, usual thing, and my rent helped out.

'They said Patrice wasn't a communist but he had been faced with a rebellion and left high and dry by

154

the UN and everyone else he'd tried. What else had he been supposed to do but turn to the Russkies? They said he was a good guy who had found himself in, or rather, been *pushed* into a corner. Now, I was beginning to think I'd heard this story, or something similar a bit too often. Did I mention Arbenz in Guatemala?'

'No, you did not...' groaned Julian, eyes closing as if in denial of what he was hearing. 'Arbenz? Don't tell me he was one of yours, too!'

'I don't know what you mean by *one of mine* but I was there, observing and reporting. When he got pushed out his people blamed the CIA. I thought his main enemies were United Fruit – they were the ones financing all the opposition to him. But, you know, you can only hear the CIA being blamed so often and – you have to think!'

'You do,' said Julian. 'But you weren't to know that United Fruit was more or less owned by the CIA, or the Dulles brothers, were you?'

'No kidding? I knew something stank there. So when it came to Lamumba I was more cautious. Even when I eventually met him, through my teacher friends, I didn't report back straightaway. I gave myself time to get to know him. He was a really good guy. Not a hoodlum like I'd been told, at all. He cared about people, the ordinary folk. They were dirt poor most of them but back in Leopoldville there was so much money around! The white folk, of course, in the mining industry and so on – they were still there. But black people, too. It was all bribes and corruption at the top and the poor folk didn't get a look in. It's a rich country. They've got gold, diamonds, everything. There should've been enough for everyone. And that is what Lamumba thought.'

'You didn't share this information with your bosses?' asked Julian.

155

'I did. I carried on with my reports – but I always used mailboxes in Leopoldville or Brazzaville, or well away from wherever Lamumba was, at least. I told them he seemed OK but I hadn't met him. Actually, I was looking after him, protecting him like I had with Dr King. Only this time I tried to teach his own guys how to spot trouble and handle it without drawing attention.

'The only problem was that I wasn't checking the boxes as often as I should. It got complicated dropping off my messages a long way from where I was and then we were always on the move. The guys at Base were sending messages everywhere but I couldn't use the drop-boxes I could get to easily without giving away my location – you follow me? I think that may have made them suspicious.

'The clincher was probably when Antoine took a picture of us all having a meal together. I said it was dangerous – could be used against us if it was found. But he said Lamumba wasn't a criminal, which he wasn't, and it would be something he could show his grand-children. Why should I worry if he didn't? I wasn't even Congolese. I could go back to Angola anytime. And, of course I couldn't explain to him why I didn't want pictures of myself kicking around with or without Lamumba.'

'No – a tricky one,' sympathised Julian. 'So what did they do? They called you back?'

'Yes. The instructions caught up with me eventually. I was given a rendezvous in Brazzaville and a series of dates for the transportations. You know, I seriously considered staying? Doing something with my life? I didn't want to be involved with the CIA any more. But, in the end, I'm not a Congolese or an Angolan. I'm an American. I live in a country where I am not respected but it's home – and times are changing there, too. Why shouldn't I fight for my own rights in my own home? Why spend the rest of my life fighting for Africans' rights in Africa? They let us go, those Africans. They sold us, you know. I felt at home there but I couldn't forget that. I'm not sure I can explain that to you either...'

'No,' said Emmeline quietly. 'That *is* hard for us to understand. We just don't have that experience in our history. When all this is over, perhaps you can try to explain. It's not something most of us here ever think about. We should. We've got black people here, too. People whose ancestors came from Africa. I've never given any thought as to how they might feel about that side of it.'

'Anyhow,' Tony went on, 'I'd met Dr King and others like him. I could pick up with them and fight for my own people. Plus, think of this. I was used to films and football and all the other things that make life fun for a guy in his early twenties, fresh out of college. Pretty shallow it seems now but that's how it was. That was my world.'

'So you went back?' asked Lewin, who had been watching and listening intently but, so far, in silence.

'I did. I wasn't about to tell them all that stuff, of course. I wasn't sure how I was going to handle it but I knew I wanted to get away from the project. It didn't cross my mind that they might not want to let me go. Stupid.'

'I don't expect they reckoned they could afford to,' said Julian. 'How could they let you run around knowing all you knew? Not that that doesn't apply to the rest of us here now, too.'

'I thought that was what the psychiatrists were for,' said Lewin. 'At least I think it is here.'

Emmeline nodded. 'I reckon that must have been the set up there, too. That woman who tried to kill Dr King. Didn't you say there was something odd about her? Her gun or something? And didn't you say she

157

started claiming that she had been betrayed, that she'd been looking for him for years? For years? Across the years? From years? Who knows what she really said. A diagnosis of paranoid schizophrenia and none of that mattered. She was effectively silenced.'

'Joan Danes.' Lewin looked troubled.' Do you really think that is what she'd do if she had to? Is that what you are saying?'

'She doesn't contribute much, does she?' said Weatherspoon.

'No. She takes part in the initial assessments and can be called in at the debrief but, no, she doesn't say much. But I've known her for years. I never got the impression that she was an *uncaring* woman.'

Julian shrugged. 'Maybe she doesn't think she is being uncaring. Maybe she thinks that being certified might be the best of several options if someone seems a little *flaky*. Or maybe she reckons that just the threat of the ECT or being locked away for a few years might convince someone to keep quiet for their own good. They'd know that, even if they ever got out, there would always be the risk of being readmitted if they stepped out of line again. There'd probably be no need to actually *do* anything to them.'

Maggie was looking puzzled. 'So if Professor Lewin is right and your bosses at the Base had the same way of dealing with people, why didn't they do that to you, Tony? If they were suspicious? Why send you on another mission?' Lewin stared out of the window; Emmeline was absorbed in inspecting her fingernails; Weatherspoon was sitting back with his eyes closed.

'Honey, they were suspicious all right,' Tony said, 'and I've had fifteen years to work out how and why I was sent on another *mission*, as you put it. Why didn't they lock me away like that poor black woman? I don't know. They knew what I'd been up to and that they had lost me. They knew the places I'd been, the things

I'd seen, the things I'd done, Lord help me. Maybe I knew too much for them to take the risk or maybe they just weren't about to let me off that lightly. Don't forget, I'm black A nigger from the South – I should have been darn grateful for what they had done for me, not coming over sassy!'

'So what did happen then?' asked Lewin.

'I had my debrief – I expect you guys do that here, too. I said I hadn't managed to get close to Lamumba but that he seemed a popular guy – that kind of thing. Told them a bit about some other people they were interested in, what I had heard about them. I said about all the money being made by the guys at the top and how it all seemed as corrupt as hell. Suggested they might want to think of supporting the opposition. They said yeah, maybe. Then Ely says "Hey, you look beat, Tony. Go get some shuteye and we'll carry on tomorrow". So I head back to my quarters.

'Then Frank comes along. "That Congo does *not* look an appealing place, bud," he says. "You're back in civilisation now, though, or as near as it gets this side of Reno. How about a beer?" Well – I'm too keyed up to sleep so we go along to the bar. I had enough sense to keep quiet about Lamumba but then he started telling me some stuff that had been going down in Ecuador that he'd been involved with through another of my original classmates from training. Said this guy had had enough and was leaving the organisation. I guess I must have looked a bit too interested, I don't know. Anyway, after a couple more beers I went off to the bathroom and when I got back he'd got in some bourbon. A final night cap, he said. We both had a long day ahead. He was right there!'

'And then?' asked Lewin, not really wanting to hear the answer.

'Well, I sure don't remember finishing that drink. I've no idea what the time was when I came round but

159

when I did I was in the lab. Ely was there with Andrews and I was in the machine. My hands were strapped together behind my back and everyone looked kind of weird. Hard to explain, like their faces were melting or something. I started laughing and it all just got funnier and funnier. Then Andrews says, "Keep laughing, boy. It's time to go home!" And that's it. I was still laughing when I landed in an olive grove in Mauretania.'

There was a shocked silence, broken by Maggie: 'Hey, Mum, are you OK? You look like you're going to faint! Here, put your head between your knees. Can someone get a glass of water?'

Lewin looked at Emmeline in concern and went to get her the water. After a moment or two she sat up and shook her head.

'So sorry. That's some story. I – I wasn't expecting that.'

It was a subdued company that parted an hour or so later. Tony promised that he would provide Emmeline with a written account of how he had got from a Roman enclave on the Mediterranean to a remote headland in the outskirts of the failing Empire. He left with Maggie.

Emmeline stayed behind as was now her habit.

'How are you feeling now?' asked Lewin.

'I'm fine, Roland. Really. I don't know what came over me. It was the shock, the enormity of it–'

'–and you were thinking of Emmy Lou, coming back from the Mojave and disappearing, weren't you?'

'Maybe I was. I think about her a lot. If there is a connection between the Mojave Base and our little Project here – and I think there obviously is...' She shook her head as if to clear it. 'What do we know about the Janus Foundation, anyway?'

'Not a lot. It's a private Foundation registered in

160

America – makes the requisite number of grants to various charities. Accounts straight, as far as I could see, but obviously no mention of us. Anstruther showed me all that when he first approached me. There are differences in the nature of our project and Tony's lot, though, aren't there? Tony was a kind of secret agent for someone or other; I'm not sure who, but Florence? The Ice Age? It's not like MI5 or the CIA can have an agenda there is it? Or big business? Our destinations are really only significant *academically*, wouldn't you say?'

'So far, maybe. But what about Emmy Lou? Can you remember why it seemed a good idea to send her to San Francisco at that particular time? I can't.'

'Actually, I'm not sure I can now. Somehow these decisions just get made, if not at our group meetings then later–'

'–when you have your little get-togethers with Anstruther?'

'Yes, you're probably right. I have been asking myself recently how certain decisions got made. Anstruther never actually says "This is how it is going to be" or "No – we won't do that". It just happens.'

'Clever man, I'd say.' Emmeline laughed a little shakily. 'Sounds a bit like my grandmother – always got her own way – we were never sure how.'

Lewin smiled. 'You look shattered. I'll pour you a wee dram and I think you'd better be off to bed.'

It was some time before he went to bed himself. He felt that he had taken on a responsibility for the group and the volunteers and no matter how hollow that now seemed – he had to stick with it. But how?

17
Confession

London
1981

The next full meeting of the Committee was scheduled for April, the delay being accounted for by the need to find and vet potential volunteers for future trips. It was also delayed, ostensibly, to provide time for all the members to think about what their priorities should be in terms of future expeditions.

The inner circle met at Lewin's house the week before. At first the conversation was all about the rioting in Brixton that had dominated the weekend news.

'And I thought London was different,' commented Tony. 'This guy Powell I was reading about – he'd feel right at home where I come from!'

'I think we thought it was different here, too,' sighed Emmeline.

'But we all made it. I think we need to get on.' Julian brought them to order. 'I'd like to tell you what I've been up to and ask for some advice.'

'We're honoured,' muttered Emmeline.

'Yes, well... I've been warned off my campaigning. That's the first thing. I've been told that my activities are being seen as counterproductive to the national interest and my support of the ladies at Greenham Common is potentially treasonous.'

'You're a supporter of them?' asked Maggie, distracted. 'I didn't think they would have been your cup of tea at all – or you theirs!'

'I don't know where you get your opinions of me from, Maggie. Most unfair. However, it is true that they don't actually know it's me funding them. I didn't think anyone did apart from my solicitor who handles it all on my behalf.'

'Who warned you off, then?' asked Lewin 'If no-one knows?'

'That's the crux of the matter, I'm afraid. I was approached by a war correspondent I used to know, the same chap who introduced me to your lot in the first place, albeit indirectly. I'm pretty sure he has government connections, if you know what I mean.'

'Which government? Ours?' asked Lewin.

'I'm assuming so. I don't really know. And there's another thing. Anstruther got in touch again and repeated his offer to get me back on a trip to the future. Just between ourselves, like he offered to before.'

'What are you getting at, Julian? I'm confused,' said Emmeline.

'I'm wondering if Anstruther is trying to go behind Janus's back, as well as behind the Committee's, possibly acting on behalf of the Mojave people, whoever they are, or someone else entirely. I'm also wondering if I should consider taking him up on his offer to try and find out exactly who he's working for and why.'

'No!' Tony and Emmeline spoke simultaneously and for a moment their eyes met.

Tony's eyes widened for a fraction of a second.

'That's two who think you very definitely shouldn't,' said Lewin, 'and I agree with them.'

'I wonder if Anstruther is just on some kind of fishing expedition,' said Maggie, who had not missed the curious exchange between Tony and her mother, 'just to see how Julian responds to the suggestion? Is he getting suspicious, do you think?'

Lewin nodded. 'Possibly. There was something else, too, that I was going to mention today. Something or nothing. It might be relevant. Anstruther told me that he'd bumped into some people in the corridor and had had a feeling they'd been down in the basement. He asked me if I thought the machine was safe down there.'

'Ah. What did you say?' asked Maggie. 'I think that was probably Tony and me. There was this guy there.'

'I did wonder if it'd been you two,' said Lewin. 'It must've been around the time you came back. I asked if he had checked the locks – he said he had and that everything seemed OK. He'd even been down into the room and had a look at the machine.'

'We scrambled the settings like you told us to, Professor. And we hid our Roman clothes right out of sight – but even if he did see them, they'd have looked like fancy dress. There's all sorts of junk down there.'

'I know. He did say it was probably just a courting couple. They'd made him jump. That was probably all it was, he thought.'

Maggie remembered the expression on his face. 'We did make him jump! He looked like he had seen a ghost!'

'Maybe he thought he had,' said Julian. 'You have a bit of the look of that girl who disappeared. Maybe he thought for a moment she had come back to spill the beans. Guilty conscience.'

'Be that as it may,' said Emmeline, 'why do you think the British lot want to shut you up, Julian? Or the Americans or Janus? Why did Anstruther want you off the committee in the first place? There doesn't seem any reason for any of it.'

'I think I can help you there,' said Tony. 'You guys are now oil producers, correct? Your government is going to have money to burn when the taxes start coming in – and those oil and gas companies are going to make a fortune, too. We know about oil companies in the States – they pull everyone's strings. If the government there did anything to affect their profits, well, that government would be out. Julian's already told us how the CIA was rooting for big business just as much as hunting commies in the sixties when I was, as I thought, working for my country. The world won't have changed that much. And what do you actually *know* about Janus? Are you sure they're so altruistic? They do employ Anstruther, remember.'

'You think they might be part of it all?' Lewin sounded troubled.

'*I* certainly do,' said Julian. 'I believe it was primarily business interests operating the unit you were part of before, Tony, probably with CIA help. It could be that history is repeating itself here, but with the goal of controlling knowledge about the future, rather than manipulating history. Or else with the goal of exploiting what we find out about the future for their own advantage.'

'They tried to get rid of Tony, Professor. They thought they had! These people are powerful and totally unscrupulous.' Maggie sat forward in her chair earnestly.

Lewin sighed. He felt it was time to bring some perspective into the discussion.

'I'm not sure that's very likely to happen here, now, though. You're talking about America nearly twenty years ago, Maggie. Before Watergate. Before all the other scandals emerged about Hoover and so on. At the time our own Secret Service was actually run by commies, as Tony calls them. If the CIA was run by the capitalists – it's just an ideological distinction. But we have enquiries and investigations into everything now. I'm sure they do, too. This is all a bit *paranoid*, don't you think?'

165

'But if Anstruther's connected to the people who got rid of Tony to protect Area 51 in the sixties and he was trying to shut up that girl, Emmy Lou, who found out about them, doesn't that worry you, Professor? Mum?'

'Hang on, Maggie,' said Lewin. 'Perhaps Anstruther did give Emmy Lou some money and persuade her to disappear before she could report to us, or even threaten her with sectioning but that's not quite in the same league as sending someone back to re-write Roman history, is it?'

'It wasn't Reculver they sent me back to,' said Tony carefully. 'They sent me to 5th century Africa. They probably thought they were sending me to West Africa, in fact, where I would have lasted two minutes in those days. They made a mistake, I guess, and I arrived further north in a part of ancient Mauretania where I stood a chance of surviving, as I did. I wasn't meant to survive, that's for sure.'

'No, maybe not,' Lewin conceded, 'but I still can't see that happening here. Now.'

He looked around at the others. Weatherspoon was lying back staring at Tony thoughtfully; Tony, himself, was leaning forward, frowning; Maggie sat, head bowed, her hands buried in her hair; and Emmeline – Emmeline! She was sitting bolt upright, her eyes closed.

'Roland,' she said, 'I can't let this go on. There are lives at stake now.'

'What do you mean?' he asked. He felt cold.

'I've not been totally honest with you, Roland – with any of you. You need to know about Emmy Lou.'

'Then tell us, for God's sake, Emmeline!' Lewin pleaded 'I knew there was something... I even thought... well, you know what I thought!'

'That she was my daughter? I know. And I was telling the truth when I said she wasn't. Although

166

there is more than a passing resemblance between her and Maggie. That's what Anstruther saw, I think. Maggie, I always intended telling you this first, but I postponed it and now – well, it's too late. I'm sorry.'

To Roland's horror he saw a tear roll down Emmeline's face. Maggie moved over to the sofa beside her and put her arm round her mother.

'It's OK, Mum. Nothing about this is ordinary, or normal. Just tell us now.'

Emmeline pushed her away gently. 'This is a bottle of whisky story, Roland, I think you'll find. You do the honours and then I'll take up the story of Emmy Lou where the tape left off.'

167

18

Emmy Lou

Emmeline, glass in hand, took a deep breath and looked around the room as if wondering where to start and whom to address.

'I think we left it at the point where Emmy Lou asked Anstruther what his name was. Well, he told her. And he knew immediately, I suppose, that he had made a mistake. Emmy Lou tried not to show any reaction – but she must have done so. She said yes to a drink and they set off to the Red Lion for a couple of beers. Before they left the hospital, she popped into the Ladies, where she left the tape hidden behind an old-fashioned cistern high up on the wall. Anstruther seemed relaxed and cheerful in the pub and, well, Emmy Lou decided to go along with it. They talked about San Francisco, music, the space programme – you name it. She began to wonder whether she had been worrying about nothing. Two pints led to a third and she excused herself to go to the loo again... is this story sounding familiar?

'The last thing she remembered was the whisky waiting for her on the table when she got back. Anstruther raised his glass, "Slainte!" he said. "Welcome home!" And that was it.'

Emmeline looked around at their pale, appalled faces and carried on.

'The next thing she knew she was in a field, lying on the grass, looking up at the stars. It was weird – funny – she got the giggles. Eventually, she got up and walked over to the woods bordering the field. She called out: *Hello! Is anyone there?* There was no answer but she was thirsty and just kept going, blundering through the undergrowth. Then there was woman. She placed her fingers to her lips and said *Tais-toi, salope!* and beckoned Emmy Lou to follow her. They walked through that wood for half an hour or an hour – Emmy Lou lost track. She was still high and tried to talk to the woman but it was no good.

'Then she began to sober up and feel cold. They came to a village; the streets were deserted at that hour, and they walked across the cobbled square to a café; it was all lit up and laughing voices and singing spilled out of the door. The woman grabbed her arm and pulled her to one side of it, down a small alley. There was a small side door there and wooden boxes full of empty wine bottles. The woman hammered on the door. After a while it was opened and Emmy Lou, still a bit drunk, smiled and said *Hello, Bonjour!* There was a man framed against the light. As her eyes got used to the brightness she could see that he wore boots – and a uniform. She heard the clicking of high heels across the cobbles as the woman half-walked, half-ran away. And that was it – she was sober.'

'And where was she, Mum?' asked Maggie softly.

'She was in France in 1943, behind enemy lines. She spoke a little French, Highers, you know. Not enough. She was arrested as a spy. She wasn't in uniform so there was no Colditz awaiting her, no Geneva Convention. That was it. They took her off to their headquarters in the town and put her in a cell.'

'My God, Emmeline!' Lewin stared blankly at the glass in his hand as if he had never seen it before and then put it down.

'Indeed. My God. That's exactly what she thought. Nobody came to the cell until the morning – and then it started. They wanted to know who she was, how she'd got there, who she was supposed to be contacting, what she knew... you can imagine. And, of course, she had no answers. They hurt her, Roland. But it was no good – if she had wanted to she couldn't have answered their questions. The truth would hardly have helped. It went on for... a long time. She could tell day from night by a little strip of daylight under the door, but that was all. When it was dark she could hear crying and sobs from the other cells.

'Then, one night, the inevitable happened. The guard on duty came into the cell and – well – you can guess why. She kicked and fought but he seemed to enjoy that. I suppose it takes a certain mentality to rape... the next night it was someone else. In the day, the SS people came back and went over and over the same questions. They told her she was going to be shot. If she told them what they wanted to know they would let her go.

Early one morning she heard them, the shots. Four of them. That night there was silence in the cells.

'That's when she decided on her plan of action. She was no stranger to sex, Emmy Lou, hadn't been for a long time, longer than was right. She started just blanking out her mind; she knew how to do that.'

Emmeline stopped and reached for her glass in the tangible silence of the room. She gave a little laugh and continued. 'Before long, one or two officers were showing an interest in the new, passive Emmy Lou. She had worked her way up, you could say. After a while her interrogators left her alone in the day. They'd given up trying to get anything out of her – but they weren't shooting her.

'One day, a soldier came in and told her to get out of the cell. She thought that was it – her cue for the firing squad – but it wasn't. He took her round the back of the building and pushed her into the back of a car. It turned out that one of the more senior officers had heard about her and summoned her. The man had pictures of his wife and children all round his bedroom. It was odd. He wasn't cruel but he made sure she couldn't get out. There was always a guard there in the apartment and a manservant. The officer was pretty senior, like I said.

'Emmy Lou did her best and got to stay another night, and another. It was a bit like being Sheherazade. Finally, some weeks later she got her break. There was a bombing raid during the day and half the street where the apartment was, was destroyed. When it was over, the two men ran out to see the damage – and she ran, too. She ran and she ran. She reached the edge of the town, unnoticed in the chaos, and made it through the woods into the fields where she had landed. She kept going all that day and the next night and the next day until, finally, she knew she was finished. She saw a barn ahead and crawled inside.

'The following morning she was woken up by a man shaking her – just an ordinary man who turned out to be the farmer. He brought her into the house and gave her bread and eggs and some kind of coffee made out of God-knows-what. He showed her to a small bedroom where she lay on a damp, lumpy bed and slept for days. Every now and then he appeared with food and wine and then went off to work. She realised she was pregnant.

'To cut a long story short, she learned a lot about farming and earned her keep with the chickens. A few weeks after she arrived there she lost the baby. A blessing, really, I suppose. Jean-Paul, the farmer was kind and she was grateful to him. I think maybe he loved her.'

'But she got home, Mum, didn't she? How did she do that?' Maggie was gripping her mother's hand tightly.

'The war ended. The Germans left. Eventually. But even after the end of the war there was no money, no-one to ask for help. Emmy Lou began to wonder if that was it. After everything that had happened.

'Then, one Wednesday, Jean-Paul went into town to the market with some chickens and rabbits as he always did. When he came back he walked into the kitchen where she was preparing soup for lunch and gave her a wad of notes. Just like that. "Rentre chez-toi," he said. Go home. It must have taken him months to save up that amount of money – but he had worked out how she was to get to Dieppe and given her just the right amount for that and her fare.'

Emmeline looked around the room at the pale faces staring at her and shrugged as if to indicate that she had finished.

It was Tony who pushed her further. 'And what happened then, Emmeline? What happened to Emmy Lou?'

'Oh, you know fine, Tony, what happened to Emmy Lou! She went to a town where no-one knew her and got on with her life. She changed her name. She even had a baby! The father didn't stay around but that was OK. She and the baby were happy.'

'And what about her daughter?'

, 'Yes. It *was* a daughter. She grew up to look a bit like her mother, Tony. Not everyone could see it mind. Emmy Lou's hair was grey by then and she'd put on a bit of weight.'

'Anstruther saw it, though, didn't he?' said Tony. 'And you, too, Julian.'

Only then did Emmeline drag her eyes away from Tony's and turn towards Maggie who was sitting rigidly upright with tears streaming down her face. 'Come on, hen! I should have told you, I know. Can you forgive me?'

'Oh, Mum,' said Maggie on a sob. 'Oh, Mum!' She flung her arms round her mother's neck 'All my life... I

172

had no idea...'

'Roland. I lied to you, too,' said Emmeline, eventually, through Maggie's hair. 'I'm so sorry. Poor Roland!'

Lewin, still in shock, shook his head. 'Poor Roland, indeed. I thought I knew what was going on – I was prepared to take responsibility for sorting it out, even. What a fool! I didn't have a clue, did I?'

'You had lots of clues, Roland, my friend. You were just too nice, too straight to put them together!'

Maggie was still gripping her mother's hands in hers. 'We must do something. What can we do?' Her voice was shaking.

Tony answered her. Lewin couldn't.

'I'll kill Anstruther' said Tony, 'one way or another. And then I'll deal with the others.'

PART TWO

'Who controls the past controls the future. Who controls the present controls the past.'

George Orwell

19
Closing in

London
1981

The Brixton riots were still dominating the news on the day of the full Committee meeting. Lewin arrived early at Anstruther's request.

Anstruther walked in and hung his coat up carefully on the hook behind the door. Lewin stared at him as he did so. How could he have known this man so long and not seen what a monster he was? This conversation was going to be a challenge: Lewin was not a man accustomed to dissembling.

'Well, what do you make of it all?' Anstruther asked as he turned back to face Lewin. 'What are we all coming to? It makes one feel like emigrating!'

Lewin looked puzzled for a moment. 'Oh, the riots...'

Anstruther looked at him oddly. 'Ye-es. The riots... what else? You academics...!' He chuckled and shook his head.

'Yes, of course. Terrible.' Lewin agreed hastily. 'The damage, the looting. I'm afraid I just tucked myself away in Putney and got on with some long overdue reading. I've been falling behind a bit recently.'

'I don't know where it's all going to end. All these strikes and demonstrations we seem expected to put up with. They seem harmless in themselves – but it all breeds a lack of respect for the law and then this kind of thing happens. It's a logical consequence. People think they can choose what laws they want to obey; and then they vandalise and loot at will if the police

177

disagree!'

'I'm not a political man, myself,' said Lewin. 'You don't think it's all racial in origin, then?'

'What, like Powell? Rivers of blood? Well, maybe. But what's *behind* it all? I'm not sure that the rioters aren't having their strings pulled just as much as the miners and the ban-the-bombers. A friend of mine in Intelligence tells me it's all funded from overseas, if you follow me. It's a problem that no-one wants to face up to.'

Lewin tried to recall if he had had this type of conversation with Anstruther before. If he had, it had just gone over his head. How could he have been so unobservant about so many people? How could he have got things so wrong?

'Actually,' Anstruther went on, 'not entirely unrelated to that, I wanted to talk about Weatherspoon. Not that I believe he is necessarily a fellow traveller himself, unlike so many of these people he's got entangled with, but he *is* getting involved in all kinds of suspect activities from what I read in the papers.'

Lewin wondered where this was going. 'Perhaps it's a good thing he resigned then,' he said. 'I'm surprised he didn't stay on, though, especially as we were going to discuss a second visit forward for him, and also that he chose to tell you rather than me that he was leaving. What do we say to the others?'

'Well, I strongly suggest that no-one on the Committee has any further contact with Weatherspoon, for a start. If he is involved in something, it could only backfire on anyone associated with him. But, the next future visit... What are your thoughts about sending someone else forward, Lewin? That's what we are going to be discussing today, isn't it?'

'Well – it sounds a bit dangerous to me. Hard to tell

178

without knowing exactly what it was that Weatherspoon hit the edge of. He was lucky – someone else mightn't be. I don't believe we can send a young volunteer.'

'Sadly, I tend to agree.' Anstruther nodded his head in agreement.

'Another member of the team or a more mature volunteer?'

'Can't think who. Unless you are volunteering, yourself? And even then...'

They were interrupted by a light knock on the door heralding the arrival of Professor Danes, followed shortly by Carew and Emmeline. Everyone knew someone who had been in Brixton the previous week, it appeared.

Lewin called them to order. 'I think we should get on with the meeting now. Some people may have to leave promptly and the rest of us – well we can always repair to the pub if we want to when we've finished.'

'Weatherspoon not deigning to join us this time, then? Or just going to roll up late?' asked Carew with a disdainful expression on his face.

'Ah, yes. That is first item on the agenda I'm afraid. Anstruther, will you do the honours?'

Anstruther looked unhappy at being thrust forward. This was not the game as normally played. 'Yes, well, Mr Weatherspoon finds himself extremely busy with his er... latest interests. He has tendered his resignation from the Committee.'

There was an immediate outcry of indignation, enthusiastically endorsed by Emmeline. When it subsided Lewin left Anstruther to field all the questions about when and how Weatherspoon had let them know of his decision. Finally, when he thought he had discomfited the man enough, he took charge again. 'So... we no longer have Weatherspoon on our Committee and we have, at the same time, lost our

179

volunteer for a return trip to the future.'

'Do we abandon the idea then?' asked Professor Danes. 'Or do we try to find someone else and just be a lot more careful about where and when they go?'

'Easier said than done,' murmured Anstruther.

'Or my preference,' said Carew, 'which is – do we give up the whole idea and stick to our original remit of expanding our knowledge of the past? You must have some areas you would like to explore, Dr Harrison, surely?'

'Well, we never had the report back on the sixties, I suppose.' Emmeline looked up vaguely and surveyed the group. 'But we *could* find another volunteer for the future, we'd just have to make sure they're aware of all the risks, maybe ask Julian to brief them and advise?'

Anstruther looked at Lewin, who was staring fixedly ahead, focussing on a point a couple of feet above Joan Danes's head.

'Professor Lewin?' he asked pointedly. 'What do you think of that as an idea?'

Lewin pretended to snap to attention and looked around. 'Sorry. Miles away. Yes. Let's all put out feelers, at least. And a good idea to see if Weatherspoon would be prepared to advise.' He nodded cheerfully at Anstruther.

'Not much point asking Weatherspoon for recommendations or advice, I would have thought.' Anstruther was beginning to sound irate. 'I thought we had discussed this. Unreliable chap, better off steering clear of him and his crackpot ideas, if you ask me. And anyway he made it clear when he resigned that he was out.'

Joan Danes, Emmeline and Carew all turned to stare at him. It was the longest sentence he had ever uttered at a meeting. He ignored them and returned to his energetic note-taking. The moment passed. Lewin smiled to himself.

Later, in the Red Lion, when the meeting had disbanded with no further decisions having been taken and the other three had headed for home, Emmeline turned to Lewin. 'That was fun,' she said. 'A bit unfair, maybe, but fun. Do you think he suspected anything?'

'I hope not. I hope he just picked up that I'm getting fed up with doing what he expects me to all the time. Now I am aware of what's going on I can see it all so clearly, how he suggests – puts thoughts in my head – watches me make the right decisions and then waits for me to implement them.'

'Do you think we upset him enough for him to feel the need to report back to his bosses?' she asked.

'He didn't look very happy, did he? I don't think he came away convinced that no-one would contact Julian – that's the main thing. He wanted me to expressly forbid it and I didn't.'

'Neither was he particularly happy that you suggested the pub. I suppose he thought he could have another tête à tête with you.'

'That, too. Well, here's to us, Emmeline!' He raised his glass. 'I don't know how you can be in the same room as that man, though. You are an amazing woman!

It was a couple of weeks before the inner circle met again in Lewin's sitting room. Anstruther had made contact again with Julian. He had suggested the unofficial trip yet again and Julian had said he would think about it but was really far too busy. He said he knew what needed to be done to avert this disaster lying in wait for the world and going back wouldn't really help. Anstruther had accepted this gracefully – with only the merest hint of disappointment in the lack of enterprise being shown by such a renowned traveller.

'Anstruther told me that you'd all felt extremely let down by me and my activities and had made it clear that any attempt by me to contact you would be regarded as an attempt to sabotage the whole project and would not be welcomed. He is taking a chance, though, isn't he? A chance that I won't bump into any of you and get talking anyway.'

'I still don't know what he thinks,' said Tony, 'I expect he was planning on getting rid of you before you got the chance and he may still have that in mind. You need to be treading carefully. That trip of yours has opened one huge can of worms.'

'It'd be good to get Anstruther to give us some more information, if we could, wouldn't it?' Maggie suggested.

Tony had not spoken further about his plans for Anstruther, and Lewin suspected that Maggie was as in the dark as he was.

'Yes, I'm working on that as well,' said Tony. 'I intend to catch him when he's on the point of one of his trips back – I know he makes them. I might manage to persuade him to talk but at the very least I'll have him in the right place to deal with him quietly. We don't want to alert anyone to the fact that there's a problem here. Not before we have to, anyway.'

'I'll let you know next time he says he's off to visit his family,' said Lewin. 'He tends to book leave for three weeks or so at a time. If he does report to the Mojave base, I imagine that's when he does it.'

'Surely he could go, have his meetings and be back minutes after he left. He could have already gone without anyone knowing.' Maggie sounded worried.

'He could,' her mother answered her. 'But, remember, anything that happens to him there happens in real time – there must always be a slight element of risk in being too clever. You know, one minute you are as fit as a flea and the next you've lost pounds, because you got ill when you were away – or you have half-healed cuts and grazes.'

'Anyway,' added Lewin. 'Normal people have families and go and visit them from time to time. Normal people have holidays, even. At least so they tell me!'

'As soon as this is all over I shall whisk you away on holiday, Roland!' promised Emmeline. Maggie and Tony exchanged glances and raised their eyebrows.

Lewin felt himself blush but decided to ignore the youngsters, as he thought of them. 'Where to? I haven't been anywhere apart from the States and I don't fancy that.'

'The world is our oyster! Maybe we will avoid France, oh, and the Fife coast–'

'–and Florence!' added Maggie. 'Or anywhere too cold.'

'Not sure how you would cope with the amenities in the Gobi, either,' Julian contributed.

They hadn't laughed much since Julian's return from Australia. It felt good.

20

Revenge

London
1981

Guns boomed out over London and the sky lit up. The Metropolitan Police held its collective breath. After a year of riots and civil unrest, was this really such a good idea? The Queen said yes. Mrs Thatcher said yes. What could they do? London was packed with people gazing skyward at the evolving display – the biggest and most expensive in British history. The corridors and wards of St Jude's were deserted as staff and such patients who could, crowded to the windows. Tomorrow they would be glued to televisions, specially wheeled in, to watch the Royal wedding.

Anstruther checked the corridor behind him and slipped through the door to the stairs. He went down to the basement and walked through the first long storeroom to the smaller one at the back of it. He turned on the low wattage light in the corner, reasonably confident that it would not attract the attention of any stray passer-by. The machine was as he had left it. He peered forward to double-check the coordinates.

'Good morning! Mr Anstruther, I believe?'

Anstruther looked up quickly and saw a tall dark-skinned man in the shadows in the corner of the room, leaning on the wall, arms folded. 'Who the hell? What are you doing here? There is no public–'

'–access. I know. You told me that before.'

'You! Of course. I knew there was something odd

184

about that! Who are you? What are you doing here?'

'Well, I'm a Company man, of course, or what passes for Company these days. Or should it be those days? A tad unimpressed with your security round here, anyway.'

'What is this? Are you checking up on me? Has someone made a complaint?'

'You know I can't be too specific.'

'I've never met you.' Anstruther looked at Tony suspiciously.

'No? Andrews and Ely can vouch for me when you see them but I guess a bit of secrecy is in the nature of my role in the organisation, if you understand me.'

Anstruther understood. He faced Tony, defensive. 'And what am I supposed to have done?'

'Something to do with a missing volunteer?'

'Oh, that!' Anstruther snorted dismissively. 'They know all about that. It was ages ago – and it was their fault, anyway. The people here were supposed to call her to somewhere in the middle of the desert and bring her back but some idiot at Base called her into Area 51 by mistake. Didn't read the bit of her file that said she was a London based volunteer. I had to cover for them... you ask Andrews. She knows what happened.'

'She says not,' drawled Tony with a shrug. 'If there's another version of the story, I need to hear it.'

'The girl came back. I hijacked the debrief so she couldn't talk to anyone else and... made the problem go away. I sent them the tape of the debrief.'

'Yeah. Unfortunately the girl made one, too – tucked it away somewhere and, well, it turned up.'

The colour drained from Anstruther's face. This was not going well. 'I don't believe you! Turned up where?'

'You just need to know it turned up. And then you say you *made the problem go away*? How, exactly did

185

you do that?'

'Andrews knows. I told her that, too.'

'She says not. Enlighten me.'

'The bitch! I put the girl straight on to the Honeybee program. We'd talked about it in Nevada and it was on the cards for here anyway. I just brought it forward. I sent her to Occupied France in 1943. She was a tough girl, no better than she should be, if you know what I mean. She was as good a candidate as any.'

'And the outcome?'

'The bitch knows that perfectly well, too,' Anstruther said bitterly. 'It went as well as it could have – she used her talents to get out of jail as we hoped she would. Killed in a bombing raid, as it happens.'

'So you never got a chance to debrief her a second time?'

'No, but the girl hadn't exactly volunteered for that trip and to be honest, I'm not quite sure how cooperative she would have been in the circumstances. What do you think?'

'I take your point,' Tony nodded. 'Go on.'

'I had deactivated her chip from here so she couldn't come back on her own and the fact that she *didn't* come back was a bonus for Andrews! The whole experiment proved my point about Honeybee – all in all a *successful* outcome, I would have said.'

'How was that?'

'It showed that the right female can sometimes survive where a man wouldn't, especially if she's an amateur and can't tell them anything they shouldn't know. I'd been pushing to test my theory and I got the chance to do it.'

Tony cocked his head and sighed reflectively 'Well, if what you say is true, do you have any idea why the knives are out for you, then? Because they are.'

186

'You tell me. I can't imagine – or at least maybe I can. I guess Andrews and Ely are in trouble over something and they're trying to send up a smokescreen, deflect interest from whatever cock-up they've made now – I'm going to suggest the Consortium people have a long hard look at what's been going on there.'

'Interesting theory. You're perfectly sure there hasn't been anything more recently, since the girl?'

'No – and all I did there was cover for Ely's mistake anyway.' He hesitated and sighed. 'OK. There's a guy who's rocking the boat here in England at the moment. That's upset the Consortium. But he's off the program now. We've discussed losing him the same way as the girl but I was going to suggest Base sent someone back to dig for dirt in his past – there's bound to be some. Sow some seeds. You know the score. Tackle it that way. We don't want any martyrs. I'm dealing with it, anyway. I really don't know what all this is about. In fact I'm beginning to think you don't either.'

'You haven't thought of organising the dirt-planting yourself?'

'Obviously not! So far, this is a volunteer program over here. Our assets aren't agents. We can't expect them to do stuff like that – and you should know it. This whole thing is beginning to stink! Who did you say you were?'

'I didn't and, you know, I'd rather not. Names are a distraction, I find. You've been very helpful, though.'

'Well, I am sure you will forgive me if I leave now. I want to get back to the Base and find out what the hell is going on. And I'll be asking a few questions about you, mister whoever you are.'

With that Anstruther climbed into the machine and fastened the strap, tightening it with an air of finality.

Tony crossed the room in two long strides and

187

flicked off the switch on the wall behind the machine and twisted a dial. Before Anstruther could protest he called out over his shoulder, 'You can come in now.'

The door opened and Emmeline Harrison walked in and approached the machine.

Tony looked down at her. 'You heard enough?'

Anstruther's eyes narrowed. 'A set-up. Very clever. Dr Harrison, you have no idea of what's going on here, what's at stake. Whatever you thought you heard, it was only part of the whole story. The story where your life and your country is protected by men like me. That girl – she provided useful information on her first trip and *also on the second*! You get collateral damage, sometimes. You must surely understand that!'

As soon as he said it, he realised he had made a mistake.

'*What* damage?'

'Dr Harrison, you're dealing with Official Secrets here. If you even think of talking about any of this they will throw the book at you. Or worse. Look, I'll go back to my base and suggest they disband this part of their work. I'm off there now. Emmeline, please. Just walk away.'

'Is that right?' she asked turning to Tony. 'He's off back to the Mojave?'

'Oh yes, Emmeline. He is. Not quite *when* he was planning, of course. But – that does happen from time to time, as we both know. We'll save the *when* as a surprise for him – but it's all for the greater good, I'm sure. He may survive, you never know. He may manage to give us some valuable first-hand information on how climates change over the ages. Stuff like that.'

'Emmeline! You're a reasonable woman. He's planning to kill me! Can't you see that? You can't let this happen!' There were beads of sweat on

Anstruther's forehead.

'Can't I? You didn't get rid of me, Anstruther. This problem, this – this bit of *collateral damage*, has come along here tonight to throw the switch, I'm afraid. Tony took some persuading but, well, I insisted. I'm older and wiser, Anstruther, but still no better than I should be, it seems.'

Emmeline waited until she saw the dawn of realisation in his eyes – and threw the switch. There was a whirr and a shimmer and he was gone.

'OK, Emmeline?' asked Tony putting his arm around her shoulders.

She nodded slowly.

'I don't know. I just feel flat,' she said with a grimace. 'Is this how it feels? Oh, that's unfair, I know.' She paused. 'Yes, I'm OK. I think the world is a better place, isn't it?'

'It is. There are others though. It's like a hydra. Chop off one head and another will take its place.'

'So there was no point apart from my need for revenge, then?'

'That was important, Emmeline. Don't you ever doubt that. That man did you harm. You couldn't just let that lie.'

Emmeline turned to him and put her hand up to his cheek. Standing on tiptoe she gave him a quick kiss.

'Harm... yes. Thank you. Let's get out of here. Maggie will be at the Red Lion by now and she'll be wondering if we're all right.'

A man squatted on the ground and sifted the sand through his fingers. It was still warm from the heat of the sun but the night would be cold. He touched his finger to his mouth: it tasted salty. He was wearing the tattered remains of a pair of trousers and a cloak made from the pelts of the small rodents that lived in the desert. It would do. He had three bags tied at his waist: one contained the slivers of bone and rock that were his tools, and the other two water. He had walked for two days to get back here. He wasn't sure why unless it was to remind himself of who he was. Sometimes in the silent emptiness of the desert it was easy to forget, to become an extension of the landscape. He fingered the metal medallion on the chain around his neck...

21
Hydra

London
1981

The meeting in Putney, a week later, was a subdued affair. Tony provided the briefest of summaries of what Anstruther had had to say and sat back.

'So – we are minus Anstruther now, I guess,' said Julian finally. 'We continue the meetings?'

'Why not?' asked Lewin. 'I don't think we need to update Carew and Professor Danes just yet – they probably won't miss him. As far as they know, he was the assistant who just sat there most of the time. I can make up some story. While I'm about it, I can say you've changed your mind and are rejoining us, Julian. I think we need to keep the team going.'

'Yes, I agree with that,' said Tony. 'The guys in the Mojave won't know what's happened to Anstruther but they may be able to monitor usage. We need the machine if we are to kill the hydra and we can't risk them deciding this part of the project has been compromised and sending someone in to close it down, something they'd probably do with extreme prejudice, as they say.'

Maggie looked worried. 'Do you really think the Committee members are in danger?'

'It'd be stupid to deny that possibility, Maggie,' Tony replied. 'We do all need to be careful. They don't know about you and me, though, because Anstruther didn't – and so far, they've no reason to suspect anyone on the Committee might know of the other travellers or of them, themselves.'

'But that still begs the question, doesn't it, of what the people in America are currently doing with this technology.' Emmeline had been sitting quietly next to Maggie who was holding her hand protectively. 'Anstruther was dealing with the same people that Tony and I knew in the sixties by going back to that time. We know that because, from what he said, my going to Haight Ashbury and France was still relatively recent news for them. So what's going on *now* in 1981? Is there another lot somewhere sending people back to change their present? Or is the focus of the people right at the top just on us now and our researches?'

'And why Haight Ashbury, anyway? Why the 15th century? Why a cave in the Ice Age, for God's sake! That's three more questions begging answers at least!' Julian sighed. 'And, assuming Janus has been in charge all along in one form or another, who are they and what on earth is their *agenda* here? That's the big one for us.'

'OK, Emmeline. OK, Julian!' Tony sat forward in his chair hands raised as if addressing a group of children. 'I can answer some of that and maybe guess the rest. Firstly, Anstruther talked about a consortium, a group of companies or businessmen. My guess is that they are now calling themselves Janus. Forget the charitable foundation thing.

'Secondly, why Haight Ashbury? I think that's straightforward enough. That was my era. The CIA were definitely involved there; they were doing all sorts of experimentation with all manner of drugs then, not just the kind of drugs they dished out to Emmeline and me. They had a couple of big names in on a program to do with LSD, for example. These guys volunteered to be guinea pigs and report on what happened to them. There were rumours at the time that they wanted to know how bigger groups would react, as well. Not psychiatrists and so on but Joe Public en masse.

'Anyway, Emmy Lou was set up as an insider. And, of course, all the people she met – you met, Emmeline – things they got up to in their youth – you would have been debriefed on that, I'm sure, if things hadn't gone wrong for them. They would see that as an investment. It was what they sent me back to do, after all.'

'But *I* didn't *make* anyone do anything,' protested Emmeline, 'or even encourage them! But carry on...'

'Yeah, well... the 15th century? The cave in the Ice Age? If you think about it, those trips did have you all convinced that what you were taking part in was *academic*. And, as far as they were concerned, they had a bona fide scientist on board, an anthropologist whom nobody could suspect of being anything other than an egghead, a ditzy historian and a shrink who was prepared to play the game. Not too sure why she agreed but she was necessary. No-one would suspect you because you were all straight up. Maybe a couple of new people would have joined you before long – their people. Meanwhile, if anyone else picked up on Lewin's early research, as they did, or got curious about the anomalies – well you're the perfect cover story.

'As for how it all relates to the Mojave folk now – what they're up to – that I haven't figured out yet. It's like you were operating as a cell buried in the future, their future. Maybe Julian going forward was planned to be part of that only he went evangelical and it all began to seem counter-productive.'

'Ditzy?' Emmeline raised her eyebrows. 'I'll have you know, I have a PhD, young man! I'm not saying they sought me out across continents but when they picked up the bait I left in various articles, *they*

193

approached *me*. Or Anstruther did, now I come to think about it. I have an extremely solid, non-ditzy reputation.'

'OK, OK – not ditzy!' Tony smiled at her. 'They should've been terrified of you, *we* know that!'

Emmeline blinked and looked as if she had been slapped. Lewin glared at Tony.

'You're brave and a survivor, Emmeline, that's what I mean,' Tony added hurriedly.

'And I may be able to help with the other question,' said Julian, 'what they're all doing nowadays. I'm just flying a kite here – but there's a hunk of history you've missed, Tony. You've never even heard of Watergate, have you?'

'No, can't say I have. You mentioned it but I kinda forgot to ask!'

'Richard Nixon, the President in the early seventies was, I believe, a CIA-backed and backing man. He was as anti-Red as anyone you've described. His team was into every kind of dirty trick – maybe they all were in those days – but he got caught out. It's a long story but he ended up having to resign over that and all the lies he told to cover up. There were a couple of investigations and first one and then the other laid open this whole can of worms you were talking about – what the CIA got up to in other countries and at home. That, or some of it, is common knowledge now. The CIA was pretty damaged. I think the FBI may have put the boot in, too.'

'I'll bet they did! Tricky Dicky got to be President – and he *resigned*? Hey, you *are* going to have to catch me up!'

'I shall,' Julian reassured him, 'but the outcome was that the CIA had to make all sorts of undertakings not to go around assassinating foreign leaders and running these covert programs to subvert other governments. They and the FBI got read the riot act about dirty tricks on US citizens, including what they tried to do (and maybe did) to Martin Luther King. But, before you say anything, yes! I'm sure they'll have picked up a lot of those pieces again. But possibly not all of them. Who knows what eggs were broken back then? It's only five or six years ago.'

'You're right. You may have more than you think there. If the shake-up was bad enough and the Base was closed it might not have had time to re-build yet. Who knows? That might be another reason for your cell, of course. Anstruther sent forward, as a safety net, to set up a permanent link with a machine here. Maybe, in time, a new permanent base. And, you reckon the other players apart from the CIA, may have got to walk away from it all?'

'I think they must have. If Anstruther answers direct to them, as he seems to, they may have just laid low and waited a few years.' Julian ran his hands through his hair and frowned before continuing. 'Janus may be the current cover for those people but, after all this time, would they be the exact same people? I doubt it. I wonder if the Consortium or Janus is some kind of association or even family-based organisation that just goes on and on?'

'I guess the baton *must* get passed on – maybe has ever since the days of the robber barons before the war,' said Tony. He tapped his fingers on the arm of his chair and stared out of the window, lost in thought.

Lewin looked around at the others as they struggled to work out the possibilities, too. Not for the first time he thought how lucky they had been to find Tony when they did. They had been marching forward blindly into something so much bigger than they could have ever imagined.

'Isn't this what you've been looking for, Tony?' Maggie asked eventually. 'A way in to break the

195

hydra?'

'Put it this way, Maggie, I know what I have to do next. Julian, I'm going to needs names and dates – all you can lay your hands on.'

'I think you have most of the names and dates you need... I suspect it's more a case of you casting your mind back and then making sure the information gets to the right people. I'll help as much as I can.'

22
Area 51

Mojave
1976

The sterile collection of buildings known to some as Area 51 was in a state of confusion. There was a pall of smoke from bonfires and scraps of charred paper were drifting up into the cloudless sky. Gym equipment and office furniture were piled in the dust in front of the Reception area awaiting the trucks which would take them away to other bases in Nevada and California. The accommodation block was empty, the beds and bedding long gone. Only the machine repair room and Ely's own sanctum remained untouched and it was the future of the machines that exercised the three people sitting around a table in a 27-foot Winnebago parked by the guard house.

'Look, Errol, we can't delay much longer. Our guy's told us that time is running out. They could turn up at any moment.' Miss Andrews was addressing her husband, known generally as Dr Ely. 'There's no point in our having burnt all our records and clearing all traces of a special training unit if they get their hands on the machines, is there?' Her frustration was evident.

'They need to go somewhere, Celine. We can't just destroy them. I made history with that machine – in more ways than one. We have agents back in time depending on us – think of them.'

'Since when have you worried about the agents! Anyway, you'll still have one machine, won't you, in

197

future London? And not that far in the future, either.'

'I know we have, in theory, but we seem to have lost contact with Anstruther and we don't actually know what's going on there.'

'But we know the machine has been used recently,' his wife argued. 'Who do you think is using it, if not Anstruther?'

Frank Lundin, the third man in the Winnebago, looked thoughtful. 'We can't tell for sure from here. That's the problem. We can only hope the others involved don't know about us and that the coordinates are still the same if we try to send someone there to find out. The good news is that Anstruther was always adamant that no-one suspected that there might be any other machines or any other travellers. The only person that side who knew about us – well he dealt with her before she could talk to anyone else.'

'Oh, yes. The hippie queen. I remember her and her motorbike.' Andrews laughed. 'Not one of his brightest choices!'

'I'm with you, anyway, Erroll,' said Lundin. 'I don't see why we can't just stash the machines away somewhere until the dust blows over. The Company isn't finished for good and I doubt the Consortium is. They will be re-grouping as we speak and when they're back they'll be knocking at our door.'

'You may well be right,' said Andrews. 'But the FBI is having a field day at our expense at the moment and they may even have some idea by now of what we've been doing here. Do you want this all to fall into FBI hands?'

'I don't really care,' said Ely. 'We were always out on a limb – deniable and expendable as far as the CIA were concerned. That was made clear. Hell, most CIA people didn't know about us at all and only a couple of the ones who did had any idea of what we were actually doing. If the FBI does come here, or anyone

198

else, for that matter, well – does it really matter who we work for?'

'You'd swap sides? That's a thought!' Lundin laughed. 'But, I dunno – so many things we thought were under wraps have been coming out in the last five years I don't know that we can assume anything. The FBI is in as bad a way as us. Leaking like a sieve as far as I can make out.'

'And it's intelligence guys like Pyle spilling the beans,' said Andrews. 'I really don't get that. The guy spends his life as a military spook and then has to go public with it all? Don't you reckon someone leaned on him, Frank?'

'What? A journalist who just got lucky? I think it would have had to come from someone who really had the low down on him in the first place – so maybe we should be looking at one of us.'

'By *one of us* do you mean a Company man?' asked Andrews. 'Most of them wouldn't know about our existence here, as Errol said. Or do you mean one of *us?* That would be another matter altogether!'

They sat and considered this possibility in silence.

'I thought you dealt with all the flaky ones,' said Ely eventually.

'*We* did, *all* of us did, if you remember,' Lundin replied pointedly. 'But we have to face up to the fact that these journalists, Sy Hersch and the like, have been getting their information from somewhere. And it's been good information. And those Washington Post guys and their Deep Throat – even if that really was a government man, as they say it was – why was he *doing* it? I reckon he was leaned on, like Pyle, by someone who knew where the bodies were buried. Who better than one of us? And can we take the chance that it wasn't? We have to get the machines out now. Because we might be the next revelation. No-one will believe it, of course, without the machines. With

199

them? Who knows what will happen? Everything is out of control right now.'

'Well, that is what I am saying. But they need to be actually physically destroyed, too,' Andrews sighed. 'Unless there is visible evidence of their destruction, no-one who knows about them will ever let us be or stop looking for them. Can't you see that?'

'Well, if this person *is* one of us and knows about the machines, why hasn't he brought the FBI here already?' her husband asked, exasperated.

'Maybe they don't know what to do with the three of us,' said Lundin. 'If they bring us down personally they'll have an unusable asset on their hands. The most valuable asset any government or private agency could possibly want. That's going to need some thought, for them. It's a big deal – or the guy may be working on how he can get us on side,' he went on. 'Big bucks would do it for me whoever he is and whoever he's working for.' Lundin sat back, the idea appealing to him more and more.

Andrews could feel the case for destroying the machines slipping away from her. 'This individual, if it is an individual, who has set the whole ball rolling – Rockefeller, Church and the rest – what if he's on some kind of mission?

'How about that as a possibility? Maybe he found Jesus or something. That's the impression I'm getting anyway. He or she won't be happy until the whole thing is blown wide open. They won't be offering us money, Frank, they'll be locking us up!'

'I've just had another thought,' said Ely. 'Anstruther. He went forward to London in the mid seventies and built a machine there, with this guy Lewin who was already more than half-way there. Sets up an academic team as a cover and starts sending out amateurs. Nobody over there but him knows about us, right?' The other two nodded their agreement.

'Suddenly, after five or six years of regularly keeping in touch and coming in for debriefs – one day, in 1981 their time, 1970 ours, he just disappears. And *that* is just about when Pyle and the other tale-bearers start getting going. A couple of years later and the police just happen to roll up at Watergate when the President's plumbers are there. Some bad luck for the President, don't you think?'

Andrews put her head in her hands. 'You think it could be *Anstruther*? That is unbelievable, Errol, even if he always was a kind of outsider as far as we were concerned. But, on the other hand, what about Dr King? Who started leaking rumours on our surveillance and involvement there? Who leant on James Earl Ray to retract his confession and feed the conspiracy theorists? After all, where was it Ray was arrested? Heathrow! Why did he go there? Whose idea was that?'

'And all the interventions in South America, added Lundin. 'Everyone at the top knew about them from Eisenhower to Johnson via the Kennedy family. Why did that all come out when it did? Someone has been putting that information into the wrong hands and turning the tables on our guys. We know that. Could it really have been Anstruther?' asked Lundin. 'Do you reckon it was on his own or on orders from the top? Where's the Consortium in all this? And why?'

'Because of that guy who went into the future?' Andrews speculated. 'We thought Anstruther was going to drop that line–'

'–hold it! What's that?' interrupted Lundin. 'There's a bike coming down the track.'

He opened the door and peered out at the approaching dust cloud. 'Who the hell...'

'If we've left it too late to destroy the machines, Errol, God help us,' snapped Andrews 'All your ifs and buts could have cost us everything!'

'Oh, cut it out, Celine! It's only a motor bike, one guy!'

'Two,' said Lundin. 'There's a passenger.'

A tall slim figure in leathers slipped off the pillion of the bike as it drew up outside the Winnebago and came up the steps to the open door. The bike veered away towards the buildings at the rear of the compound.

'What do you want?' demanded Lundin. 'This is a High Security Zone. Scram! I can see you're not one of ours.'

Maggie removed her full-visored helmet and let her long hair fall to her shoulders in an auburn cascade. She tossed her head a couple of times.

'No – I'm not. Well-spotted! I'm Maggie. I've come from the London group, Anstruther's people. Do I get a cup of coffee?'

'Please... do come in. Was I forgetting my manners? Or should you have informed us you were coming?'

'Now then, don't be sarcastic! You must be Frank.' She stepped past him into the camper and smiled at his companions. 'Dr Ely and Miss Andrews, how do you do? My name is Maggie. We haven't met.'

'And where, may I ask, is Anstruther? We were expecting him to have the courtesy to come in person, you know,' said Andrews.

Maggie was reminded forcefully of her mother's description of Miss Andrews.

'Oh, he's around here somewhere,' she replied vaguely.

'Really! I think he has some explaining to do. Will he be joining us?' asked Andrews.

'Oh no, it's only me and my friend out there *now*! I can see you aren't expecting company, I must say. More like you're doing a flit! Is anything wrong?'

'A flit? Christ. Yes, there is a lot wrong, as you put it – and we were hoping Anstruther might be able to enlighten us about one or two things.'

'For a start,' said Ely, 'we need to know how the three of you got here from London, if that's where you've come from, and how long you've been here before condescending to contact us.'

'We came with the machine, of course. I've only been here a matter of days myself but my friend has been backwards and forwards over the last few months – or do I mean years? These questions are always a bit confusing in the circumstances, though, aren't they?'

'And Anstruther?'

'Oh he's been here for ages!'

'I see,' said Andrews. 'He's been here for *ages* and has chosen not to contact us. I wonder what on earth he can have been doing! And what is *your* role in this, exactly? You and your friend? Have you come as tourists to gloat over the destruction of the project? You do realise that my husband here is the brains behind it? Anstruther and Lewin are nothing.'

'The most significant and important scientific project of the millennium, at least, is going up in smoke here,' added Ely. 'If you don't help us it will be lost to the world, possibly forever.' He was almost begging. 'We can still salvage it, though, if the base in London is working. Is that why you're here?'

'I don't think it is.' Lundin had been watching Maggie thoughtfully. 'Although I'm not too sure what you do want, Miss – Maggie. That isn't a name I recognise from Anstruther's reports, incidentally, but what is your interest here?'

'My interest is in what kind of people you are to use these machines to manipulate history – using them for short term advantage and profit for yourselves and your bosses, eliminating anyone who gets in the way, your own people included. Not that we haven't been doing similar things, of course. My friend out there has been busy sowing the seeds of your destruction for quite a while. I'm sure you've worked out that somebody has. And when we go home we're going to be using our knowledge of the future to try and change it, just like you did, but for everyone's benefit. It doesn't look like much is going to survive for long in London the way things are going – so your experiment would have reached its end at some point anyway, if it's any consolation.'

'Maggie,' said Lundin reasonably, with a world-weary smile. 'Maggie, you're a kid, you don't understand. How could you? We've been at war, fighting for democracy and our American values. In wars you get casualties.'

'And our own people that we had to let go, Maggie,' added Andrews, 'we just moved them. We didn't kill them. Where *is* Anstruther, though? We really do need to talk to him personally.'

Maggie sighed theatrically. 'I can see I'm not going to get any coffee, we might as well go to the machine room. My friend has been following Lewin's instructions on setting up the machines – he seems to think you have more than one ready to go.'

'Yes, we do,' said Ely. 'We had considered leaving, of course, but needed to know the status of the London base first. Once there, we can discuss where we go with the technology and provide some obviously-needed explanations. I presume Anstruther will be with us by then? If it's a deal you want,' he looked sideways at Lundin, 'we can talk deals then, too.'

Maggie threw her hands up in the air. 'OK – you win. All will be made clear. Come along.'

She led the way out of the Winnebago towards the buildings where the bike had disappeared. They found it parked outside the machine room but Tony was nowhere in sight. Inside the room were three units, all wired up with lit panels. Ely went across and glanced quickly at the settings.

'They're fine,' he reassured the other two. 'They're set for London. I don't know what Anstruther's game is but I guess he knows what he's doing.' He turned to Maggie. 'I get the impression you Londoners (and Anstruther, I assume?) want some changes made. That's OK. You're making the right decision here, though. You'll take charge of destroying these machines when we've gone?' he asked as the three of them took their seats.

'We certainly will.'

'Thanks, Maggie, whoever you are,' said Lundin. 'I hope we can get together in London – put this awkward start behind us. Maybe I can take you out for a drink one day – try some of that warm beer you English like so much?'

'Oh shut up, Frank! Get yourself strapped in!' snapped Andrews. 'The sooner we leave here the better.'

'How about going for a pint with me instead, Frank?' said Tony as he came into the room, pulling his helmet from his head. 'Maggie's Scottish anyway, as she would no doubt have informed you, given a chance. Not the same thing at all.'

Frank was staring at Tony, slack-jawed.

'Ah, not sure you recognise me? Bit grey round the edges? A lot's happened.'

Ely and Andrews sat pale and still.

Ely was the first to move; he leaned back and grabbed the lever. 'Just do it, Celine. We can't trust him!'

There was a shiver of light and he was gone. Followed by Andrews.

Frank Lundin sat back and looked across at Tony

steadily.

'I don't know how you did it, Tony, but I'd guess they're not in London, right?'

'You'd be wrong. They are. Just not the London that has pubs – or buildings, for that matter. Not the London Maggie and I'll be going back to. We have a road trip planned first – I think my ma and pa will like her, don't you? They'll be a bit shocked, of course, and not just by the way I've aged. Then it's London and fighting for a future. Something worthwhile, Frank. Don't you wish you had lived for something worthwhile?'

'You mean, don't I wish I was about to die for something worthwhile?'

'Nos moritori te salutamus! Is that how it goes, Maggie? Speaks fluent Latin, Maggie does – we both do! Who'd a thought it? That's how we met in a way.'

Lundin sighed. 'OK. Where's it to be? Get on with it!'

'The surprise is half the adventure, don't you think?'

An hour later, the flying saucer watchers of Nevada were rewarded with an explosion that lit the sky and was visible for tens of miles in all directions. The imaginative reported seeing saucer-shaped vessels ascending to the heavens. The less imaginative reported a motorbike heading through the desert towards Reno.

23
Explanations

England was reeling from the shock of being a nation at war again. The Argentine invasion of the Falklands hadn't been an April Fool's joke after all. Overnight, Maggie Thatcher had become Britannia with a handbag. Carew, too, was reeling from shock. He turned down Julian's offer of a lift with a distracted wave of his hand and walked blindly towards the river. He turned to his left and walked along the path under the trees until he found a vacant bench. The sun was already low over the river. Dark clouds boded an end to the unseasonably hot weather of the last week but promised a spectacular sunset.

He had been surprised to receive the invitation to lunch at Lewin's house but, seeing an opportunity to push his request for an expedition to an Iron Age Settlement in the Outer Hebrides, he had decided to go. Nothing had been resolved at the previous meeting at St Jude's, whether because of Anstruther's absence or Weatherspoon's presence, again, he didn't know. The man was still obsessed with the implications of his trip to the future. Carew's need now was for space to digest everything he had heard today.

The small sitting room was already full of people when he'd got there, people sitting on stools and on cushions on the floor. Space was made for him on a small sofa beside Professor Danes, who had been looking as bemused as he felt. They had been introduced to a young girl, who was apparently Dr Harrison's daughter, and a tall black man whom he thought he might have heard of before, but couldn't quite place. He had bridled at the thought that the Committee had been extended in this way without consultation.

'This must seem strange, Philip,' Emmeline had said, as if reading his mind, 'but we have a lot to tell you and I really hope you can understand why we've been so slow bringing you and Joan up to speed.'

'Better be good,' he'd muttered ungraciously.

It had been – if good was the right word, which he doubted.

First of all, Emmeline had introduced herself as Emmy Lou – a shock in itself – and given a brief account of what she had seen in the desert; and of what had happened to her on her return. She had skimmed over events in France but concluded her tale with a shrug. 'I wasn't supposed to survive, you see. If it had been known that I *had* survived I suspect I would have been dealt with some other way.'

'You're looking unsure, Dr Carew,' Tony had said, 'but perhaps my story may convince you. I worked at the base that Emmeline went to in the Mojave. I was a time traveller myself until I started questioning things.'

The story had got more and more fantastical. He heard for the first time about Weatherspoon's second trip to the future and the events that had led to Maggie's rescue mission to Reculver. Tony had then given a brief account of his own career in the shadows and his recent attempts to sabotage the CIA project in Washington and the Mojave.

Carew and Professor Danes had sat in silence throughout.

'Good thing you had the chicken pox, Emmeline,

208

wasn't it?' Joan Danes had commented, at the end.

'Yes. Well – I didn't, of course. I couldn't get my head around the implications of meeting myself and knowing that I couldn't warn me!'

'But why couldn't you?' Professor Danes had asked.

'What we do next is important, Joan. I'm here and I've been able to help put right some wrongs and play a part in dealing with Anstruther – and maybe even improved the future for everyone. If I had by some miracle succeeded in changing things for myself, would we ever have suspected what Anstruther was up to? And Maggie! What about her? Would she have ever happened? Remember I had the benefit of hindsight to some extent.'

Tony had nodded. 'And I would still be speaking Latin – and the unit in the Mojave would probably have gone from strength to strength.'

Lewin had taken up the tale again. 'We decided that something had to be done to stop what was going on – how the machine was being used. We had no recourse to law – we were unsure of what MI6 would do, even if they believed us, and weren't convinced that they wouldn't be tempted to pick up where the CIA left off, themselves. And, this is the point: we decided on a line of action that some might consider wrong. We felt we had to act quickly and couldn't take a chance on having our decision vetoed in the Committee or one of you deciding you would rather trust the police.'

'And bearing in mind what we had discovered about Anstruther and that Emmeline has been less than truthful,' Weatherspoon had added, 'maybe we were over cautious about you, too, about how much you knew and where your allegiances might lie...'

'Julian!' Lewin had said, frowning. 'That's not helpful.'

'Yes, it is, isn't it Philip? Neither of you are stupid and we still don't really know how you got involved.

It's just that we've decided to put our cards on the table and trust you now. We have to.'

Carew had felt his face flush with indignation but, as the enormity of it all sank in, he had sat back and nodded. 'Thank you for that, at least. I can assure you that I am exactly what I appear to be and very dull that now seems. I don't think I want to know what line of action you took but I assume Anstruther will no longer be joining the Committee meetings. Do I assume, also, that we are now in charge of the whole programme on both sides of the Atlantic?'

'As far as we know we now have the only machine,' Tony had said, 'but we didn't give the Mojave people time to notify operatives in the field of what was happening before we blew up the base and there may well be time travellers out there still. We don't know when or where – or whether they were told of the political threat to the programme. For all we know they may be trying to undermine what I did in Washington in the seventies as we speak. Neither did we get to the backers of their project, the people they referred to as the Consortium.'

'But you don't think they'll succeed in undoing your work in the Mojave?' Carew had asked.

'No, I honestly don't. If the project had continued it couldn't have been kept under wraps forever and we know from Julian that a hundred years from now no-one has heard of the technology.'

They had all fallen silent as this sank in. No-one seemed inclined to break the spell but Carew had become aware that the focus of attention had now shifted to Joan Danes who was staring blankly out of the window.

Eventually, she had shifted in her chair and looked around her at the waiting group.

'Oh,' she had said. 'My turn. Just to reassure you, I had no idea about Emmy Lou or CIA involvement, or about other time travellers, for that matter. But, like Philip, I won't take offence at your caution.' She had paused for a moment. 'I did know that Anstruther was pulling the strings in the Committee. I could see how he manipulated the meetings and, of course, it was he who approached me to join it in the first place. He said, or implied, he was MI6. You may have been right to be cautious about contacting the authorities here – I don't know.'

'It was Anstruther who explained your role to you, then,' Emmeline had said softly. 'Why did you agree, Joan?'

'That's a good question – the sixty four thousand dollar question, as they say. I'm qualified enough. I worked for the SOE during the war when I was a student – I helped set up the psychological assessment programmes for their operatives. I'm afraid even now I can't tell you the kind of things we were doing then. One of my jobs was to convince the candidates who didn't get accepted to keep quiet about what they had learned in the assessment process. They were tough times and tough things had to be done. It made me the ideal candidate for this, I suppose.'

'You didn't have to take it on, though, did you?' Emmeline had asked.

'No. I could have said no – but some of things we did in the war, some of the things I did, don't sound so good in peace time. I would probably have lost my job if word had got out... I don't want to retire just yet.'

Weatherspoon had cut to the chase: 'You were blackmailed, then.'

'I suppose I was, in a way,' Professor Danes had replied, 'but, you know, Anstruther never asked me to do anything against my better judgement. Those youngsters needed to be psychologically suitable, just as the ones in the war did. I played my part in that. I was never asked to collude in keeping anyone quiet – the situation didn't arise.'

'But you made sure they knew the score before they went...' Carew had said. He hadn't seen why she should get off lightly.

'As did we all, directly or by our silence,' Lewin had said firmly. 'We all shut our minds to things we didn't want to face up to. That's collusion in itself, Philip. But we are where we are and the question now is where do we go from here?'

'The next Committee meeting at the hospital is already fixed for June,' Emmeline had reminded them. 'I think we all need to give this some thought; I don't think we'll be using young volunteers again so if you want to withdraw, Joan, you can. And you, of course, Philip – although we still have the option of continuing a research programme. Nobody has to decide anything right now.'

People had started to drift off soon after that.

Carew sat on the bench by the river letting everything he had learned sink in. The last walkers had passed him on their way back to the road and the last rowing boat had found its way to shore by the time he realised, with a shiver, that it was time to go home. He had missed the sunset. He pulled himself up stiffly and made his way back to Putney Bridge and the District Line. He had much to think about and decisions to make.

24
Fundraising

London
1982

The war was over by the time the Committee next met at St Jude's. Nine hundred men had died, three hundred and twenty when a nuclear-powered submarine sank the *Belgrano*. Eighteen hundred islanders could now sleep easy in their beds and Britain celebrated. Julian was evidently less enthusiastic.

'There were 750,000 of us at that demonstration against nuclear weapons in Central Park in New York,' he said, as they waited to see if Joan Danes would arrive. 'I come back here and all people can talk about are our marvellous nuclear-powered submarines. I don't think they'd have cared if we had actually nuked Buenos Aires!'

'It doesn't seem right, I know,' said Emmeline.

'What we need now is a major nuclear accident to counterbalance the impact of victory, isn't it?' said Carew.

'Yes! That is, no, of course not. We just need a bit of publicity about the number of minor accidents there have been with these submarines and with the warheads but *that* is an official secret apparently. The Russians haven't been so lucky in keeping things under wraps but our attitude is "Oh dear, poor sailors dying of radiation – but what can you expect when Russians have this technology!" *Everyone* will have this technology if it is allowed to continue. What

213

makes us think we will have any say in safety rules and quality of construction in the future?'

'And it's not just poor Russians, is it? What about the poor fish and the other fish that eat them? Don't they get poisoned, too?'

They all turned to look at Maggie. Lewin wondered, not for the first time, what got into Emmeline and her daughter sometimes.

'Save the pilchard?' asked Julian who, Lewin had noted, seemed to have a soft spot for the girl. 'It doesn't have quite the same ring as Save the Whale, does it? But you may have a point. I hadn't thought of that.'

'I'd put the thought on hold, anyway, if I were you,' laughed Emmeline. 'I'm not sure the world is quite ready for that yet, hen, and we've enough on our plates without worrying about pilchards, in a potential pickle or not.'

There was a single knock on the door. Joan walked in and looked around the room. 'Well, I'm here if you think I can be of use. I wanted you to know that I'm behind you, anyway.'

Lewin stood. 'I am so glad. We did want you and Philip with us – but I know we handled it badly. That and so many other things.'

'Never mind. I did understand. I'm sorry I'm late.'

'We were just discussing the possibility of polluted Polish pilchards getting in a pickle, Joan,' said Julian with his most charming smile.

'Best place,' said Joan arranging her bony form elegantly on the chair that had been left vacant for her.

'Ignore him, Professor. I try to.' Maggie looked crossly at Julian. 'Very funny!'

'Let's move on, can we?' asked Lewin. 'Julian. You've raised the possibility of someone going back to Australia, a few years later, and making their way to

Britain, if your friend can swing it. Why not go straight to Britain in the machine?'

'I think it would be a good idea to be part of a properly equipped team to start with. The Australians are learning more about radiation protection all the time,' replied Julian. 'And I think the journey itself would be informative. There would be a lot of stopovers, I imagine. It's a matter of judging when those flights will start and hoping that Bill is still around! He seemed to think they were nearly there.'

Tony looked unconvinced. 'Taking a bit of a chance, then. The later you leave it the less likely you are to have a contact there.'

'Bill's not that old and things were moving quickly but, yes, you have a point.' Julian replied. 'I'm not necessarily talking about me, anyway. There are other things we need to do here and there's the question of radiation exposure, too; we don't know enough about it yet but I've already had quite a bit. It's going to be important for people to go to the UK and the US at some point to find out what went wrong – what the political and economic background to it all was as well as what the results were, so I think we need to be cautious about exposing them to other journeys to even a mildly radioactive world until we know we will get maximum benefit...'

'And didn't you say that China figured in all this, Julian?' asked Emmeline.

Julian nodded. 'I did, Emmeline. And it is starting to happen right now – old economic practices changing and so on. China is already on the move.'

'So you want someone to see what the damage is in the US and find out who was responsible for what went wrong so you can target them or influence them in some way now. Sounds familiar!' Tony sighed.

'It's right up your street, Tony,' said Maggie. 'It's what you are good at – but this time for a good cause.

I could come, too! You never know when Duke of Edinburgh skills will come in handy.'

'A good cause...' said Tony, ignoring her offer. 'Where have I heard that before? It was *always* for a good cause! The protection of civilisation and life as we know it–'

'–but you can't possibly think that what I saw in Manchester was in any way desirable,' Julian interrupted urgently. 'Maggie's right!'

'No-one's suggesting we're going to assassinate anyone or set them up in any way, Tony,' said Lewin. 'I think it's more a case of finding out what we should be concentrating on *now* in terms of campaigning, funding research and so on. At least I sincerely hope that's what we're all talking about.'

'Yes, of course it is,' said Julian, 'although, talking about funding...'

'Yes, that's another thing.' Carew leant forward. 'Who exactly is funding all this? Who is paying the piper now? Can't be the NHS, surely.' So far he had been sitting back, arms folded, an expression of disapproval on his narrow face. Lewin had been waiting for his objections.

'Of course not,' said Lewin, 'although this room and the basement room come for free on the back of my hospital research. The costs of making and running the machine have been funded by Janus, via Anstruther. They've also been backing my medical research. So it's a good question, Philip. That cash is presumably going to dry up now. I assume you've been paying for your activities from your own money so far, Julian?'

'I have, but my resources are finite. We can hardly apply for funding from anywhere else, can we? Even the research into the past has to be hush hush, assuming we do go on with that.'

'This really is not a problem, guys,' said Tony. 'A

short trip back with some horse-racing results – or anything else people bet on – and we'll be sure-fire winners, won't we?'

'Somewhat immoral, Tony,' said Emmeline, 'but not a bad idea, at all. We'd have to shuffle the money about a bit or it might look as if a bunch of gamblers had suddenly developed planet-sized social consciences. But do-able.'

'Yes. That could work,' said Julian. 'But have we decided yet on who's going where?'

Lewin was the first to speak. 'Sounds as if Tony with his CIA skills and Maggie with her, er, Duke of Edinburgh skills might be our best bet for the US. You've definitely decided against Australia, then, Julian?'

'I'd like to see old Bill again, it's true, but I've plenty to do here – quite apart from the radiation thing. It would be my third trip into the future and I told you what they said about me being a walking a miracle. Maybe the time travel protected me in some way. Who knows? I can do the fund-raising trip, though. I've probably led a more disreputable life than most of you and would know where to look. I might even deposit some money in an Australian bank for future use. As far as I could see, their financial services were still operational over there.'

'Gold and jewellery are good, too,' said Tony. 'Divide it up and bury it somewhere and we should get most of it back.'

'Sounds like a plan. And I'll give a bit of thought to the impact of the time travel on radiation poisoning,' said Lewin, feeling quite excited at the prospect of this new avenue of research. 'With some funding I could set up a separate research project. Depends how much money we get. And I'd need to get help if I'm going to keep the day job going. But what about you, Philip? Have you anything you would like us to be

217

considering?'

Philip nodded. 'Well, I had had my eye on an Iron Age Fort and was going to see if we could arrange for Darren to go back there. He'd need to know a bit more about what is going on now, though. We seem to be expanding our numbers – how about him? We'd have to explain everything to him, of course.'

'How reliable do you think he is?' asked Emmeline. 'I agree that we should be upfront with everybody involved now so we'd be admitting him to the Committee.'

'I trust him,' said Carew. 'He is a solid academic and he's managed to keep quiet about the source of his thesis so far. More of an artist these days, though. He might not even want to go.'

'Sound him out, then,' suggested Julian. 'Any other ideas?'

Carew hesitated for a moment and cleared his throat. 'I was actually rather wondering if I shouldn't do some travelling, myself. Nothing too ambitious. I'm not the derring-do type, obviously.' He looked around defiantly.

The room fell silent.

'I think you've taken us all aback, Philip,' said Lewin, 'but why not? Are you sure you want to? Where to?' He could not imagine what had got into Carew and his face must have reflected his amazement.

Carew bridled. 'I'm no CIA man – or boy scout for that matter – but I think I could manage to go back a few years and make an investment to help us with funding now. Or even put money into some up and coming company if you point me in the right direction.'

'That's not a bad idea.' Emmeline was looking impressed. 'It would spread the *luck,* so to speak, and draw less attention. Thanks, Philip. Did you have any idea of when and where?'

'Oh, I don't know. I was thinking of perhaps going back ten years or so from the date we all got going here. 1966? Oxford is a place I know my way around.'

'Any good sporting events to bet on then, I wonder. How do we find out?' Lewin was frowning. He wasn't at all sure Carew was the right man for this job.

'Give me strength!' exclaimed Julian. 'You might not get great odds on the World Cup but it would be criminal not to place the bet! You'd do better on the Grand National: I seem to remember the winner was something of an outsider that year. Go mid-March their time.'

'You seem very, knowledgeable,' Lewin commented drily. 'Who would have thought it?'

Carew was sitting forward, hands clasped in front of him, as if unsure of what he had agreed to. *Why had he?* wondered Lewin, but Carew offered no explanation and made no further contributions to the discussion. Maggie, too, sat in silence. Lewin thought she looked a bit subdued.

As he walked to the station Carew was planning his conversation with Darren when he heard a soft footfall behind him.

'May I join you?'

He turned to see Professor Danes.

'I... er, yes, of course.'

They walked along companionably for a while.

'Interesting meeting,' Professor Danes observed eventually. 'You certainly surprised one or two people.'

'But not you?' He had to ask.

'No, not me.'

Carew felt the euphoria of the last half hour drain out of him, leaving him once again the calmer, lesser man he knew himself to be. 'Why is that, if I might ask? Superior psychoanalytical powers?'

'No. Just a good set of case notes.'

Carew stared at her.

'You know what my job was. It wasn't just the students, you know.'

'You missed Emmeline...'

'I did. She had an amazingly well rehearsed backstory, for an amateur. I was right about her positive qualities, though. Not a person to be underestimated.'

'Unlike me...'

'Your qualities are not the issue here, are they?'

'I don't follow...'

'Yes you do. How will Dr Pargetter react, do you think, when you turn up looking like your father one day and back to normal the next?'

'Not quite my father...'

'Close enough. It won't do, you know.'

Carew sighed irritably. 'If you say so.' He knew she was right.

'I do understand why you want to. Anyone would in your shoes.'

'If you know so much then surely you can see why I must... Or would it be meddling with history? Is that what you're afraid of?'

'No. I'm not that high-minded. Just practical. If you took Darren with you, could you take him into your confidence? I'd feel happier if you had him covering your back and maybe doing the actual bet placing and so on. You could give him all the local information he'd need. I have to say, though, that I believe you may well be disappointed and that concerns me. We don't really seem to change things that much at the end of the day – as far as we can tell, at least.'

'So you'll let the trip go ahead if I do it your way? If I keep out of sight and take Darren with me? You won't tell the others?'

'No. I won't tell. Confide in Darren, though.'

They had reached the bridge by now. The Professor

stopped and turned to face him. 'I'll leave you here. Different station. Have a safe journey home, Philip. The proposed timing is perfect, isn't it? Seems meant to be.'

She left as quietly as she'd come. Philip Carew watched her for a moment and then carried on across the bridge. Once on the train he sat back in the companionable fug of the over-crowded carriage and reflected on their conversation – and then on everything that had led him to this point.

25
Carew

Oxford
1966

Carew had never been what you would call a club-able man. Neither did he have a local pub where he could be sure to meet up with the chaps on a Friday night. At school he had been the swot, the outsider, last to be picked for any team. At university he had been studious and intense – not one for serenades and gaudies or drunken excesses of any kind. He had moved smoothly up the academic ladder, regarding colleagues as objects of suspicion rather than as like-minded men and women – let alone potential friends.

There was, however, a Mrs Carew. He was never quite sure how that had happened. One minute he was relatively content in his bachelor rooms near the university and the next he had found himself engaged to Dr Pargetter, a lecturer in Medieval French whom he had met at an inter-college dinner. She was an earnest lady in her late thirties (he was forty two at the time). They got on reasonably well, if by that it's meant that they seldom disagreed about anything and never argued. They both continued with their Oxford careers after a honeymoon in the South of France, where they managed to take advantage of academic contacts to add depth and interest to a trip that might otherwise have been a mere round of auberges and eating.

In the circumstances, perhaps the most surprising thing that happened in the early years of their marriage was the arrival of James. Carew watched his burgeoning wife with a detached interest bordering on revulsion. He didn't find the scrawny red baby much more appealing when he eventually materialised. He smelt of vomit and had a piercing cry – a cry that was calculated to drive Carew out of the house. Mrs Carew, as she seemed to have become, did not mind at all. She took James in her stride and juggled nappies and marking with her usual uncomplaining equanimity. With her unparalleled organisational skills she had produced James a couple of weeks into the summer vacation and had found a reliable childminder by the time the college term began again.

When colleagues asked about the baby, Carew was always faintly surprised and would reply with a vague, non-committal remark that cemented his reputation as a cold fish. It was not until James was two that Carew started to notice him. His own primary academic interest had always been in language development in primitive societies and here he found he had the privilege of watching the process of language development in his own home. He observed, made copious notes, and spent more and more time with the earnest little fellow who was always so anxious to please him – and whose rarely-bestowed smiles were like the warm sun on a winter's day. Over the next two years, Carew felt his heart begin to thaw. The job had not been completed when fate took a hand to see it never was.

One day James awoke with a cold. He was miserable and snotty and cried a lot. The childminder reported back that evening that he had been a bit better in himself but had now developed a cough. She didn't think it was anything to be worried about. Or so Mrs Carew told her husband over supper.

'I'm sure she knows what she's talking about, dear.'
'Yes. I do trust her judgement. She's so patient.

And I've got a tutorial first thing. Fellow's going to miss a Second if he's not careful!'

However, the next morning James was still listless and feverish and Mrs Carew, having been up and down to him all night, did take the day off work – something she had only ever done once or possibly twice before. Carew was never sure he approved of her lack of professionalism but James was her department, after all, and he was happy to let her get on with it.

When he came home that night it was to a cold, empty house. There was a note on the table: *Taken James to doctor's.* He sighed and went into the kitchen to put the kettle on. He opened the fridge and found some bread and some eggs. He stared at them for a moment wondering, irritably, why she hadn't put a time on her note. How long did a doctor's appointment take, for heaven's sake? Why hadn't she left earlier if that is what she was going to do? He shut the fridge. It was unlike her to be thoughtless over such things. There had probably been an exceptionally long wait at the surgery. They would be back any minute. He went through to the sitting room and turned on the radio to listen to the 6 o'clock news. It was past 7 o'clock when he heard the key turn in the lock.

'I've come to pick up some things,' said Mrs Carew. 'The doctor has arranged for James to be admitted overnight for observation.'

'He's only got a cold, surely.'

'It's gone onto his chest, apparently. He's given him antibiotics.'

'That's good. I wonder why he wants him in hospital as well.'

'Observation, as I said. I'm going to ask if I can stay with him, anyway. They'll probably say no but I might as well try.'

224

'That won't be necessary, surely? I'm sure the last thing they want is parents under their feet.'

'All the London hospitals welcome parents these days.'

Carew was not impressed. 'Well, I think it sounds like you don't trust them. How would you like it if mummy and daddy sat in at the back of the lecture theatre?'

'He's four, Philip!'

Carew threw his hands up. This was beginning to sound uncomfortably like a disagreement. 'You do what you think is best, dear. What would you like me to do?'

Mrs Carew ran her hands through her hair. 'Oh, I don't know. Can you make yourself an omelette or go down the road and get some fish and chips? I must get a move on.'

'No, I'll be fine. I didn't mean that. Just give me a ring when you know what's happening, will you?'

'Of course. Thanks.' His wife hesitated a moment by his chair and then, to his surprise, leant forward and gave him a swift kiss. It was the last time she was to do so.

In the end, it was Mrs Carew who took care of all the paperwork and appointments. Philip Carew just drifted through the next three weeks doing what he was told at the right time, unable to fully take in what had happened. He was glad she was such a competent, sensible woman. It made it so much easier. For himself, he had never been an emotional kind of chap and generally ran a mile from emotional displays in others.

The coroner said that everyone had done what they could – pneumonia was a silent killer and cruel. Dr and Mrs Carew bowed their heads, gravely appreciative of his consideration. The funeral was on a

Thursday. Carew was surprised to see the departmental secretary, Marian, there and a couple of junior lecturers. Marian was dabbing at her eyes with a white lacy hanky. He didn't really see why as, to the best of his knowledge, she had never met James. A woman introduced as the childminder was there, too, red-eyed and sniffing. It seemed his wife had quite a few friends whom he had never met: everyone looked tearful and distressed. He himself felt little.

He and Mrs Carew carried on as normal, throwing themselves into their work and spending whole evenings in different parts of the house. They had little to talk about, so they didn't. At the end of that year his doctor, the same one who had treated James, suggested that he consider taking things more easily. He had been having chest pains. Out of the blue, he would experience a sensation as if his chest was about to explode. He would find himself gasping, almost sobbing, to relieve it. The medication prescribed helped with the pains but, after a few days, left him unaccountably sad and depressed.

Then the job at University College in London came up. It was a demotion in academic terms but he could pursue his research in a more relaxed atmosphere with fewer departmental responsibilities and, if he was honest, it was a relief to be away from the constant reminders of James. He was not surprised when Mrs Carew decided to stay in Oxford. She phoned weekly 'to see how he was' and in the first year he went back to Oxford once a month. By now, that had become an annual visit in the long vacation. He would browse the bookshops and catch up with some old colleagues – find out what they were up to and so on, and deal with any matters pertaining to the house. Mrs Carew, now Dr Pargetter again, had found herself in a position to take on the mortgage and general expenses herself but nevertheless welcomed him and looked after him well for the week or so that he was there. They seldom mentioned James. It was better that way.

If he woke at night occasionally with his heart thumping and an acute sensation of emptiness and panic, he would get up, make himself a cup of tea and get on with some work. It was after a bad patch of these disturbances some ten years after James died, that he bumped into Gerald Hathaway, an acquaintance from his own student days. Now some kind of civil servant, Hathaway had asked him if he might be interested in a little part-time job. Good money for a few hours a month – a kind of consultancy. Hathaway was a bit vague on the details – he himself had been contacted by a chap in another department, *all a bit hush hush, you know*. His contact had actually mentioned Carew by name, something Hathaway had obviously found a bit odd.

He didn't think too much of his fellow committee members, a second rate historian, a psychiatrist of questionable ethics, a *writer*, for heaven's sakes, and a couple of bumbling scientists. No-one seemed to understand the enormous academic opportunities presented to them for research into the origins of man and prehistory. Darren Blythe had been a find. He was a Grammar School lad, as Carew had been himself, and Carew recognised the burning curiosity and dedication that can sometimes override parental and societal expectations and launch the most unpromising material into academia. Darren had been nervous, of course, but he had that *desire to know*.

Darren's dissertation, the year following his trip to Moravia, had been a tour de force. A lot of what he had learned was unusable, of course but, having chosen the title: *The role and significance of Ice Age art with special reference to the archaeological finds in Moravia,* his interpretations of these and other

227

finds elsewhere made so much sense that his First was a foregone conclusion and he had had several invitations to extend it into a PhD. He had opted, rather, to develop his own skills as a sculptor and painter. Disappointed, Carew had nevertheless stayed in touch and had high hopes of Darren returning to the academic fold. He had matured into a thoughtful, intelligent young man and actually became a kind of *friend* – a novel experience for Carew. He wrote a note to Darren that night, inviting him round to his flat the next Saturday.

'So you see the offer is there, if you're interested. If not – that's fine. I understand. It would only be for a couple of weeks, though, at the outside...' Carew tailed off apologetically in the face of Darren's silence.

It must have been fully a minute before the younger man looked up and met Carew's anxious gaze with his own cool grey one. 'Oxford in the mid-sixties. Some interesting people around then, I imagine, but not quite as exciting as last time...'

'Well, you could look on it as a way back in. They've said they're still interested in historical research and you would have shown yourself to be a prime candidate. Although if it's excitement you are after you might be able to get involved in the other stuff. Not that I'm convinced that *that's* likely to get very far, personally.'

'Do you think they might let me go into the future? I'm not sure what I would have to offer but that really would be an adventure worth having.'

'We can always ask.' Carew sighed. 'Does that mean you're not interested in the Oxford trip, then?'

'Oh, no. It would do me good to get my hand in. I'd have a chance to find out more about the Committee and, well, become one of the team, don't you think?'

'Exactly. And although fund-raising doesn't seem

very exciting in comparison, I'm sure you can see how necessary it is.'

'Who actually knows about the Committee now – apart from the people in it?'

'Good question, Darren, and one no-one else seems to be asking. The Janus people, obviously. The contacts Anstruther used here to recruit people must still be around. Don't know what any of them will have made of his disappearance but, then, we don't know how much they knew in the first place, either. Anstruther's own people in America... well, they went up in smoke back in the sixties – quite literally, I gather.'

'You'd think the modern CIA would have some record, though, wouldn't you?' mused Darren. 'Do you think they might have a list of Committee names handed down from those days?'

Carew shrugged. 'Seems likely, doesn't it? No-one talks about that, at least, not to me. I suppose we hope that they'll think it's all quietly collapsed. Being financially independent will definitely help to keep us under the radar from now on.'

'The most promising clue must be no-one else now or in the future seeming to know about the technology. But aren't people concerned about the possibility of more Bennetts and Emmy Lou's floating around? And those other agents from Nevada, some of them may well be around in the present now, if you think about it, whether they were in the field at the time or on leave.'

'You'd think so. I'm so glad you're going to be joining us, Darren. It's about time somebody was asking those questions.'

26
Evolution Enterprises

London
1982

It was a crisp autumn day when Lewin next welcomed the Committee to his house in Putney.

Julian had bounced in looking pleased with himself. 'Well – it worked!' he said, sitting back with a satisfied grin. 'We're rich – or richer than we were at any rate.'

'Thanks to you and Darren, Philip,' Emmeline added. 'It all sounded very complicated, what with currency changes and so on. Tell us about it!'

'Darren – you go ahead. You were the one who spotted the pitfalls in time and researched a lot of the bets, after all. Decimalisation coming in the middle complicated things, for one.'

'OK.' This was only the second time Darren had met the entire Committee and he seemed eager to make a good impression. 'Well, it wasn't really the decimalisation that was the problem. It was the change in pound notes – new designs and so on. Taking and leaving cash was out of the question, really. Tony transported some gold back to Philip's garden shed for just before we arrived. So we had a good start.'

'That was how we used to fund people for their first trip in the South America days,' Tony shrugged. 'It was much easier this time with a safe shed to aim at.

In the old days I guess quite a few lucky people found caches of gold in strange places and never knew where they came from.'

'Probably blamed the pixies,' shrugged Darren, 'but anyway, we sold it all to fund some short term bets and build up the capital. Then we placed bigger bets on Anglo at 50 to 1 to win and Forest Prince at 100 to 1 for a place in the Grand National – and something on the Cup Final for good measure. We had to do a return trip to get the pay out on that, of course. There were some other big bets as well – we didn't want to influence the odds on any one event after all.'

'And how did you get the money back here?' asked Emmeline.

'Philip opened Post Office Accounts for himself and me out at Abingdon, where he was less likely to bump into someone he knew. He bought Premium Bonds in my name and some shares. We arranged with a firm of solicitors that we know is still in Oxford in 1981 to use their address and keep correspondence in storage for us. We didn't want to spend our windfalls before we got here, if you follow me. I knew I'd never checked on Premium Bonds and neither of us would have thought we might own shares. And we bought some gold and buried it. Amazingly, it was still there when we went back to look.'

'I recommended the shares and they've done pretty well, as you can imagine. It all went like clockwork,' Julian chipped in, not to be outdone, 'and now, as you know, we are all trustees of a wealthy registered charity called Evolution Enterprises.'

'And you managed to avoid anyone who might have recognised you, Philip?' asked Emmeline, something that had been worrying Lewin, too. 'It was a high risk strategy, you going back then, wasn't it?'

'Maybe. It was fine, though.' Philip dismissed the question with a motion of his hand. 'I wore a hat –

different glasses and so on – and kept away from my old haunts. I don't really look much like I did in those days, anyway.'

As he seemed to have nothing else to add, the conversation moved on to future plans.

The trip hadn't worked, of course, from Carew's point of view. Part of him had known it wouldn't. He had taken a chance on ringing his wife up on the morning of James's last day at home, his last day ever, and suggesting she took him to the doctor to get him checked out as soon as possible. She had said she would and had asked if Carew was coming down with a cold, too (he was sounding 'strange', it seemed), but she had still waited until the late afternoon before taking James. Maybe that was the first appointment available. She had never mentioned his call, back then, or told him why she waited: he hadn't asked, of course. How could he have when he knew nothing about it *then*, himself? He took a chance now and watched them as they left the house and went up the road, following them at a distance and drinking in every last view of James's pale face that the little boy's hat and scarf permitted. After their appointment Mrs Carew and James had taken a taxi to the hospital and he had done the same. He had kept watch outside while his wife went home to get her things. He wanted desperately to go in but knew that that was far too much of a risk.

He looked up now to see Joan Danes regarding him with a concerned expression. He smiled and shrugged. She had already grilled him, of course. Psychologists! Always looking for problems!

'And what about you, Darren?' Lewin was asking. 'Has your trip whetted your appetite?'

'It has. I want to talk to you about that. About what, you know, opportunities there might be to, well, go again. Not to Oxford, obviously, but somewhere else. Some other time?'

'I imagine Philip has told you that we're thinking of sending someone back to future-Australia to find out exactly what the state the rest of the world is in,' said Lewin. 'It looks as if international travel was almost, but not quite, a possibility when Julian was there. We have a good contact – but we can't obviously be sure how long to leave a return journey to get the full benefit of it. We've also discussed coming back directly to this country at a later date from Julian's disastrous trip to Manchester. And Tony is planning on going to America to see what happened there.'

'And I would be up for any of that but I did have another thought...'

'Thought is always welcome,' said Julian with a smile. The older members of the group, at least, seemed to have warmed to Darren.

'Well, I don't know much about the background,' Darren went on, 'and may be completely out of line – but wouldn't it be better to go back to just *before* the disasters struck? You would still be able to identify the poor decisions that were being made and it'd probably be safer.'

'Yeah,' said Tony, who had been sitting quietly in the corner observing Darren closely. 'Not a bad idea for my next trip, at least. I can pick up on the key players just as easily then – maybe better. And do something about it. I reckon I'd be more likely to get to the bottom of it at home than here.'

'Mmm,' said Julian. 'I'm not sure what you mean by *doing something about it*. We might have to discuss that. But we could certainly see what's happened to the anti-nuclear movements – and that would help us plan the right way to go now.'

'Could be a bit discouraging, don't you think? What if everything you are doing now comes to nothing?'

233

asked Carew.

'Then you could say *I told you so,* couldn't you, Carew? At least one person would be happy!'

Carew flinched and looked quickly at Darren. It was as if an unspoken message passed between them.

Emmeline, oblivious, sighed. 'We're working on the assumption we *can* change things, though, aren't we? Create a different, alternative future to the one we will see on these trips? I must admit, it's hard to get your head round all the permutations of possibilities. It was easier when we told ourselves we couldn't make any real difference to anything and actually found that reassuring. But it looks as if Mark and Darren probably *did* make a difference in the art world; without my own experience we'd know nothing about what Anstruther and Janus were up to. Tony made a difference in Africa and South America, for better or worse – at least the CIA thought so – and the money you raised, Philip, is *really* making a difference to what we can do now, isn't it?'

Carew nodded slowly and shrugged. 'OK. I suppose so...'

'But, anyway, what about you, Maggie?' asked Lewin. 'You were looking forward to going into a post-Apocalyptic America, weren't you?'

'Not to the point of wishing the Apocalypse on us! I just want to maximise our chances of making a difference.'

'I think this is a solo job, anyway,' said Tony firmly.

Lewin looked at Maggie, anticipating a reaction, but she was studying her fingernails intently.

Darren continued: 'I *could* go to Australia to carry on the research into alternative power sources, and maybe get to fly over to check things out in London. Or I could do the direct British trip. I could go to the post-Apocalyptic time, as you call it, but much later so as to avoid the worst of the impact of it all. Maybe twenty or thirty years after Julian went. We could find out how people are surviving, and where, with a view to investing in help for them now – to give them the best chance if things do go wrong and we can't stop it. I'd guess somewhere fairly rural.'

'You still can't be sure what you'd find,' said Emmeline doubtfully. 'Are you sure you'd be OK doing that?'

'He survived the start of an Ice Age, for heaven's sakes,' snorted Carew. 'It was actually the most successful trip, if you remember. I think he's pretty well qualified, myself!' He looked at Darren. 'But you don't really *want* to do it, do you?'

'Yes. I think I do. And, for that particular trip, I've probably as good a background as anyone here.'

'But have you got a Duke of Edinburgh award?' asked Maggie with a bat of her eyelashes. 'Pretty essential, I'd say.'

The girl didn't give up, thought Lewin. You had to give her credit for that.

'Certainly more use than Latin,' Julian mocked. 'Not sure how much more use, though.'

Maggie settled back in her chair. 'Good. That's settled then. I'm coming, too.'

27
Circles

Wiltshire
2110

It was that time of the morning when the sky is beginning to lighten on the horizon and a monochrome world is becoming tinged with colour but is not quite there yet. A damp mist swirled around them and the knee-high grass, blue-y black in the dawn light, threatened to soak the legs of their jeans if they moved. Darren tested the ground with his foot. Maggie was less cautious. 'Yuk – landed in a bog. Great! Whose idea was it to come here? Whose idea to wear jeans?'

'I don't know the co-ordinates of every bog in the area, unfortunately. And what did you want to wear? A wet-suit?'

'OK, OK, where do we go from here?'

Darren looked around, frowning. 'It's hard to see anything in this mist – but hey – there it is! Look over there.'

Maggie peered in the direction he was pointing. 'What the hell is that?'

A small group of ruins was taking shape against the skyline, tall and angular.

Darren laughed and turned to her grinning ear to ear. 'I knew it would still be there. Totally indestructible! The best view in England. You must have been here before, haven't you?'

Maggie stared at the structure again. 'No,' she said eventually. 'But I have been to Callanish. That's

Stonehenge – we've arrived. Right place but could be any time in the last few millennia, am I right?'

'That's the other thing, of course. But there's no reason to suppose we got the time wrong.' He peered around. 'Stonehenge was pretty well looked after in our day, or at least, this close to it was. The farmland in the area was neat and well-maintained. It looks as if people might have other things to think of now.'

'So – do we get going then? The road is next to the stones, isn't it?'

'It is, or at least it was, and from there we can head towards Salisbury. Yes, let's go.'

They squelched their way to the edge of the field and scrambled across a broken down barbed-wire fence. There was an air of desolation and abandonment all around and their initial high spirits lowered as they trudged on. Neither of them had said a word for about ten minutes when Maggie, in the lead by a few yards, reached the top of a gentle slope and crouched down. As Darren drew level he realised that she was looking down on a long, low building, partially hidden by pine trees and the slope of the landscape.

'Well, that wasn't there in our day... there was nothing around the Henge for miles.'

'If there are people there, they might still be in bed – a good time to investigate, don't you think?' Maggie had visibly perked up.

Darren nodded his agreement and they walked quickly across the open ground towards the shelter of the trees. From this distance they could see small shuttered windows set into the wall. The walls themselves were curved both horizontally and vertically, so that the roof was an untiled concrete continuation of them.

'Weird,' frowned Maggie. 'Let's do the circuit and see if we can see a front entrance – or a window we can look in. No sign of people from here, that's for sure.'

Pine needles crunched underfoot as they made their way round to the other side. Sure enough, there they saw a large glass double door. They went up to it and peered inside. A shiny counter stretched from one end of a large entrance hall to the other. To one side was a stack of plastic chairs.

'Do you see what I see?' Darren whispered.

'Yeah. Candles. Lanterns. And over there in the corner, see, boots!'

They looked at each other and grinned.

'What would the Duke of Edinburgh do now, Maggie?'

'Oh, I think he'd knock on the door and stand to one side to get a view of who comes to answer it before they saw him.'

Darren knocked as hard as he could on the glass. And again.

It was a couple of minutes before they saw signs of movement at the back of the entrance hall. First to emerge was a large lurcher, straining at the lead. It was followed by a square-shaped, florid woman at the other end of the lead and a slightly taller, skinny man with wispy grey hair, carrying a shot gun.

Darren and Maggie stepped forward putting their hands in the air as one, just to be on the safe side.

'Sorry to be bothering you,' Maggie shouted through the glass. 'We're lost and wondered if you could help us.'

'Git!' shouted the man, cocking the shotgun. 'I got ammunition!'

The woman let go of the lead, leaving the barking and slavering dog to jump up against the window, and opened her other hand to display a couple of cartridges. Maggie shrugged and waited a moment, giving them her best smile to no avail.

238

'I think that's a no, Maggie,' said Darren pulling her out of the direct line of fire. They crossed the open ground to the trees opposite keeping slightly to one side of the doorway and came to a wide gate giving access to a track. As they looked back from the gate, they could see the pale faces behind the door still in the same positions.

'Hey, look up there,' said Maggie pointing upwards. Overhead was a metal arch. Gleaming lettering spelt out: *Welcome to Stonehenge Visitor Centre.* The two travellers set off in the direction of the circle itself, still a good half mile away.

'So we know what that funny building is,' Maggie continued, 'and we know the natives are hostile – what else?'

'Lots. We know there's a Visitor Centre. Last time I was here there was nothing. And it's all looking overgrown and decrepit. We know people are frightened and feel the need to protect themselves with shotguns and dogs. We know that ammunition is hard to come by and they are refilling the cartridges they have. Did you notice that? And this is rural Wiltshire – still rural, as we can see. Hard and dangerous times, I'd say. Oh, and that sign isn't any metal I know – look how it's still gleaming.'

'Well done, Sherlock.'

They carried on in silence. By the time they reached the stones the sun was already dispersing the distant mists and shining warmly on their faces. They stopped to drink some iodised water from their bottles. Short of walking round in lead suits, iodising their water was all the radiation protection they had been able to think of. Maggie left Darren sitting with his back against the altar stone, eyes closed, while she went off to explore, scrambling up onto stones and giving a running commentary on what she could see.

Eventually Darren stood up and stretched. 'Come

239

on, girl scout. Miles to go before we sleep.'

An overgrown dual carriageway, devoid of cars, ran from east to west and they set off towards the ascending sun.

'We're heading for Amesbury first,' said Darren. 'It's the nearest small town, or was. We might get all the information we need there, who knows. I'm not quite sure how we'd get to London, anyway. I know you wanted to, but there's no sign of vehicles – electric, steam or otherwise. We seem worse off than Australia in that.'

'Remind me why Amesbury? Checking out Roman forts?'

'More like Iron Age but no, it isn't that. Not that I'd mind checking the archaeology out... it's an interesting area. There are some Bronze Age barrows completely vandalised by farmers some years ago – but who knows what they've discovered by now – it's a work in progress.'

Maggie rolled her eyes.

They walked on in companionable silence until, before long, they were approaching Amesbury from the north, cutting across fields and keeping as close to the hedges and trees as possible. It was a while before they saw any sign of life and then they saw a man with long hair of indeterminate colour and wearing dirty overalls walking away from them down a track at right angles to their own path, pushing a squeaking wheelbarrow with a spade on it.

'Hello there,' called Darren with a wave. 'We're lost. Can you help us?'

The squeaking stopped and the man turned, picking up the spade as he did so. He had a lined, weather-beaten face and could have been any age from thirty to fifty.

'Whoa!' said Maggie with a comical expression. 'We

come in peace! Where are we?'

'Amesbury,' the man replied helpfully, pointing at the houses.

'And? What's there? Anywhere to stay?'

The man snorted. 'Anywhere to stay? You are joking? You'll be lucky not to get shot if you just go wandering up there. What planet have you come from?'

'Planet Earth – but not from round here,' said Darren, thinking quickly. 'We're from... Tintagel! We're from Tintagel – and it's not like that there.'

The man looked curiously at them. 'Really? What's it like there then?'

'Well, people don't point shotguns at you when you knock at the door – or set their dogs on you.'

'Oh! You've been up the Visitor Centre! Old Daniel Moreton and that woman of his – that's who you met. Not that there aren't plenty like them.'

He looked them up and down. 'I can't say you look like you've walked from Cornwall. But it's years since we've seen a strange face round here. You walk ahead of me where I can see what you're doing and we'll go to my place. That house just there.' He pointed at a semi-derelict stone building a couple of hundred yards further on.

'Oh, thank you,' glowed Maggie. 'I could murder a cup of tea! I'm Maggie and this is Darren.'

The man shook his head. 'A cup of tea? I think I'll have to go to Tintagel myself – sounds more like Camelot. My name's Coram – like the superhero.'

Maggie frowned and opened her mouth as if to ask a question – Darren gave her a nudge and glared at her.

Once in the front room of the cottage, Coram bolted the door and set about lighting a fire in the open grate. He hung a blackened kettle from a hook above it. 'I broke into the museum and got this stuff before anyone else thought of it,' he said with pride. 'You'll have to make do with nettle like everyone else but I put lemon verbena in mine. It's OK.'

'You're a bit of a gardener, then?' asked Darren. 'Is that where you were on your way back from?'

'What if it was?' Coram looked at them suspiciously. 'I may have bits of garden, as you call it. All well-camouflaged. *You'd* never find them.'

'Oh no,' Maggie reassured him, 'we don't want to find your gardens. But why camouflage them? I'm curious.'

'Huh – they'd nick the lot round here. Or burn it all.'

'They?' she asked.

'The toe rags who can't be bothered or don't know how to grow anything. My mum loved her garden and I know how, see? I trade stuff and I'm better off than most. They can't stand that.'

'What about livestock?' asked Maggie. 'We haven't seen any of that around anywhere. Darren says he thinks the area was once famous for its bacon.'

Coram narrowed his eyes. 'Is that what you're after? My chickens are mine and I'm not saying where I got them or where they are. Maybe some people saved pigs when they were told to kill them down Cornwall way – but not here. We were a Grade Two area. Everyone knows that. It was all over the news. And they made sure we killed the pigs round here, at least.'

'We were babies at the time, living out on the Scilly Islands,' explained Darren. 'I'll be honest with you – we got a boat across and travelled up to Tintagel just a few years ago. We were brought up in a community on St Agnes that didn't believe in televisions and books or – er, computers. Transcendentalists, you know.'

'Ah, right! That explains the funny clothes and

accents... transcendentalists, eh?' He sounded impressed.

'Are you from round here originally,' asked Maggie. 'Your accent seems a bit different...'

'Born and bred. Nothing wrong with *my* accent, if you don't mind my saying. Now you just hang on and I'll go and find some more mugs in the lean-to. Don't touch anything, mind, or get up to any funny business. I still got my gun.'

Darren turned to Maggie when Coram had left through a small door at the back of the room. He shrugged. 'That's what a hundred years of MASH and The Waltons will do to you,' he muttered. 'And there's a bit of Dame Edna there, too, if I'm not mistaken.'

'There's a thought. The catastrophe wasn't all bad news, then.'

When Coram came back in he had two mugs of herb tea for them and a couple of tired looking apples.

'Oh, that's great,' smiled Maggie. 'I'm starving!'

'Amesbury,' Darren frowned. 'Isn't that near where the boffins had a research station?'

'It is. More's the pity. You've heard of them, at least. That's something.'

'Is that why you were a Grade Two, then?'

'Yeah. They had some radioactive stuff there that started leaking around the same time as the power stations. That's why they had to kill all the animals and anyone with kids moved away. Dunno where they went. Hinkley was as bad as us. My folks stayed put.'

'And what happened to the boffins?' asked Darren.

'Dunno. They said they were all leaving apart from a skeleton staff who would keep an eye on things. To start with I remember people in protective suits coming and going and knocking on doors telling everyone to move away – but that stopped. They're still there at the research place, mind, but they come and go in the night in these covered wagon things, like the Wild West, and you never see them. Why?'

'I just wondered why they didn't they come up with something to protect us from nuclear fallout when it all started to go wrong, that's all.' Darren shrugged and hoped he wasn't showing his ignorance again.

'In my dad's day that sort of question would have had you locked up. Maybe still could – I'd be a bit more careful how you shoot your mouth off. In the bad old days they might have been better prepared, I guess,' Coram went on, 'before the Nuclear Weapons Freeze. I reckon they didn't see the point after that. But we didn't need a war, in the end, did we? We done it to ourselves. No-one saw it coming, did they? Not the boffins, not anyone else. They dished out iodine tablets here for a while but that was mainly for the kids – and they stopped years ago.'

'They still put iodine in the water in Tintagel,' Darren nodded knowledgeably. 'But I don't think we had it so bad there.'

'Odd, that, with Boscastle on the doorstep.'

'Isn't it?' said Maggie, quickly changing the subject. 'Anyway, Coram, if you know somewhere we can get something to eat, we'll get out of your hair.'

'Something to eat... that'll be here, I reckon. I've got beans and potatoes out the back. You sit tight and I'll get them in the pot. You can stay over tonight and carry on tomorrow. Safer in daylight. Where did you say you're off to next?'

'No real plans – just kind of exploring,' said Darren. 'We thought we might carry on to Andover and then maybe set off in the direction of London. Or go to Salisbury first. What's Salisbury like these days?'

'That's it. Why we were better off staying here. It's full of gangs, Salisbury. When the army moved out the gangs took over. Although they say they're mainly made up of ex-soldiers anyway. Police didn't stand a chance in these parts. That's between ourselves, mind.' Coram's gaze flicked around the room suspiciously. 'I don't know why I'm telling a couple of strangers this. I keep myself to myself. Best that way.'

'We don't know anyone round here,' said Maggie. 'No-one to tell if we wanted to. Don't worry about us.' She smiled at him.

'And what about London?' asked Darren.

'What about London? How would we know? Nobody here's heard a dicky bird since the fuel finally ran out. Ashamed of themselves, I should think. They had all those smogs, didn't they for a while? Maybe it killed them off. Serve them right for hogging what fuel there was right up till the end. Anyway, I'll go get the spuds. Back in a minute. Then you can tell me about Tintagel.'

Maggie sat back and breathed a sigh of relief as soon as Coram was out of earshot. 'Do you actually know anything about Tintagel, Darren?'

'I went there once. Bronze Age barrows – ruined castle. Roman remains up to the fifth century, Tristan and Isolde, King Arthur. Not that King Arthur *was* born in that actual castle – it's medieval.'

'That isn't really the kind of information we need now, Darren, is it? And anyway, sometimes these legends *are* true. Think of the Roman castle at Reculver!'

'True. But I'm pretty sure that if Tintagel was a tourist trap in our day, it will still have been one a hundred and fifty years later. Never would have imagined they'd put a power station at Boscastle, though. Thanks for changing the subject. Quick thinking!'

That evening Coram interrogated them at length about their time in Cornwall and they found it hard to know which fabrications might be believable and

245

which not. In the end, they pleaded exhaustion from their long journey and settled themselves to sleep on an array of cushions and blankets in front of the fire. Going to sleep was easy but when they awoke in the small hours of the morning they were cold and aching all over.

Darren sat up and stirred the embers of the fire remembering another cold hard floor in another age and another girl by his side. 'You all right?' he asked Maggie.

'Yeah. Sort of.' Maggie stood up and stretched. 'It was that research place that brought us here presumably? What's the plan?'

'Get inside, I suppose.'

'That sounds like an excellent plan. Deceptive in its simplicity.'

'Now, now. Less of the sarcasm, woman,' Darren laughed. 'How would the Duke of Edinburgh tackle it?'

'Hmm. If I know the D of E, I think he would go along under cover of darkness and see what he could see – without being spotted himself, of course – for a couple of nights and hope to get an idea of what these wagons are. Daylight might be better for ordinary travellers but not for us.'

'Do you want to hang around here today with Coram, drinking nettle tea, or find somewhere else to hide out until nightfall?'

'I'm sure you could find us a nice barrow to hide in nearer the research place – and it is hard work avoiding saying the wrong thing with Coram. We could leave him some of our iodine tablets and just sneak out now, couldn't we? It's still dark.'

Darren shrugged. 'Why not? I think it'd be getting light by the time we got to Porton Down itself, but we could get through Amesbury and as far as Porton Village before people are up and about maybe. There's bound to be somewhere to hole up round there even if

I can't produce a barrow. Worth a shot.'

There was an ominous silence.

'Why? What's wrong now, Maggie?'

'*Porton Down*? Really? Now you tell me. Thanks a bundle... even I've heard of that place. It's bloody toxic. Chemical warfare. People dying in mysterious circumstances.'

Maggie kept her voice low but her anger was palpable as she ran her hands through her long tangled hair in a futile attempt to restore order and stomped out of the door, slapping a packet of iodine pills on the table as she went.

Darren caught up with her as she strode down the track in the direction of the town, hugging herself to keep warm or control her rage. He wasn't sure which. He walked beside her in silence for a while until they approached the first row of houses where, by unspoken consent, they moved into single file and walked as close to the walls as they could. No glimmer of light came from the houses and clouds obscured the stars. Every now and then Maggie produced a torch from her pack and flashed it briefly so they could make sure they were still heading in the right direction. There were heaps of rusted metal in the road that looked as if they might once have been machinery or even cars. Between the houses piles of rubbish spilled forward towards the road.

'I wonder if the sewers are still working,' Darren murmured.

There was no response; he sighed and they carried on.

The built-up area extended much further around Amesbury than on the maps he had memorised back in London but eventually they found themselves walking alongside fields again.

'We can't be far from Porton now,' Darren said, 'but

it'll start to get light soon so I think we should skirt round the outside and then find somewhere to lie low.'

Maggie shrugged and gestured for him to lead on.

'This is ridiculous, Maggie,' he said at last. 'You're being childish. You left it up to me to make the decision about where we landed up while you scooted off God knows where with Tony and I thought this looked like a good idea. And you now have the hump because you didn't bother to ask me for the details.'

'I didn't think there *were* any details other than what we discussed originally – why would I? We left it that you would chose an area you were familiar with that was unlikely to have had a nuclear power station built on top of it – and that's it. Then it turns out there's a research station here and then that just turns out to be Porton Down! Did you let the cat out of the bag by mistake? Were you really going to push me over the wall without telling me?'

'Of course not – that is, I'm sorry. I assumed you'd be all right with it. I wasn't sure Porton Down was still here, even. The last I heard, the military were decommissioning it. It's obviously too good an opportunity to miss now we know it *is* still here, though. You have to admit that. It could be dangerous. True. But you don't have to go any further if you don't want to. OK?'

'Not OK. The only bit of that that was remotely OK was the apology and there wasn't much of that.'

They walked on. A gate, much repaired, appeared on their left and Darren clambered over it. Maggie pulled herself up on to the top bar and jumped lightly down on the other side, ignoring his outstretched hand.

It was getting light by the time they reached the village. Their track took them to a road on the outskirts.

'What a lot of bungalows,' commented Maggie.

'And do you notice something else?'

Darren closed his eyes in a swift prayer of gratitude. With a bit of luck, the storm was over. 'What? The rubbish and the wrecked cars?'

'Exactly. Where are they?'

They walked on down the street, hurrying past driveway openings and keeping their heads lower than the overgrown hedges. Every now and then they stopped, looking about for signs of early risers getting up and drawing their curtains – or even a dog or cat. There was nothing and, after a while, they strode on with more confidence.

Road after road was the same until they came to the church. Everything was overgrown but the boarded up windows of the church and surrounding buildings showed none of the casual vandalism that had added to the sense of desolation in Amesbury.

'Once we leave Porton we'll be more exposed, I should think,' Darren said quietly. 'Let's stop here now.'

Maggie sighed. 'OK. We can go into the graveyard and find a corner, I expect. If it warms up I could do with a kip before we set off again, anyway.'

There was a heap of ancient gravestones piled up in one corner of the graveyard, sandwiched between the wall and an overgrown yew tree. They looked around and, having reassured themselves that they were out of sight of the road and the windows of the neighbouring houses, settled down on the grass.

'You know I *am* sorry, Maggie, not to have been more upfront with you,' Darren said after a few moments had passed in silence. 'I've never had to consult with anyone about what I do and I was a bit, well, high-handed, I suppose. I can't stand this silent treatment – and I need your help here. We're going to have to think about how we get to look inside, for a start. I do need you to forgive me! Friends? Please?'

'Just a bit high-handed?' She shrugged and sighed. 'OK. You're right. We'll start again.'

The day was warm and they talked and fell silent, talked again and took turns to nap in the sun. Maggie spoke about growing up with Emmeline, just the two of them moving down from Scotland to first one university town and then another – and how she had sometimes wondered why they had no other family, why she had no grandparents, no cousins, no aunts or uncles. Darren told her about his own restricted childhood with ageing parents, separated from early friends by being sent to the Grammar School in the next town where he was singled out yet again for his broad Yorkshire accent. He told her about his trip to Moravia and the art he found there and, eventually, he told her about Mouse.

'Wow, that was some footprint, Darren. The blue-eyed boy outdid us all.'

'I don't know about blue-eyed boy – you didn't do anything too awful, did you?'

'Maybe not, but the future of those Romans might have been different if I hadn't gone back for Tony. Who knows, there might have been a Roman cohort at the Battle of Hastings – and then what might have happened?'

'Especially if Harold had had explosives at his disposal. The Bayeux Tapestry would have been a bit different, that's for sure. And probably the outcome. But what *about* Tony?' he added hesitantly. 'Were you disappointed not to go off to America with him? Or that he didn't want to come here?'

'There was no real choice for him, was there? Getting in with the movers and shakers is his metier. America was the right place for him and I would have made him stand out like a sore thumb with my Scottish accent, even if the colour combination didn't make any difference then.'

'That's not exactly what I asked.'

'No, I know. You're fishing, just like Mum and Julian did when we got back from the Highlands. I like him, right? We get on well and had a good laugh. And I *was* put out he didn't want me there. But, I don't know. Maybe it was a good thing. To be honest, Darren, he's a man on a mission. And he's lived so many lives already, somehow. It's all made him how he is. He's kind of–'

'Old? Ruthless?'

'Not old. Ruthless, I guess. You should have seen the way he despatched those men in the Mojave.'

'But he had cause. Like your mother...' Darren stopped, not sure how or whether to continue.

'He did have cause. Heaven knows. And so did Mum. But Mum was bitter. No... not bitter. That's not her style. *Angry.* And, you know, I don't think Tony was. He was kind of *mechanical* – like it was just a job that had to be done. There's no way it was his first time. Put it that way.'

'I don't suppose that's the kind of question you can ask.' Darren looked thoughtful for a moment and then smiled and gave her shoulders a quick squeeze. 'I don't feel quite so bad now about being an artist who's never knowingly run over a hedgehog. I think I might have been feeling the need to compete with Tony, on some level. He's a bit of a hard act to follow.'

Maggie laughed. 'That's silly. Although if you *had* knowingly run over a hedgehog, that would be that. I'd be back in London before you could blink. Future of the world be damned!'

28

Porton Down

Wiltshire
2110

They waited until the last light had disappeared before
setting off across the open land towards the high walls
that surrounded Porton Down. Fortunately, the land
was as unkempt here as elsewhere and there was
plenty of cover for them as they first stooped and then
crawled as near as they felt they safely could. Finally
they collapsed onto their stomachs and peered across
the dim, shadowed scrubland. The wall loomed white
except for dark shadowy vegetation extending against
it at intervals and the tops of trees on the other side.

'Ivy,' Maggie stated with satisfaction. 'And
something to climb down on the other side.'

'Can't see any light coming from in there. You'd
think someone would have a fire lit and some form of
lighting. I wonder if it's empty.'

Maggie picked up a stone and threw it hard
towards the wall. A dog barked.

'Cut it out!' a man shouted, his voice carrying
clearly in the night air.

They lay still, holding their breaths, but the night
fell into silence again, with just the sound of small
animals scurrying about their business to disturb it.

An hour or so later there were shouts and sounds of
general activity; a gleam of light appeared. Darren and
Maggie scrambled round the base of the wall, keeping
as low to the ground as possible, until they found
themselves near the south-west corner of the

rectangular complex. Peering round the corner, they had a view of the approach road and it was along this that they soon saw a small caravan of vehicles and animals approaching.

There were two large, rectangular, canvas-topped wagons, each being pulled by a pair of Clydesdale horses. Ahead and to each side rode horsemen wearing pistol holsters; there were larger guns strapped to the sides of their horses. The most immediately striking thing about the men was their clothing – white boiler suits and masks with filters attached, giving them the appearance of spacemen or aliens.

'Did you ever watch Dr Who?' murmured Maggie.

'And where the hell did they find those horses?'

They moved nearer so that they could see the gate as it opened spilling light onto the horsemen, who had surged forward ahead of the wagon.

'Do you think we could make it to the wagon and hang on underneath like in the films,' whispered Maggie hopefully. 'Or do you think I could just wander up and smile nicely at the soldiers like I did in Reculver? I could sneak back and let you in later.'

'I don't think there's any need to throw yourself under any wagons, Maggie, let alone under any soldiers. Let's get back to that ivy and take advantage of the distraction here at the gate to climb over as in Plan A.' Darren closed his eyes for a moment as he realised what he had said.

'Boring, but if you say so...' said Maggie after a split-second pause. They retraced their steps to the rear wall and headed for a particularly solid looking mass of ivy. 'I'll go first. I'm lighter and can give you a hand in case the ivy weakens.'

Darren hesitated instinctively and then thought better of it. There was only so far a man could push his luck. 'That makes sense. I don't suppose there's a wire cutter on that Swiss Army knife of yours, is there? You don't know what you'll find up there.'

'Of course there is – and I'm putting my coat round my waist, see, so I can get at it in case there are glass shards up there. At least it's unlikely to be electrified.'

Maggie's climb in the bright moonlight seemed to take an eternity – although, as Darren told himself, it must have taken less than ten minutes in actual fact.

A soft 'All clear!' was his cue to follow, tracking her ascent as closely as he could. While he was on his way up Maggie busied herself cutting through the coiled barbed wire that lay along the inner edge of the top of the wall and pulling it away. That done, she hauled herself onto the top and, leaning forward, grabbed at a branch of the large chestnut tree the other side, swinging herself lightly across the twenty foot drop beneath. She made way for Darren to follow and they sat side by side looking down at the research centre.

They could immediately see why there had been no lights. All the buildings were blacked out and windowless corridors linked one building with another. The only lights to be seen were at the far side by the gate and looked like torch beams.

'Some electricity, then,' said Darren.

'Yes. Just look at the roofs of these buildings – they're shiny! They're covered in panels just like the ones Julius saw in the Gobi. The bastards! They're sitting here with all mod cons while everyone outside is expected to live like, like savages.' Maggie was indignant.

'Looks like it. Let's get down there and see if we can see what's being unloaded.'

They clambered down and followed the main wall to the front again, keeping to the trees until they reached a point where the trees had evidently been chopped down to create an area of more open ground. At that point they ran across to the buildings to get

254

what cover they could there.

The white-suited arrivals were carrying large crates into the first building, Darren and Maggie could see vegetables in some and slabs of meat in others. The men had removed their masks and were joking amongst themselves as they worked. Finally large barrels appeared and were rolled across into the same building. The caravan's escort then returned to the wagons and Darren and Maggie were about to retreat to somewhere they could talk safely when half a dozen men in military uniform appeared from within the buildings, carrying a different set of boxes and crates over to the wagons for loading. Eventually, the wagons were unhitched and turned and the horses re-attached. Head-coverings went back on the horsemen and gun holsters were re-adjusted; the wagons headed off the way they had come, towards Salisbury. The gates clanged shut.

As soon as all was quiet and dark again, Maggie and Darren retreated away from the main door.

'That stuff coming out looked like radio equipment,' said Maggie, 'and those canister things – what was in them?'

'Chemicals? Medicines? It is a laboratory after all. Used to specialise in biological and chemical warfare, didn't it? Maybe they still do. That was no skeleton staff.'

'And interesting how all the riders took their protective gear off when they were out of sight of the road. Quite a good cover to clear the village and fields in the neighbourhood and stop people being too nosey – you just say there's an exceptionally high level radioactivity here.'

They returned to the shelter of the wall of the building and walked back to the front gate, now in darkness again. From here they slipped through into a central open area surrounded by buildings.

255

As their eyes adjusted to the gloom, their suspicions about the true quality of the air seemed borne out when they came across vegetable beds. Maggie took a chance and flicked her torch over them.

'Cabbage and broccoli coming up and, look, some kind of parsley – very nice! And what's that over there?'

At the far side of the vegetable beds they could make out a high wire fence with a gate in the side and wooden structures just visible at the back.

Maggie walked across and peered in, shining her torch to the back. The beam of light was greeted with sleepy cackles as it penetrated the slats in a row of hutches.

'Shh. Come away, Maggie!' hissed Darren, reaching out to grab her backpack.

'Yeah, come away, Maggie,' mocked a male voice behind them. 'But not too quickly. I have you both covered and, trust me, there is no shortage of ammo here!'

They turned slowly, hands in the air, to face the soldier standing behind them in the gloom. They hadn't heard him approach and had no idea how long he had been watching them.

'Don't know who you are but you're coming this way. Slowly. Hands where I can see them. That door over there.'

He gestured towards a door in the nearest building with his torch and, at the same time, raised his free hand to his mouth; a metal object in his hand glowed momentarily. 'Wilson here. Two tourists coming up to garden door. Support required as far as Room 16.'

There was a soft click and the glow faded. Almost immediately the door opened and the scene was illuminated by a shaft of light. A dark shadow emerged from the door, gun in hand.

They moved forward slowly.

'Oh well, it's one way of getting inside, I guess,' muttered Maggie.

'Silence!' snapped the second guard.

Maggie gave him her brightest smile as she passed him. 'So sorry. Of course.'

Room 16 was a bare, windowless room containing a table, half a dozen chairs and a third armed guard standing to attention in the far corner. The heavy metal door with its food hatch and small window marked it as a cell.

They sat with their hands in plain view on the table, as instructed, and waited. And waited. They lost track of time.

'Do you know who or what we're waiting for?' Maggie asked at one point.

The guard shrugged. 'You got an urgent appointment somewhere else? Shame.'

'No. Not at all. I'd like a glass of water, though, and maybe to stand up? I'm getting stiff.'

'Shame,' repeated the guard with a smirk. 'Now shut up.'

Maggie shut up.

An hour, or maybe two, later the monotony was broken by the sound of approaching footsteps and then the clang of a bolt being pulled back. The door opened outwards to reveal yet another armed soldier. 'Colonel Lazenby's ready to see the prisoners,' he said, looking at them curiously.

Their guard gestured them towards the door with his gun. 'Move. Hands over your heads as you go. You go first with the girl, Kel, and I'll follow with this moron. One step out of line and we *both* shoot. You understand?'

They did – and proceeded in single file down the corridor, hands elevated over their heads. They passed one numbered room after another until they finally

257

came to a door with a nameplate. *Colonel Lazenby.*
The first soldier rapped on the door and entered
without waiting for a response. They filed in and
found themselves facing a large desk and a short, red-
faced man in uniform sitting behind it, peering at a
folder through thick round lenses. The soldiers
retreated to either side of the door.

After a while the colonel looked up and sighed
wearily. 'OK. I want to know how you got in and what
you think you are doing here. I'm sure you know
perfectly well that this is an unsafe area. You have
both been exposed to extreme radiation already.'

Maggie looked across at Darren and nodded for
him to do the talking.

'Thanks a lot, Maggie! Well, no, sir,' said Darren.
'We don't know anything. We're new to the area –
from Cornwall. We saw the wagons arriving and
followed them in. We've been on the road a long time
and thought we might get some clean food here.'

'You did, did you? Just trotted in after the trucks
and no-one noticed you, eh? Mistook us for a
restaurant. Easily done, I'm sure. And what made you
decide to then go skulking around?'

'It – it wasn't what we'd expected, sir. No-one was
wearing protective gear inside the gates and then
there was the veg growing out in the open... we
wanted to see what we'd got ourselves into.' The best
lies, Darren had once heard, contain as much truth as
possible.

'And you know now, do you? Enlighten me – I'm all
agog.' The colonel's mouth set in a thin wide line that
might have passed for a smile had his eyes been less
cold and fish-like.

Darren shrugged and scratched the inside of his left
arm as if thinking how best to continue. 'I guess it's
some kind of barracks here and you're not going to
give us any food. We're sorry, right? We'll get out of

your hair as soon as possible when you've finished what you have to say to us.' He looked over at Maggie and saw her nod her head, almost imperceptibly.

'I can't imagine what would make you think you're going anywhere.' The colonel widened his eyes as if amazed at their temerity. 'I'm sure you've heard of Porton Down even in Pixieland. National security dictates that some matters remain secret, you know, even now and you two – you've been caught spying at a military installation for God's sake!'

'Well, that's a bit strong,' protested Maggie. 'All we've seen so far is that there's hope. You've got the technology for light, warmth and communication – and it's obviously possible to grow food outside now. That's all good news, surely?'

Lazenby turned to Darren. 'Are you as naïve as your girlfriend? I think not. Tell her.'

'This technology isn't available to the general public, Maggie. I think that's what he means. The army, the government, the scientists – they're looking after their own. Why, I don't know. There's been plenty of time to roll it out more widely after all. Maybe by now they're just afraid the sick and hungry people out there might turn into an angry mob if they find out what's been kept from them all this time.'

Lazenby stood up; his face was now a light shade of puce. 'Sick and hungry, my arse! Have you *been* into Salisbury? It's a jungle! You know damn well it was a jungle even before the contamination. Drugs, gangs – the flotsam and jetsam of the whole world ending up on our shores. A decision was made at the very highest levels... Anyone who is prepared to knuckle down and work hard can survive perfectly well. They're doing so all over the country in small communities that look after their own. If they can do it in Scotland and Wales and, yes, even Cornwall – they could damn well do it here.'

259

'That may be true,' agreed Darren calmly, 'but I expect everyone would find survival a bit easier with electricity and clean water. Not to mention some of the drugs we saw being crated out. Was this *highest level* the highest level of the army, by any chance? Or were any elected politicians involved?'

Colonel Lazenby's eyes bulged and his face got redder. 'Impudence! In an emergency someone has to step up to the mark – and we did. Defence of the realm is the first responsibility of government. Didn't they ever teach you that? We were not in the business of taking a show of hands on it or giving a carte blanche to terrorists – and we still aren't! And that goes for you lefties, too!'

Getting into the spirit of the thing and, as she admitted later, curious as to what colour he might go next, Maggie decided to chip in. 'Where do you keep the breeding pairs, then? How's that going?'

'Enough! I don't know who sent you but, rest assured, we shall find out. No Geneva Convention here, I'm afraid. And no chance at all of ever getting out to spread misinformation and speculations just to stir up trouble in the country. We can all do without your sort. Sergeant! Separate cells for these two, please. Be prepared for an escape attempt and ready to fire. Get them out of here *now*.' The soldiers cocked their pistols.

'What? *Now?*' asked Maggie, looking at Darren.

'Yep. NOW!'

There was a shimmer and a pistol report – and then nothing.

29
Getting There

London
1982

She was on a ship. It was warm and stuffy and the drone of the engines was hypnotic. She was in a saloon bar. The rows of Formica tables were bare and the bar closed up. She walk through to the right of the bar. A corridor stretched ahead. There were pictures and safety instructions on the walls but no-one to ask for directions. At the end of the corridor was a broad red-carpeted staircase. She walked up it and came to an area with corridors leading off in two directions, two to the fore and two to the aft of the boat and another staircase going up. A higher, shriller note now entered her awareness. She walked down one of the corridors heading aft, believing herself to be already towards the front of the boat. The corridor was identical to the other and led into an identical saloon. She carried on through that and down another corridor. The high pitched note had become piercing and seemed to penetrate right into her brain. There was a lift. She knew that if she wanted to find the source of the noise she must go up. She went up two floors and got out. More corridors. Another saloon. This time there were three men in it drinking beer and playing cards. They looked up at her blankly as she walked past. The noise was getting painful now. The next corridor led to a junction. She had to go left or right. Her legs were tired and she

261

had had enough walking but she chose left and laboured on. Her head was exploding. That corridor, in turn, led to yet another bar. The Formica tables were empty again but now there were disco lights, flickering and changing colour. Nothing for her here.

As she walked down the next carpeted corridor dragging one foot after another, she realised that only grim determination – or bloody-mindedness, as Emmeline would call it – was keeping her going. She thought about her mother. Where was she? What was she doing? Somewhere between the engine drone and the shrieking noise she heard voices murmuring indistinctly, uttering unintelligible nothings. Any feeling of panic or urgency had dissipated and she knew the voices for auditory hallucinations. As the noise got louder and louder the murmuring voices got louder, too, and more excited. She heard herself scream and then felt herself fall backwards into the welcoming green water. She floated for a moment or two and then sank into the blessed peace and quiet.

When Maggie next surfaced the noise had gone and she found herself floating on her back looking up at the disco lights again but now they were softer and their gentle, multicoloured flickering enchanted her.

She must have died and this must be heaven. She was content for it to be so. When the white-robed angel with the golden hair appeared she was sure of it and, then, when her mother's smiling face drifted into her line of vision she smiled up at her and said, 'Hello, Mum. Are you here, too? That's nice.'

It was an anxious group that Lewin welcomed to his office at St Jude's two weeks later. It consisted of Lewin, Weatherspoon, Carew, Joan Danes and Darren. The office heater really was totally inadequate, Lewin had to admit, but this time not even Julian complained; instead he demanded the latest news of Maggie the moment they were all seated.

'She's fine,' Darren reassured him. 'Or will be. She's alive, anyway, and able to do a bit more every day. She came out of intensive care last week and visiting hours are much easier now, thank God. Professor Lewin wangled a private room for her.'

'Emmeline's there now – they've been doing shifts,' Lewin added.

'What exactly happened?' Joan Danes looked around at the assembled company. 'Remember I was away on holiday when they got back...'

'We'll be writing up a full report as soon as Maggie's a bit better but I can summarise for now,' said Darren. 'I keep going over and over it in my mind: I know it was my fault.' He looked tired and drawn; Lewin knew the lad had had little sleep since his and Maggie's precipitous return.

'We had a good trip to start with,' Darren went on. 'Interesting. We learnt a lot. I'll come back to that. But before we'd been there more than a couple of days we got caught in the military research place at Porton Down. It was my fault. I wound up the bloke in charge and then, when he told the soldiers to take us to separate cells, I shouted to Maggie that it was time to go and they shot at us. A bullet got Maggie just as we left.'

'She must have already been on the move but still with some material presence there,' Lewin frowned. 'The bullet was found in her head but should, according to the doctors, have gone right through. They're puzzled and we can't explain what happened, obviously. Even if we understood ourselves.'

'And the bullet itself?' asked Julian. 'Has that raised any issues?'

'It might if they analyse it. I don't know,' said Darren 'There was evidence of some more advanced technology around, odd alloys and so on but, generally, the world seemed to have taken a few backward steps if anything. So maybe... if and when it gets analysed... who knows?'

'No questions being asked here at the hospital about what's happened to her?' Joan Danes looked enquiringly at Lewin. 'I'm sure hospitals have to report bullet wounds to the police.'

Of course, this is her sphere, thought Lewin; he should have brought her up to speed sooner. 'We had to say we found her on the street,' he replied, 'and we don't know what happened to her. We don't think she said anything too revealing as she came to but, to be honest, she was talking such nonsense it probably wouldn't have mattered. She was high as a kite for hours after they brought her round. Spouting Latin, the nurse said, and going on about her garden. Emmeline and Darren have managed to fend off the police so far and I think Emmeline has talked her through the story now.'

'Good,' said Carew from his chair in the corner. 'I wonder how soon Emmeline can get her out? It's all a bit worrying.'

'Our first concern is her health, Philip!' remonstrated Lewin. 'At the moment, she's paralysed on her right side. The physio's only just been this morning and there's also some kind of residual bleed which they don't want to get worse. I just wish my day-job research was a bit more advanced. Proper magnetic resonance imaging would be really helpful – but we're not quite there yet with brains.'

Julian raised an eyebrow. 'Are you fishing for a future trip yourself, Roland?'

Lewin shook his head. He had, of course, considered it but by the time he had done a trip, found the information he needed and, above all, applied it back home, it would be too late to benefit Maggie. In the scientific world you couldn't very well come in with a finished product having missed out the middle bits and expect cooperation from your medical colleagues. He only wished, for Maggie's sake, that his research had been just a couple of years further on.

'When I looked in a week or so ago, her post-op hairdo was a bit extreme,' Julian continued. 'I hope she doesn't find that too depressing when she gets to a mirror.'

Darren laughed. 'Don't worry. One of the nurses has already offered to give her an Annie Lennox and she's looking forward to it.'

'OK, that's good to hear,' said Julian, leaning forward in the armchair, his hands clasped between his knees, 'but, more importantly, tell us about what you saw in 2110.'

'Generally, much more primitive than Australia as you described it,' replied Darren. 'It seemed to be everyone for themselves and there'd been a complete breakdown in law and order. Or at least that's what we were told. We didn't actually see any gangs and rioting ourselves – just scared people waving weapons around and trying to protect what they had. No running water, no electricity or shops. No schools or clinics. No regular communication between different parts of the country, as far as we could tell. We weren't there long, as I said, and I just assume the rest of rural Britain would be fairly similar. People we did speak to implied the cities were some kind of no-go areas.

'The main thing was our trip to Porton Down. That's still going strong. It's got electricity, weapons, well-fed soldiers. We saw them bringing in food from military transports and sending out what looked like radio equipment and medicine. None of that stuff was available to anyone else, it seemed. Just the select few. The guy in charge gave us the impression it was a deliberate policy – like there was some kind of military-run state within a state and some pretty fascist politics going on.'

'Who were they blaming, then?' asked Julian. 'Fascists always blame someone. Was it the nuclear industry in general or anyone in particular? The Chinese?'

'I don't know. We didn't really meet enough people to generalise, but those we did meet seemed frightened of gangs and the colonel guy did mention immigrants and terrorists. I guess terrorists would be an excuse for a military takeover, wouldn't they?'

'And immigrants always get any flak going when things get tough. Where does that leave us now, though? Does it change what we should be doing, do you think?' Julian was frowning.

Darren nodded. 'I've had some time to think about that, sitting in the hospital. It does, really. We do still need to be investing in alternative technology research, of course, for transport and so on, and upping awareness of the risks of the nuclear power stations – but it seems to me that we also need to be getting information out into small communities at a very basic level. Solar panels seem quite simple – and potassium iodide. Cheap to buy and just about possible to make yourself if you know how. People shouldn't need to be dependent on the central government for that kind of thing. And if the soldiers were growing their veg out of doors – why were they telling everyone else that *they* couldn't? Were they treating their own soil with something or just scaremongering? If the ordinary population had had more accurate information, been better educated, I think it would have made a difference. Made them less easy to fool, anyway, if that *is* what had happened.'

'More information at a grass roots level, then. Self-sufficiency, basic skills... do you think it would catch on if there's no immediate need?' Julian was thinking hard. 'How can we make that fashionable? Bring back the hippie communes?'

To everyone's surprise, it was Carew who responded. 'We could use some of our cash to invest in a more modern type of self-reliant community – ones where they make their own electricity and transport rather than ones that pretend we can do without the 20th century altogether,' he said, flushing as they all turned to look at him. 'Give prizes for inventions – stir up interest that way.'

'Not a bad idea, Philip,' nodded Julian, impressed.

'No need to look so amazed – I do have ideas, you know. And maybe we should be encouraging better health education? People these days are becoming so dependent on their doctors that they don't think for themselves. In a few years they'll be totally helpless on their own.'

'They'd still need the medicines, though,' said Lewin.

'Not as much as you might think. In the past people used herbs and poultices, that kind of thing. Everyone had some knowledge.'

'That's true,' said Julian. 'They certainly did in Mongolia. They even used the minerals and rocks but I don't know that they'd ever really forgotten, over there. Putting the clock back *here* on that stuff might be harder than the rest – but worth thinking about. Perhaps we can work on this together, Carew.'

Lewin stood up and stretched. 'Well, I suggest we all give that some consideration over the next few days and re-convene in a month. With a bit of luck, Tony will be checking in with us just before Christmas for a few days and, by then, Maggie will be home and Emmeline can join us, too. Maggie's going to come and stay with us initially so Emmeline can keep an eye on her.'

The others exchanged glances. Julian raised an

eyebrow and opened his mouth as if to speak.

'The pub, I think!' said Joan standing up quickly and putting her hand on Julian's arm. 'You can tell me how you got on at that conference in Seattle on the way.'

Darren arrived back on the ward just in time to see the nurse sweep up Maggie's russet curls. He bent down and picked one up and looked at it. He smiled at Maggie and nodded his approval. 'That's better! It really suits you. Makes your eyes look positively huge.'

'Your hair will grow again, won't it, love?' Emmeline stood up and gathered her coat and bag ready to go.

'I expect it will, Mum, if I let it...'

'Now you are just being provoking. That didn't take long.' Emmeline bent over and planted a kiss on Maggie's forehead. 'Over to you, Darren. I think she's decidedly better this afternoon!'

Darren let Emmeline get past and took her place in the chair beside the patient. He took Maggie's hand and gave it a squeeze. They waited until Emmeline and the nurse had gone.

'So how are you, really, Maggie?'

'Fine. At least much, much better. Look.' She picked up a notebook from the tray table in front of her and showed him her scrawly attempts at writing her name. 'I couldn't even hold the pen yesterday. I've got my exercises and I stood up this morning. *And* they've reduced the painkillers to almost nothing. Now tell me about the meeting.'

'Well, they all asked after you, of course. I gave them a brief summary of our trip. Julian is making plans for sponsoring self-sufficient villages and it looks like Carew has taken up an interest in herbalism. They want to make sure everyone has access to the basics at least, even if we don't manage to change anything.'

'Sounds like a case for the Duke of Edinburgh.'

'Doesn't it? I nearly said so but I thought I'd leave that up to you. Do you fancy yourself as an Akala?'

'Wrong lot – but it might be worth getting them interested, too.'

He glanced quickly towards the door. It was closed. 'I know your mum has told you what we decided had happened to you for the benefit of the nurses and police – but how much of what really happened can you remember?'

A crease appeared between Maggie's eyebrows. 'I can remember the cell and that man going on about national security and so on. And he was getting redder and redder in the face. And that's it, really. I woke up here. Mum says the official version is I'd arranged to meet you all in the Red Lion and when I didn't turn up you all started off for the station... and found me. Is that right?'

'Yes. And from your point of view, in that version?'

'I was thinking about the pub and being late – may have noticed some men out of the corner of my eye but not sure where or when, and then – I was here. I tried it on the nurse who said it was quite understandable, that I wouldn't remember much and all these gangs are a real menace.'

'And you will be going *home* to Lewin's when they let you out? That's what he told us.'

'Oh, did he?' Maggie laughed. 'That must have been funny. Poor old Mum. Mind you, it's nice to have all the speculation about someone else for a change. I'm saying no more!'

Emmeline had told her of the plan earlier, saying that she and Roland had been decorating the spare room and clearing a bit of space in the cupboards for her clothes.

'There's only one bed in there, isn't there, Mum?'

Maggie had asked innocently. 'What will you do?'

Her mother had blushed and then laughed. 'I'm sharing with Roland, of course.'

'About time too, I say!'

'I know, Maggie. It's been a challenge! I've never met such a *gentlemanly* gentleman in my life. I'd almost given up until all this happened.'

'Glad to have been of service.'

Maggie smiled at the memory of the conversation and then, seeing that Darren was still looking at her expectantly, said 'What? Oh my goodness, and they say women are gossips!'

'Not at all. And you will be right on hand for our next meeting – when it seems Tony may be joining us.'

'Oh, that'll be good. It'll be great to see him again and find out what he's been up to. Do you think he'll tell us everything?'

'I suppose so.' Darren hesitated. 'Exactly how delighted do you think you'll be, Maggie?'

'On a scale of one to ten? Maybe eight or nine? Why?'

'That's high. I'd kind of hoped to myself that I might have grabbed a bit of advantage on our trip... but just wishful thinking, really. Silly.'

'And that's what you'd wish for, Darren? What you'd like?'

'You know it is! But I'm a realist. You are a beautiful free spirit and I am a pretty boring kind of feller – who just ended up in this un-boring situation. I sometimes think I'm a younger Carew – but I don't want to make his mistakes and end up wishing I'd said things, when it's too late.'

'You're nothing like Carew. That trip to the Ice Age was far the bravest thing any of us have done. You knew what you were getting into and still did it – and I wouldn't have been with anyone else when we got arrested!'

'Really?'

'Really. And, when you walked through the door today, you know, seeing you rated eleven out of ten, at least.'

Darren looked at her suspiciously to see if she was going to burst out laughing at him. You never knew what Maggie was going to find funny.

She sighed theatrically. 'Oh, come on, Darren. When a lady says nice things like that you should at least kiss her. It's only polite.'

He leant forward to her as she lay propped up on the pillow and did kiss her. And then he kissed her again and then they talked for a while and went back to kissing each other.

The nurse had to cough loudly a couple of times to attract their attention when visiting time was over. 'Tomorrow's another day, children. And did you want me to throw away that curl you picked up with the others, sir, or...?'

Darren looked a bit sheepish as he removed the curl from his pocket and looked at it. 'No. It's all right. I think I'll keep it. Bye then, Maggie. Sleep well and I'll see you tomorrow – and you, too, nurse. Thank you.'

After he'd left, Maggie and the nurse exchanged glances.

'I don't know what's wrong with Mum and me – we both seem to be losing our touch. But we get there in the end.'

30
Cartels

London
1982

Lewin looked around his crowded sitting room. They were all there, including Tony who had arrived the previous day. It was good to see him.

'Well, it seems a long time since we were all together here. Bit squashed, isn't it?' he said by way of welcoming them.

'It is a bit,' said Joan. 'But I understand we've found a new home for the project and it's all happening really quickly.'

'Yes, it is. Courtesy of our new-found wealth. Completing next week. On Christmas Eve, in fact. I'll have a few days off over the holiday to clear things out of the hospital, with a bit of help from anyone who can spare the time, I hope.'

'*I* hope the new place will be a bit warmer than your old room, Lewin,' grumbled Julian, 'and have fewer stairs.'

'Oh, I always rather liked it,' said Emmeline. 'I'll miss our meetings at St Jude's.'

'We have to do it, though. No choice. There are a lot of changes in the offing at the hospital. Re-organisations, new buildings... We can't wait until someone decides to clear out the basement – and I can't imagine I'll be able to keep my cold little eyrie

272

forever, either. I might have to move hospitals. I might even lose my job in the reorganisation... it's all up in the air. It seems a certain charitable organisation that was contributing to funding my particular line of research has withdrawn.'

'Janus!' said Tony with a shrug. 'I guess I'd better stay until the machine is set up in the new place in case there's a problem. I'm not sure I'm ready to be permanently uprooted yet again by taking chances. So I'll be able to help you with the move.'

'You will go back, though?' asked Julian raising his eyebrows.

'Yeah. It's the place for me to be. I'm getting to grips with what the problem is there – but doing something about it has been harder. I need to work on it a bit more.'

'I can help with the move, too,' offered Darren.

'And me!' said Maggie, passing round a plate of wizened mince pies.

'No, you can't!' said her mother and Darren together.

'No heavy lifting, no driving or operating machinery, no tiring yourself out – which bit didn't you understand, Maggie? I give up!' Emmeline sounded exasperated. Maggie looked crestfallen.

'She can always keep us supplied with tea and mince pies, Emmeline, can't she?' suggested Darren.

Julian tapped his mince pie with his fingernail. 'I haven't tried the tea yet, of course, but rather you than me,' he said.

'Let's get on with the business at hand, shall we?' suggested Joan. 'Tell us about America, Tony. First of all how was it for you going back? You didn't turn up for our psychological debrief.'

Tony smiled and shrugged his shoulders. 'I guess I'm a lost cause, Professor Danes. I'm quite used to this stuff, you know. Anyway, I went and got myself one of those little computers while I was there – tablets, they're called – and I spent some evenings looking up what happened in the sixties. You can type in people's names and get the low down on them if they're famous enough. And some events, too. Dr King and Lamumba are there, for example – but when I looked up the Mojave in 1976. Zilch. That was some cover-up. We never did know anyone's real names so I couldn't look up any info on the other agents and travellers. Like Julian and Maggie and Darren, I couldn't see any obvious signs of the technology being there in a hundred years' time, but when I checked out the business histories of certain of the big players, they did seem to have made a lot of real clever investment decisions at the right times. Makes me wonder if the Consortium or the Foundation isn't still helping out, somehow; maybe through the agents who were already in the field when we blew up the machines. I don't know.'

'What about Chinese-built reactors, though? Did they have them in the States the same as the rest of the world?' Julian never strayed far from his preoccupation with nuclear safety.

'No. Not directly, anyway. You know how it is in America. Money talks. Big business shouts. They broke up Standard Oil decades ago but the bits each seem to have, have grown to the same size as the original. Seems it's all got as out of hand as it ever was. It's even got so it's business tycoons running the government, picking the President, filling all the senior posts. They've managed to convince people that voting for them is the way to get to be millionaires themselves. Businessmen don't thrive on making other guys millionaires, though, do they?'

'Wouldn't have thought so,' said Julian thoughtfully. 'But they provide an attractive model of success, I suppose. Appealing to people confused by

274

the messy demands of the real world.'

'Maybe. Anyway the worst of them all have been the oil companies and what they now call the media – newspapers, films, computers and so on – and they're in cahoots. The oil companies got control of the car industry and the plastics industry and they blocked any attempt to develop alternative power sources and materials right up till recently – even when everyone knew the oil and gas were going to be running out.'

'What happened to the nuclear industry you had? They've got power stations and so on now, in the 1980s, after all.'

'I know, Julian. And haven't you been pointing out the dangers yourself? The radiation leaks and the nuclear accidents causing meltdowns?'

'Well, yes. People need to know.'

'Well, it seems the leaks and accidents are gonna get worse and worse. Mostly down to human error, they claim, but helped by freak weather and waves on the west coast causing problems for the ones using sea water to cool them down.'

'I thought as much!' Julian look almost pleased at this catalogue of disaster.

'Yeah, but... did you think it through? Who's going to benefit? The American oil and gas people had the market in their pockets after all that came out. No-one wanted to know about nuclear. Some of the trouble was genuine, I'm sure, but there was a bit too much *human error* for my liking. But then I guess I'm paranoid.'

'I doubt it, Tony,' said Emmeline. 'You know better than anyone–'

'–about dirty tricks? I know enough. Anyway the Americans seem to have gone on driving and burning and lighting places up like there was no tomorrow. They kept finding new sources of oil, going further, digging deeper – long after everyone else was pulling

275

back. When little countries like Greenland started reining in the supplies, well, our government backed the oil companies and money changed hands – you can imagine. It seems the Chinese had Africa by the balls and the US the rest. But, in the end, even they couldn't ignore it any longer. We were the only people left burning oil on just getting around and living. There were wars anywhere there was oil left, as you can imagine.'

'So they had to look for alternatives in the end?' asked Darren.

'Yes. And what have they gone for but nuclear. The other alternatives that Julian and the rest of you are looking at don't lend themselves to anyone making big profits. It's too hard to corner the market in that technology but nuclear – well, that's different, I guess. At the moment, only the government has the dough to invest in reactors, certainly in the numbers the US now needs all at once. But big business *is* the government and they're getting the contracts. They haven't stopped for breath.'

'But do they actually know what they're doing? Has there been any research going on at all? Any improvements?' Lewin asked, frowning.

'Has there hell! No, nothing and none! They've fallen back on the old designs from the last century and maybe they have pinched some from the Chinese – wouldn't put it past them. And this time there really *are* no experienced personnel. People cut corners and then, when things start to go wrong, they don't know what to do. Some incidents get reported but a lot of people think it's happening much more than gets out. And no-one knows what to do with waste, either. No-one wants it and no-one's prepared to pay to get it properly stored. Every now and then you get a local demo – but people only hear what the government wants them to hear in the main. The news on the

276

internet and TV is controlled by the big guys, after all, just like it is in the papers.'

'The internet?' Carew sounded puzzled. 'Julian mentioned that and I've heard the word since – but can you explain what it actually is?'

Tony laughed. 'Don't ask me. Somewhere between TV, a conversation and a newspaper. It makes what the Prof here does look like building blocks. I'll entertain you with that over a pint later, Dr Carew, if you're interested.'

'Well, I am. Communication is always of interest. It leads the way in human development, you know. The rest follows.'

'You may well be right, but in what direction? Something has happened to Americans. They seem more ignorant, not less. More easily led and misled than ever they were. They just get the facts people want to give them. I've been in towns where they tell me about a plant accident and someone in the next county won't know anything about it – *or believe you when you tell them.* They say if it was true they would have heard on the TV or internet. And then rumours of things that *aren't* true fly around and no-one seems to care that there's no evidence.

'There's more. You know we've always had our religious nuts and sects. We were founded by them, if you think about it, but that kind of thing is more extreme and widespread than ever. You'd think it would be less. There are communities that live 'off the grid' as they call it now – no TV, no internet – but they're not hippies any more. They tote guns and I sure as hell couldn't join one.'

The group fell silent. Somehow this was not what they had expected. Whatever had gone wrong in Asia, Australia or Britain they had nurtured a conviction that the Americans would have coped better, that the Americans would provide the light at the end of the tunnel.

'And you *really* want to go back?' asked Emmeline, eventually. 'What can you do?'

'I don't know, but I have to do it. What I need from all of you are ideas.'

31
Crystal Palace

London
1983

It was the New Year before the group met again – this time in the new premises in Crystal Palace. It was a detached Victorian house, tall and narrow. It had a basement and three further floors with an observatory on the top. Almost a folly, as Julian commented.

'There are quite a few of these eccentric looking houses round here,' said Lewin. 'It's perfect for us. There's plenty of room for the machine and my other research in the basement; there's this room and a kitchen here, two bedrooms and a bathroom upstairs and then another big room on the top floor – that one's got a spiral staircase up to that totally useless observatory. The youngsters are going to have rooms here to keep an eye on things – and there's a bed for anyone else who wants or needs to be around at any point. As far as the neighbours are concerned it's a student house-share and the coming and going shouldn't attract the attention it was beginning to in Festing Road.'

'You've all been busy with the paint pots. It's looking good,' said Julian looking about him with a critical eye.

'Yes, well, to be honest it was good to have something to get on with,' said Maggie. 'I think we all felt a bit gloomy after the last meeting.'

Joan had been looking out of the window but now she turned to face the room. 'I don't think changing world history was ever going to be easy for half a dozen people in London, you know.'

'Bloody impossible, if you ask me,' snorted Carew. 'Did anyone come up with any ideas at all? I know I didn't, apart from what I said last time.'

'Yes, we have some ideas,' Maggie replied tartly. 'Darren and I have been thinking of ways of spreading information about survival techniques for if the worst happens. Might just help the people like the ones we met in Wiltshire and stop the others taking control so easily. Julian is working on how to encourage model villages that don't need external fuel sources. He reckons he can get some influential people involved...'

Julian nodded. 'I'm even thinking about sponsoring projects for architectural students in the universities. Maybe setting up an Award scheme. I think we can make living without oil and grid electricity fashionable if we try. And there's still time for that to percolate down to ordinary people before 2080. We'll need more money, though. Lots. So there's a job for you, Philip.'

'And I think we should be actively promoting more research into the safety of the nuclear plants,' sighed Lewin. This was, he considered, the crux of the matter. 'So much of what gets published now is funded by industry – the very people who have an interest in getting the answers they want. I never thought I'd hear myself say that but, from what Tony has been telling us about what's happening in the States, we need some independent voices and we need them to be heard.'

'Particularly in the States, of course,' added Tony, 'but maybe it would be easier to start over here, or in Europe, at least.'

'But if it's China that is going to present much of the problem worldwide, what do we do about that?' Julian shrugged 'How does what we do here or in America help that?' He was, as ever, resistant to the idea of any cooperation with the nuclear industry being included in their planning.

'If we invest in our own industry we wouldn't be so dependent on them ourselves, would we?' objected Carew. '*We'd* be better off, at least.'

'And there's something else,' said Darren, changing the subject before a fully-blown row could develop. 'While we were painting, Tony told us more about the internet. It does seem to have a huge impact on how people think and learn things in the future – more than newspapers, even – and it's kicking off now. At the moment, here, it seems to consist of companies and governments sharing information between their own computers within their own networks. By the time we get to when Tony was in America, people can buy into it like we would buy papers and they get their television and films through it, too. That's why the companies that own it have so much influence. But maybe we could try and nudge things along now, here, with a view to opening it up more. If we can keep ownership of that technology out of the hands of the old cartels that seem to be controlling it and everything else in the future – well, who knows?'

'Do you think there's any chance of doing that?' asked Lewin. 'How?'

Tony answered. 'That's the problem we need to be working on. When I go back, I could try to identify key areas and centres of research that might have been significant. I could bring that information back for you guys to kinda help the right people along. Speed things up for them and give them the edge.'

Carew looked thoughtful. 'I've still got contacts in Oxford and they tell me there are computer boffins and computer courses in all sorts of departments. Bit of a computer science hotspot now. If I were to just go back a couple of years or so I won't look much different from how I do now and I wasn't living there at that time, so I wouldn't meet myself. I could take Darren, and if I could find out who the latest whizz kids were, I could point him in their direction. They'd be more likely to pay attention to someone younger, I suspect, and Darren has actually used a computer, it seems. While I was there, I could make a couple of investments, like before, and we'd be in a position to offer some funding as well as research tips.'

Joan lifted her hand to speak. 'Funding in the right places to help keep the research independent is great but wouldn't it be better to bring back more detailed technical information to give them?'

'Well, yes, Professor,' agreed Tony. 'But this stuff is really hard to get a handle on. At least I find it so. I last went to school in the fifties and sixties remember!'

'If I could get the right person in Oxford interested,' said Darren suddenly, 'I could always see if they'd make the journey themselves...'

'Whoa...' said Julian. 'We'd need to think about that, Darren.'

Lewin agreed with him.

'It's a desperate situation, Julian,' said Maggie. 'We were all of us trusted once and this time whoever it was could go with Darren – and Tony would already be there to show them the ropes. It would all be much better organised and safer.'

Emmeline nodded. 'I agree. I think we all sat around over Christmas feeling fed up and stuck. This looks like a plan with real possibilities–'

'–and, if you let *me* finish,' Joan interrupted, 'I might be able to help with the technical side, myself. I've been building a little personal computer, a Nascom 2, at home. It's a kind of a hobby, you understand, now I've semi-retired. I've always been interested in them, ever since I met this man in the war. Bit of an unsung hero, really. Dead now. Cryptologist. Anyway, I've had to learn some basic programming and I do understand some of the technical language they use. I could go with Tony to New York and pick up enough to whet someone's appetite for travel at least – and vetting prospective travellers is my job here after all.'

'Good god! Whatever happened to cross-stitch?' asked Julian.

Emmeline and Joan looked at him coldly.

Emmeline sniffed and pointedly addressed Joan: 'Thank you, Joan, that's a good offer and I, at least, am impressed. So, to summarise: we seem to have decided that influencing the spread of knowledge is the way forward generally. Even if the world does run out of fuel and we can't use the nuclear power plants we've got, with the right skills and knowledge, people will stand a better chance. Humans do have a history of picking themselves up from disasters. And, although I don't think any of us are expecting you to bring down the cartels single-handed, Tony, you've identified their weak link. If we can get the internet thingy to be more open, less of a closed shop, independent scientists and research institutions might stand a chance of being heard in time–'

'–and, with the internet thingy, as you call it, more open we can make sure accidents and problems don't get brushed under the carpet quite so easily.' Julian stretched and stood up. 'You're right, Emmeline. It looks like we have the beginnings of a plan. Where's the bar in this establishment? I need a drink and this could be something worth drinking to!'

Later that evening Maggie and Tony stood side by side in the observatory, looking out over a London bejewelled with street lights and lit windows.

'I told you we'd given you the best room.'

'You certainly did, Maggie. This is impressive. Like New York without the skyscrapers and sirens.'

'We have got the Natwest Tower now, you know, as well as the Post Office Tower! You can probably see them from here.'

'It's OK, honey. I don't miss skyscrapers.' He laughed and slipped his arm about her shoulders. She leant against him companionably. 'But I *did* miss you, Maggie, when I was home. I wished I had someone to laugh at it all with. You've spoilt me for solo travelling.'

'You didn't seem to want me to go before, though.'

'I wasn't sure what it would be like – or even if there would be an America. Well, there is – even if it's not one I like much. You could come back with me, you know. Stay a bit longer, maybe.'

Maggie straightened up and wrapped her arms across her chest, hugging herself as if cold. It was a moment or two before she replied.

'No, Tony, I don't think I could.'

'Why not?'

'You know,' she said slowly as if working it out as she went along, 'when I look at all those lights in the houses and flats I sometimes wonder how many homes I can see from here. It must be thousands. Each set of windows represents a person or family. And each person or family is the centre, the hub, of their universe. Whether they know a dozen people or hundreds, it's all the same to them.'

'And?'

'And – I think this is where I belong now. The trips were an adventure but my life here can be an adventure as well. It's only just beginning. And there's so much to do *right here*.'

Tony gave her shoulders a final squeeze and

284

released her.

'Yeah. There *are* other things in life apart from time travel, they tell me. Things of great value. And of course there is – Darren.' There was the hint of a query in his voice.

'And there's Darren.'

'Does he feel the same?'

'About staying around here? With me? Yes, I think so. But in the meantime there's this trip to Oxford for him when Professor Danes gets back and then the boffin hunt and then – who knows?'

'You think he might escort the boffin to the States?'

'He might. There seems to be less appetite for sending people off into the blue on their own now.' She smiled. 'And I expect he'd like to look at the galleries. There are galleries, I assume?'

'Yeah. All that stuff. And he could have a ball between genning up on computer science and looking at Indian burial sites, if he got bored.'

'Tony, please...'

'It's OK, Maggie. If he does come I promise I'll look after him and send him back to you in one piece. How about that?'

Maggie smiled up at him and kissed him lightly on the lips.

'That would do very nicely, Tony. Now let's go and join the others before everyone gets *really* confused!'

The End

Acknowledgments

I'd like to give a big thank you to Rose and my friends at Beach Creative for their encouragement in the early days and to Andy Ochocki for excellent and much-needed editorial input and, of course, to Chris for keeping me supplied with cups of tea and the occasional timely gin and tonic while work was in progress.

Another big thank you goes to Rebecca Emin and her colleagues at Gingersnap Books for their work in turning a manuscript into a book and also to Jonathan Temples, book cover designer par excellence.

22047133R00174

Printed in Poland
by Amazon Fulfillment
Poland Sp. z o.o., Wrocław